Idol [illegible]

Rosy had m[illegible] Mel Gibson in a hotel room, if [illegible] arranged interview with tape-re[illegible] ladies running, and had fou[illegible] [illegible]urprisingly amusing.

She [illegible] Hoffman to ground in Sussex one memo[illegible] [illegible]ekend, and found him short but relatively charm[illegible]g in the circumstances.

And Tom Cruise, and Michael J. Fox, and even the ex-Monkee Davy Jones. They had all been lovely to talk to, yet they all shared one characteristic shortcoming which had subdued the privilege she felt.

Not to put too fine a point on it, Rosy was beginning to wonder whether she would ever meet a full-sized famous actor.

Some days she felt taller and more inelegant than ever.

Deborah Lawrenson was born in 1960 and graduated from Trinity College, Cambridge in 1983. From 1987–90 she was a Staff Reporter on Nigel Dempster's column at the *Daily Mail*, and from 1990–2 worked as his Deputy Editor at the *Mail on Sunday*. She lives in Kent. *Idol Chatter* is her second novel.

Also by Deborah Lawrenson
and available in Mandarin

Hot Gossip

Deborah Lawrenson

IDOL CHATTER

Mandarin

A Mandarin Paperback
IDOL CHATTER

First published in Great Britain 1995
by Mandarin Paperbacks
an imprint of Reed Consumer Books Ltd
Michelin House, 81 Fulham Road, London SW3 6RB
and Auckland, Melbourne, Singapore and Toronto

All the characters and events in the narrative are fictitious, and no resemblance to actual persons, living or dead, is intentional

A CIP catalogue record for this title
is available from the British Library
ISBN 0 7493 2024 9

Phototypeset by Intype, London
Printed and bound in Great Britain
by Cox & Wyman Ltd, Reading, Berks

To Robert, with much love – he always believes in me

1 | *The Tower of Babble*

'*I* have not ruined her life – YOU have ruined her life!' roared Anthony Sword down the red telephone.

A burst of fury exploded at the Palace end of the line.

'Just who the hell do you think you are?'

It was a question Anthony Sword had given some consideration lately. He clapped one hand on his barrel chest and smiled 'I am the most famous gossip columnist in the world, Sir!'

The most famous gossip columnist in the world – or so he had recently decided – was on top form. As a man who had invented himself, Anthony Sword was a past master of the right word in the right ear.

He replaced the red receiver with the lightest of triumphant gestures, as if it were the final piece of a house built of playing cards.

Then he jiggled his feet with delight.

Anthony Sword chuckled to himself as he turned his attention to assembling a final chump cut of prime beefing for the next morning's *Daily Dispatch*.

'The fevered fantasist on the downmarket *Daily Post* has now outraged everyone who has ever felt a pang of patriotism,' he began. His computer terminal fizzed and wobbled with creative input.

The daily butchery of his *soi-disant* rival Benedict Pierce of the *Post* had never been so bloody, nor so sweet.

'His meddlesome mendacity has stunned Her Majesty the Queen,' crashed Sword at the keyboard addressing his fabled two million ABC 1 readers from the most magnificent office suite at the *Daily Dispatch*. 'HM has sighed sadly to friends that there is nothing new in so-called revelations about difficulties between her husband and their eldest son. And she is outraged by suggestions that her thoroughbred racehorses have ever been fed anything but the finest unsullied hay, and certainly not that which has served as a barn boudoir for grooms and their amorous guests. Sadly I have to inform the deluded fool – whose tenure at the pathetic *Post* has coincided with the paper's loss of almost a million readers – that his rotten ramblings are tossed straight on to the Windsor compost heap.'

Sword paused and gave a gleeful snort.

Since his own recent elevation to Muckspreader of the Year – a historic press title of some cult prestige and distinction – he had wanted no opportunity to rub the Pierce nose in it.

Some people said that Anthony Sword was a monster.

Others claimed incontrovertible evidence of his pussy cat qualities. Either way, the gossip columnist didn't much care – just so long as no one forgot that he kept his claws sharp.

He had built a thirty-year reputation on as much.

On the wall in front of him, he could see himself – a King Kong of a *bon vivant*, roaring and uncontainable – posturing on a hundred party photographs. For a certain class of person, all human life was there – all that one would want to know, at any rate, in these tricky modern days of instant fame and false idols.

Anthony Sword viewed the world he had created with some ambiguity, of course; and with a detachment that might have come as an unpleasant surprise had some of those he featured in his daily renderings had a finer sense of irony. 'Who *are* all these people? NOBODIES until I wrote about them! I have *invented* them,' he would seethe and chuckle, although never in public, naturally.

Wherever he went in London, there were people who whispered his name in vain, but these were often the people who ended up giving him his best stories. There were others who would abruptly stop their whining and turn their back on him, but he took this as a compliment. There was nothing like the view of a stiff, narrow back as he entered a room to alert him to a decent exclusive.

Sword grinned – the bearded piratical grin familiar to millions from the largest picture by-line in the *Daily Dispatch* – at the dark, elegant young man who walked languidly into the room and began a critical appraisal of the evening's invitations pinned in an alcove above the secretary's desk.

Jamie Raj, deputy editor of the diary page, shuffled a few of the stiff engraved cards, then glanced at the sub-editor's computer screen in passing. He looked up and smiled. 'I saw Benedict last night, by the way. At Quaglino's with the Marchioness of Weedon. He sent his regards.'

'Gracious in defeat. I like that,' said Sword.

'Sad, though, to think he's only just got on to that old story.' Jamie slid a fistful of invitation cards into his inside breast pocket. He wore an embroidered waistcoat today, Sword noted, that implied both otherworldliness and a dangerous level of dandyism.

'So where are you off to tonight, James? ' asked the rotund inquisitor as he reached for his own vast cream jacket and made for the door. 'Or should that be, whose heart are you breaking?'

'Private view in Cork Street, then there's a British film launch. Wiser to leave that until the drinks afterwards, I think. Then dinner with a Caroline.'

'Any Caroline I know?'

His handsome deputy gave a slow smile. 'I'm working on it. What about you?'

'Thought I might force m'self to look in at a claret-tasting at the Garrick. Then off to hear a friend sing.'

Whichever way *that* turned out, thought Sword with a private chuckle.

The two men walked out of the diary office together, and took a glass-sided bullet ride down through the sub-tropical atrium of Dispatch House. To their mutual satisfaction, the newspaper's premises represented the most sumptuous high-tech in the business. The heat, in the vast greenhouse where the plants and indoor trees thrived even more glossily than the weekend editorial supplements, was stifling.

'Night, Rosy,' called Sword, as a tall young woman walked towards them in the direction of the lifts. Her long hair was the rippled dark blonde of a shelled walnut.

'Oh, er . . . night,' she returned, managing both to stride purposefully and look nervously distracted.

Sword saw how she looked at Jamie, then away again quickly as she hurried by. 'Why is she clutching two carrots?' he frowned.

Jamie shrugged. 'Another of her daft diets?'

Which either meant he was playing it very cool, or hadn't seen much of their former colleague lately. Sword thought it highly unlikely that Rosy Hope had got too big for her boots since her transfer to by-line status on

Features. Of all the young women who had ever worked for him on the Sword's Secrets column, the gossip columnist regarded Rosy Hope with something dangerously close to affection.

She could do the job, for one thing.

And she could *keep* a secret, too. Even if he had discovered that too late.

There was a pause for a nano-second.

Sword watched Rosy disappear above the tree-line in one of the glass lifts, and wondered whether the time had come to call in favours.

He and Jamie parted outside the building, where the warm roar of rush-hour traffic on the Embankment cut between them and the glistening river. Sword took a lung-full of brown evening air and felt the rise of his trademark girth.

The royal rant returned to him. 'Just WHO do you think you are?'

Should Anthony Sword ever confront that question – and he was being pressed ever harder to do so – he was well aware that it could be the biggest story of his life.

And people had been asking whether he was all he seemed – ever since Rosy Hope had blundered into his world and opened that can of worms.

2 | *Their Carrot-Crunching Colleague*

Rosy Hope's flirtation with the *Daily Dispatch*'s gossip column, which inevitably included Jamie Raj – and *that* aberration was absolutely over now – was limited these days to creeping in to beg or steal useful telephone numbers.

Her beat on Features, as might be expected, was the Celebrity Interview. That was OK. In many ways that was more than OK. It was miraculous.

After eight months last year working on Sword's page, it felt like mainstream journalism again. She still went out to meet all the same people, of course, but now they didn't duck when they saw her coming or turn white when she asked them if she could check a few tiny facts. She even had the glamour and kudos of her own picture by-line once in a while.

Her parents could hold up their heads once more in Chislehurst.

She had managed to get Mel Gibson in a hotel room, if only for a pre-arranged interview with tape-recorders and PR ladies running, and had found him short but surprisingly amusing.

She had run Dustin Hoffman to ground in Sussex one memorable weekend, and found him short but relatively charming in the circumstances.

And Tom Cruise, and Michael J. Fox, and even the ex-Monkee Davy Jones. They had all been lovely to talk to, yet they shared one characteristic shortcoming which had subdued the privilege she felt.

Not to put too fine a point on it, Rosy was beginning to wonder whether she would ever meet a full-sized famous actor.

Some days she felt taller and more inelegant than ever.

She could have done without seeing Jamie Raj and Sword. It was the end of a long day. She was starving, feeling grubby and unkempt, and she had less than an hour to breathe some life into a suffer-fest of Dead Rock Star's Wives. The planned feature on golf widows had been pulled at the last moment, due to an unpleasant incident at Wentworth. The features editor's ensuing panic had seen off footballer's floosies and snooker spouses as alternatives. The only option which found favour was an old piece by a freelance – a bundle of copy which had done service as a drawer-liner and draught-excluder and whose time had now come to save the day. It had fallen to Rosy to revive these tales of leopardskin and woe, and she was scurrying back to her desk with sustenance when she ran into the gossip columnist and his cohort.

The good news was that they were heading out, leaving the coast clear for a telephone numbers raid.

In a perverse way, Rosy found herself fond of Anthony Sword. Why that should be, when the man was renowned throughout the newspaper – no, the industry, the *country* – as a volcanic-tempered ogre, she was unsure.

His notorious outbursts of fury regularly reverberated around the *Dispatch* building. He was renowned as a hideous enemy and a formidable operator. Yet for whatever reason, Anthony Sword had been a strangely avuncular figure to her. She wasn't about to forget that it was he who had given her her big chance on what had once been Fleet Street, just when her courage was failing in the *Daily Dispatch*'s notorious newsroom. Sword had plucked her from the terrifying footsoldiery of General Domestic Tragedy in the nick of time and sent her out on the party circuit.

On any other paper the transition might have looked like a soft option.

When Rosy had started working for Sword she had been the girl who knew nobody. She knew better now.

She had stayed with Sword for eight months, chasing stories, charging around London in a taxi to drink other people's champagne at parties. She'd dealt doggedly with the column's persistent old theatrical tipster Eva Coutts, who rang in dozens of times a day with gossip about actors and actresses. When she'd done her best for Sword – and Rosy *always* did her best – she'd written feature profiles of the famous people she'd met through him. In her own time. Until finally – and not without a few operatic furies for general effect – the gossip columnist had allowed her to take the Features job she'd been offered.

Rosy hadn't looked back since – except to pass on stories she'd been told during the course of her celebrity interviews. Not off-cuts exactly. Just stories she reckoned the gossip column could do more justice to than she could. That she preferred to leave the salacious stuff to them, she realised, was a measure of how clean she kept her hands these days.

When Rosy ran into the Sword's Secrets office to grab the most famous address book in London, she found it in the unsteady hands of Pearson McKnight. The column's countryman elder reporter was hunkering down inside his rotting tweed jacket. His face was ruddy and a pall of cigar smoke hung over him.

Rosy knew the signs. He had the unmistakable air of a man who had sneaked back into the office too late to make the point that he had actually returned from lunch.

'You can stop working on your excuse,' said Rosy. 'They've already gone.'

'Rosy!' he breezed. 'What's this, keeping a horse these days?'

Rosy smiled and did a cutesy wave with the carrots she was holding. 'The antidote to eating like one, I'm afraid. It was this or sausage and chips at the canteen.'

The senior hack pulled an expression of distaste at her choice. 'When are you coming out to lunch with us? Haven't seen you properly for ages.'

'Mmm,' said Rosy. 'Pearson, I'd love to chat . . . but I've got a rush job on. I couldn't see the book, could I?'

'Be my guest.'

She gutted it in five minutes, while her ex-colleague called an old rock contact on her behalf. He handed over the ready-made quotes.

'Pearson, you're a star,' breathed Rosy, glancing anxiously at her watch. 'Thanks so much . . . I must dash.'

'Ah, so fleeting . . .'

'I'm sorry, Pearson, honest . . . but the boss is already deeply suspicious of the time I spend chatting to you lot, not that I have for ages . . . and tonight is not the night for a supplementary fracas . . .' She bit on her lip in a gesture of hopelessness and turned to go.

'Hey, Rosy,' said Pearson, leaning back in his chair with crossed arms. 'One o'clock tomorrow. Diary drink at Scribblers. Be there.'

Rosy took a deep breath. 'Sure,' she said. 'And thanks again. I really appreciate this.'

'Any time.'

The words carried into the corridor behind her.

3 | *The Sword File*

Across town, where the desirability of an SW1 postcode was mainstream political rather than merely social, the work in progress made Crighton's back ache.

He dropped two heavy box files on to his desk. He unbent with a wince and rubbed the base of his spine. He gazed beyond the standard issue surroundings, scratched and battered as his spirit. Beyond his steel-framed window, the whole world – the bricks of the government building opposite, the road and pavements four storeys below, the clouds, the sky – was civil service grey.

There was a sudden pop.

Crighton glanced down to see that the catch on the lid of the top box had given out under the strain.

The Sword file, like its subject, was a bulging body of work.

It took him a while to find what he needed. Over the months, an astonishing array of details had been assembled. They began:

> Name: Anthony Sheridan Banks, born May 12, 1945 in Hammersmith, London.

Occupation: Newspaper gossip columnist; pen name, Anthony Sword; adopted circa 1965.
Addresses (w) The Daily Dispatch, London EC4
(h) Quornnel Lodge, Tranquil Rise, Highgate, London N6
Description: Height (approx only): 5ft 9in
Weight (fluctuating, estimate only) 13st – 15st, now 18+st
Mother, Eva Banks (see addendum); father unknown (*to be ascertained*)
Educated: unknown before part-time attendance at The LaValle School of Performance Arts, London NW1 (defunct).

Spilling from the box were the most recent surveillance notices, meticulously logged. From the control sheet compiled from these, Crighton could see at a glance that the man was a creature of habit.

He was ferried every morning from home (see above) to work (ditto) in a black taxi cab which arrived promptly for him at ten o'clock. This arrangement, it would not have required the CID to deduce, was largely to accommodate the gossip columnist's drinking – of which there was a prodigious amount during the course of a working day.

He would invariably depart from his office at around 12.30 – pitching up at one of the more expensive and clubby restaurants in the West End for lunch with one or two companions, almost always male.

Every Tuesday evening he would visit his mother in East Sheen.

There was a separate dossier on Eva Coutts, née Banks. The story was full of neat touches like that. Eva Banks, born 1924, in Mitcham, Surrey. Stage name, adopted circa 1940: Eva Coutts. Actress, entertainer and hostess. Parts of the dossier had been added from a xeroxed government Restricted Access file.

Most of the surveillance reports on the activities at her home at 2, Fairlawn Avenue, East Sheen, were dated more than a decade previously. Time had not dimmed their appeal for the dedicated conspiracy theorist.

Crighton flicked faster, more impatiently, through the papers.

Clipped to the most recent lunch log was a scrappy list of Sword's eating companions over the past few months. They were an eclectic group, ranging from theatrical agents, politicians and television executives to famous chefs, racing men and an ennobled millionaire garagiste.

From a morass of newspaper and magazine clippings came the idiosyncratic details that, Crighton knew, were the blocks from which breakthroughs were built.

When the taxi was not required, Anthony Sword drove a 1930s Bentley (colour: dark cream) and a C-registration navy blue Vauxhall Nova.

He had a standing order for stargazer lilies from the The Conservatory Flower Shop on the High Street.

His cream linen suits were bought in Italy and altered by a seamstress in Hornsey.

He was a devotee of the Divertimenti kitchen store.

He was an opera and jazz buff, and he would take friends to outdoor concerts in the grounds of Kenwood House – or had the previous summer, when the file had been initiated.

He had lately taken to near-obsessive evening visits to a restaurant in the West End called Puccini's, and this was what currently interested Crighton. With a small suck of triumph between his teeth, he fingered the notes he needed.

The sheet was headed *POSSIBLE LEADS*, with a hasty memo to self: *Yet to be contacted*. The list that followed was little more than a scrappy scrawl: Rachel Williams, Mrs M (Muriel?) McKnight, Rosalind (known as Rosy) Hope. Beneath it, marked *Contacted*, were the names Framboise Duprée (this one crossed with a line) and Lucinda Bisset.

It was time to raise his game.

Crighton stuffed the page into the inside breast pocket of his Austin Reed suit, carefully shut the door of his office as he went out, descended to the street and merged with the universal grey outside.

4 | *Benedict's Art*

If Anthony Sword were ever to get his come-uppance, his much-maligned rival Benedict Pierce of the *Daily Post* felt it was only right that he should be the one to dish it up.

He was working on it.

Face it, he had been working on it for years. But never with quite such steely determination as since Sword exposed him as the long-lost son of The Most Embarrassing Woman in London. The former Countess Mallern, ex-Lady Hartford, ex-Mrs Windophin-Lancaster, dowager mistress of Lord Spute and one-time Lady Fordcombe (née actress Bea Goff) had provided the gossip columns with decades of ridiculous stories. All of which proved the old maxim that a fool and his money would soon be married.

The previous year she had been between finding aristocratic husbands, and so she had decided to find a son instead. It was all too horribly convenient that he, Benedict, should have been that son.

If there had been cold champagne to drink, Benedict might have stayed longer at the private view. As it was, the smart polished wood and glass gallery in Mayfair's Cork Street was offering primary splodges and warm recession hock. Pierce of the *Post* well knew that a private view was of the people, never the art, yet there was still enough of the ex-City desk man about him to want to evaluate the wares.

He knew he wouldn't pay £19,000 for a trickle of black on a red daub.

Across the room was a corner devoted to human gore, several pieces of which had already appeared in a notorious exhibition described by one critic as 'relentlessly disgusting'. Once, to describe a young sculptor as having guts would have been construed as praise. Now, thought Benedict, it could be taken quite literally.

One large, jellified object reminded him uncomfortably of Anthony Sword, quivering malevolently under a spotlight. Sometimes Benedict felt that, for all his Savile Row suits and success, his skin remained as thin as that of the agonised Madonna exposed to the bone by the doorway. He felt his ambitious hairstyle shrink a little on his scalp.

In other words, he was still smarting from Sword's latest swipes.

To add salt to the wound, across the room Sword's self-assured sidekick Jamie Raj, an Anglo-Indian of the GQ persuasion, was calmly enjoying the attentions of several well-dressed blondes. His dark hair flopped à la Hugh Grant, his linen suit was creased to perfection, his waistcoat was serious shopping, and his golden skin glowed against the white background. Jamie Raj wasn't just at the party: Benedict had the impression that the deputy editor of the *Daily Dispatch* diary had carefully picked his showcase.

'Cork Street is not what it was,' said Honoria Peeke. The social editor of the *Prattler* magazine always popped up when there were contacts to plunder.

Benedict sighed. 'We're none of us what we were. Do

you realise I've begun to describe almost everyone I see as *young*? When did *I* stop being young?'

'About ten years ago?'

'I never thought you were deliberately mean, Honoria.'

'Sorry, darling – why so sensitive all of a sudden?'

'I am not old. I am forty-four,' said Benedict with dignity.

'It's not young.'

And if Honoria Peeke, with her plumped-up peachy cheeks, matronly girth and almost grown-up daughters, thought that . . . then perhaps Benedict had some unpleasant re-evaluation to do.

'At least,' he said, with a savage nod to where Jamie Raj stood with all the prettiest girls, 'I am not a danger to daughters.'

Honoria gave him what she no doubt intended as a kind look. 'Oh darling, you've been safe in taxis for *years*!'

Benedict glared.

'Have you seen your mother lately?' asked Honoria, with unexpected malevolence.

'My mother is a respectable widow in King's Lynn.'

'That was quick. Who's died on her now?'

'I am referring to the woman who brought me up, whom I will always think of as my mother. Not that – harpy who has barged rudely into my life and tried to bag herself a son.'

'Oh, darling,' said Honoria, clearly enjoying this. 'That's not very filial. A woman who has been through what she has – '

'Precisely. Bea Geoff is a name with which I do not want to be associated.'

'Last I heard,' persisted the *Prattler*'s social *editrix* with an impish wrinkle of the nose, 'our dear Bea had talked a country peer to the steps of the High Court for his divorce, all the while impersonating a Relate counsellor.

Apparently she's already wearing the most dazzling engagement ring from Asprey's.'

The age business had begun to get to him months ago. Benedict was under no illusion that that was why he had been seeing Lottie Landor.

His liaison with Lottie – a pretty, *young* actress of sufficient talent to get by – was strictly egotistical, on both sides. So long as she accompanied him prettily to events where there were cameras, and was understanding about the perennial problems caused by two grasping ex-wives, then they both knew where they stood.

When he left Cork Street, he picked her up from Pimlico – the Aston Martin Zagato was borrowed for a motoring feature – and drove her to Chelsea Harbour where they dined for free. These days Benedict was a man with a lifestyle – one which did not say Ford or Vauxhall.

He was a man who had made something of himself.

'What shall I put then – about your work in prospect?' he asked, feeling he could fudge no longer when it came to mentioning her in his column.

'Mmmm . . .' Lottie mulled it over. 'It's been quiet.'

She was not exaggerating. The quietness of Lottie Landor's career lately had lent a whole new dimension to deathly silence, as far as Benedict could see.

'It happens to lots of people when they're in the gossip columns a lot,' she explained.

'Hmm.'

'Although I did have one good bit of news I haven't told you yet,' said Lottie.

'Oh yes?'

'That film I made last year, that was always being written about but nothing seemed to happen – '

He knew only too well.

'We-ell,' she went on, 'My agent phoned yesterday to say the producers are taking it to Cannes because Matt Pyne's in it. Now Matt's got to be so famous – well, *quite* famous – they think that they might be able to persuade the Americans to buy it. And they want me to go.'

'To Cannes – the film festival?'

'Isn't it great!'

Benedict laughed. 'Well, well – bikini time.'

She pouted. 'It's not that kind of film.'

'It makes no difference, believe me.'

The light went out in her big blue-green eyes. 'It's called Chicken and Chips.'

'We might skip the title, darling,' urged Benedict.

There was a slight pause, during which Lottie turned on a radiant smile and leant forward for the house photographer.

Cannes . . .

The more Benedict thought about it, the more he was convinced it could be a master stroke.

For weeks he had been mulling over the possibilities.

The right story with the right people. Beautiful people, with beautiful money and connections. The ultimate exclusive, but not in print – *on film*.

As the literary agent had said in the Groucho Club: 'When the Prince of Wales was in Los Angeles, a marketing company showed his picture to a large cross-section of the public. The results showed that although almost everyone knew he was a big star somewhere, almost no one could name the movies he's been in.' Benedict had snorted. 'But seventy per cent were able to reply that he always plays the psychopathic husband,' continued the literary agent with heavy emphasis. 'It's already happened!'

'What has?'

'This . . . blurring of fact and fiction on our screens. The strange hybrid of the drama documentary. Can't say that any of us should approve but one must learn to . . . adapt, as it were. This, at least, would be pure.'

Pure what, Benedict did not care to contemplate.

Instead, he said, 'We're talking a *royal* story here?'

'The biggest so far,' said the agent. 'The title of the book is *Princess Laid Bare*.'

The right story with all the right people. The idea took flight in Benedict's head. A story of our times: the truth, as portrayed on film by the very people it concerned.

Perhaps the time was right.

Benedict Pierce would show Sword.

5 | *Wine, Woman and Song*

Anthony Sword scored a couple of notable St Emilions at the Garrick Club wine-tasting and was in an amicable enough mood to set out on foot for his next port of call. The thick pavement aroma of melting tar and sweating exhausts was like a navvy's embrace at the end of a long day.

He ambled past music shops and book emporia and sensed the enclosed excitement of the theatres as their shows unfolded inside. He paused once, briefly, to check on a billing outside the Phoenix, then pushed on through the strolling dusk.

At Puccini's, he ignored the queue outside and went straight in.

After a hard day as a scourge of the Establishment, the permanently peckish star columnist liked nothing better than to get within sniffing distance of an indulgent dinner and hoist a few while anticipating it. It was this unerring instinct, naturally, which had restored his *embonpoint* to its former glory after an uncharacteristically lean period the previous summer when he had attempted some physical image reinvention.

The temporary weight loss he achieved against the odds at a health farm had brought two sizeable benefits:

the pacification of his fretful doctors, and his enduring friendship with Framboise. The latter was far more important.

They took baths together – in a manner of speaking.

Inside the restaurant, he was shown to his regular table.

'My usual beaker of the warm south please, Giovanni.'

The head waiter nodded with a full-toothed smile. He returned two minutes later with a bottle of Grumello. Or his Grumbello, as Framboise called it. 'Perfect timing, Mr Sword. Miss Duprée is about to go on.'

By a tiny dance floor, originally installed only as a technical justification for an all-night drinking licence, a four-man band had begun to tune up. Framboise Duprée gave him a cheery wave from the wings by the bar and strode on. Her vast bulk rippled freely under a dress of fiery red sequins until the effect was of a woman in flames, skin black as coal under the lights. Framboise, a light opera singer only in the musical sense, took positive pride in her appearance. 'I am Round as an O!' she would chuckle, with a neat nod to her recently developed passion for all things English.

A passion which, most importantly, embraced – in the widest sense – a large, round gossip columnist.

Tonight she sported a red flower behind one ear in homage to Billie Holliday.

On the telephone that morning – he in his bath, she in hers – she had told him: 'I've got news.'

'Oh, yes?'

'Only . . . I think I should tell you face to face.'

A pause, during which his soap did a high diver's double twist and pike from his fist. He wasn't holding his breath, exactly, but the last time she'd said the gossip was too good for bathtime, the result had been two Cabinet resignations and a smoking gun in the form of a male dancer in Framboise's jazz cabaret spot.

He raised his first glass of Grumello to her, and tossed it back in hearty anticipation of a good story. Besides, since Framboise had pitched up in London from Louisiana via New York (she had arrived for a season with the People's Jazz Opera of Camden and never left) he rarely missed a performance. Her latest wheeze was packing 'em in for cabaret at Puccini's, where her rich voice and abundant good humour had acquired something approaching cult status.

Several nights a week Anthony Sword was in the audience. He had got into the habit of dropping in, at least for a nightcap, from wherever his travails had taken him.

These days he felt his evening had hardly begun until the fat lady sang.

He was distinctly dewy-eyed after her Gershwin finale. Framboise arrived at his table at the same time as a pizza the size and shape of Switzerland.

'Oi!' she said, as he filched an olive. She tweaked his beard in a gesture of affection.

Sword poured her a glass of wine and beamed expectantly.

For once, she misread him.

'So . . . Have you done it?' she asked.

Sword dragged himself out of dreamland. 'Done what?'

'*Asked* her. Asked Eva.'

The last thing he wanted to discuss. 'No, look – '

'You gotta do it, A. You said you were going to – '

'Don't *you* start.'

'Eh?'

'What is it to everyone who my parents are?' he

exploded. For weeks the *Dispatch*'s idiot features editor had been on his case. In fact, ever since he had made the misjudgement of admitting that Eva Coutts, one-time actress and supplier of gossip stories to the *Dispatch*, good-time girl and hostess of a party *at which Rosy Hope had turned up*, was his mother, people had been asking questions. He'd been positively plagued by requests for more family dirt. And not just from the women's magazines, but from Sunday supplements and even the upmarket broadsheets.

For as everyone knew, Anthony Sword was a man who revelled in other people's secrets, but had never blabbed about his own.

Framboise shrugged. 'Why do they want to know? Let's see . . . Score settling? Revenge? Divine justice? Do you want me to go on?'

'Is this what you wanted to tell me?'

She shook her head. 'No . . . but I had a call today. Some guy asking questions – about you. It ain't going to go away. You know the score.'

Indeed he did. As a man who had reached the stage of being more famous than most of the people he wrote about, Anthony Sword found himself in the intolerable position of having taught his tormentors everything they knew.

'I can see how it's screwing you up,' she said. 'The biggest story of your life, A . . . who is your father, who are *you*?'

They locked glares across the table.

'But you just don't seem to want to know. And, you know what? Someone's going to get there before you.'

From anyone else, that would have provoked purple outrage. He settled for a stern glare. 'You tell him anything – this person asking questions?' he snarled.

'What do you think?'

His response was a grudging grunt. They left the subject hanging in the air, like a noose.

'What's the difference between famous and notorious?' she asked, after some minutes of a condemned woman's attempted conversational gambits.

Sword shifted in his seat. 'Are we back to Eva again?'

'Just asking.'

'Good, because . . .'

Framboise put her head on one side in a parody of coyness. 'Famous or notorious, which are you, A?'

'I could not possibly tell. I write about other people, never myself. I merely reflect society,' said Sword, intent on piloting the discussion away from dangerous waters. 'As far as I can see, these days everyone wants fame. The criminal, the stupid, the grasping: they all rush to claim their fifteen minutes without caring about the distinction. The way things are going, I myself am heading for the day when I find myself writing about second generation train robbers and bank fraudsters. Whole showbiz dynasties of serial killers releasing pop records and showing off their telegenic dentistry on my diary page . . .'

'I *would* say, come to America,' said Framboise gaily, 'but then, as you know, Americans have no sense of irony.'

'*Some* Americans,' said Sword, a fond swell of friendship reasserting itself. 'I count you practically an honourable Brit on that score.'

'You've led me astray.'

He waited for her to explain what this was all about, but she began an assault on the south face of her mountainous pizza.

A dangerous ooze of the blues came from the dance floor, where the saxophone player in her band had clung to his spot on the stage. The audience was visibly swooning to the spell as the sax man targeted a table of three women. Framboise followed his gaze and raised her thin, painted eyebrows.

'It works every time,' she confirmed.

Sword laughed. 'Practising unsafe sax.'

They were edging around the subject, whatever it was.

'So,' said Sword eventually.

'So,' said Framboise.

She gave it to him straight, then. 'I want to get married.'

6 | *Garden Rosy*

In the words of the song playing on the car radio, Rosy thought she'd try a little tenderness. A delicately scented lily, perhaps, or a trailing petunia might make up for the fact that it was nearly nine o'clock by the time she parked her Renault 5 in Flood Street on positively her last assignment of the day.

Monday late nights at The Chelsea Greenhouse were a mecca for the urban green wellie set.

At the age of twenty-six Rosy was beginning to feel as if she were getting too old for most of the vagaries of fashion. Her innate cynicism cut in whenever she wondered what she would look like in a seventies hip chick outfit, or whether the power of crystals could change her life. The only voguish enthusiasm she had caught – and this made her feel more ancient still – was for gardening.

It had begun when she was still on the Sword's Secrets column: in the early nineties there was no telling *who* you might see at The Chelsea Greenhouse. Or rather, there *was* the telling.

Over the months, Rosy had found the Marchioness of Weedon only too willing to tell all over the jasmine officinale about an affair with her husband's estate gardener, though that was as nothing compared to the frank admission by the Marquis over the begonias that he too had done more than gaze longingly at this horticultural youth. Then there was the confirmation in the clematis corner of the Larks-Henderson's separation, and the announcement by the lobelia trays of Emily Strong's short-lived engagement to a grandfather of rock. Whether cutting loose or settling down in SW Heaven, it was hardly considered to be serious without a trip to the local garden centre for a festive fuchsia or six.

The way the wind blew in fashionable circles was effectively confirmed by the reincarnation of the modish Earl of Trent as a plant salesman. From which high office, predictably enough, he had soon become Anthony Sword's Man Behind The Hybrid Roses.

Or, as Rosy thought of him, the Bedding Plant.

Rosy had reason to be grateful to the Earl of Trent, as well as to Sword. After all, Brett Trent's impromptu attempt to blast out his own brains with a duelling pistol at Ascot the previous year had been something of a lucky break for her. The appalling scene – staged at Sword's Ladies' Day picnic at the races while she had still been a novice on the column – had provided the material for her first full-page feature in the *Daily Dispatch*. She had succeeded, in effect, because he had failed. Which may or may not have had anything to do with the difficulty of actually locating any brains to blast out, as one unkind observer had noted.

Rosy chose to forget that he had brandished the gun uncomfortably close to her as the shocked racing party had set about disarming him.

The earl's heart, at least, was in the right place – more or less – and that, Rosy was sure, was the important thing. Besides, a reporter's life was supposed to be dangerous sometimes, wasn't it?

Even *she* could think of more dangerous assignments

than marching through the tender perennials to find the earl. The soft May night filtered through leaves which promised summer lushness to come. On the way she contemplated giving a home to some more nicotiana in her dusty window-box in Fulham – an arrangement they would have to share with night stock seedlings and a sickly miniature rose. She walked on through into the office.

'Darling! Have a drink!' The earl greeted her with an affectionate Sloane brush of the cheek. His dark hair frizzed as crisply as ever from his pony tail, but he no longer affected an ancestral pallor. His inbred cockroach face glowed with a health it had never previously managed, even when he had recreated himself as a top person's personal exercise trainer.

'Hi, Brett,' said Rosy. 'Couldn't keep away. And the pansies I got last week are flowering themselves silly already. How's it going?'

'Demand is *quite* enormous, and I had to get up at quarter to nine this morning,' he replied with a lizard lick of his sharp little teeth.

'Good grief,' Rosy couldn't imagine that, somehow.

'And I went to the most marvellous party last night!'

Now that was more like it. It was still hard to picture Brett Trent as a model of sober industry. 'Anywhere I might have had to go to once?' asked Rosy with a wry smile.

'Oh, far too trendy for you.' There was, she was grateful to note, a tease in his voice. 'The film crowd, that's where it's happening.'

'I'm sure.'

'It's true. No one's going to be interested in telling their friends' stories to Sword and boring old newspapers any more. You've gotta sell the film rights!'

'Hmm,' said Rosy dubiously.

'A really nice girl was there from the *Dispatch*, though.'

'Oh, yes?'

'Mmm. *Great* girl – really you know . . . WILD. Huge fun. Couldn't work out why I'd never met her before.'

'So – who was she?'

'Lulu . . . somebody. Wonderful glossy hair and tiny skirt. Do you know her?'

Rosy nodded.

'She didn't seem to know who you were,' said the earl artlessly.

'I didn't think she would,' said Rosy.

While the earl dealt with the sale of four terracotta urns – assuring the fretful purchaser that all were indeed naturally distressed, having been discovered only recently in a forgotten Tuscan garden and shipped to these northern shores – Rosy admired the passion flowers tumbling around the conservatory office. Unlikely, she thought, that she would ever be able to grow them herself, for many reasons. She might just manage the sturdy fronds of flat parsley behind them.

'So,' said the earl, loping back towards her.

'So . . . I was wondering whether you wouldn't be just the man to help me out.'

They exchanged smiles. She had used that intro more than once before.

'The New Exoticists,' said Rosy.

'I may well be.'

'I'm writing a piece about them, along the lines of "the new garden designers who create exotic settings for the famous to forget they live in England." You know, all fronds and steam and parrot colours and compelling scents.'

'Sounds like my bathroom.'

'Huh, well . . . you may have got yourself a picture in the paper, then.'

'Exposure, how lovely! Shall I be *in* the greenery?'

'I knew I could count on you,' said Rosy.

7 | *Later That Evening*

'You what?'

'Married,' said Framboise.

Sword's throat felt as if it had just dealt with a triple strength tandoori. 'You don't go and do that kind of thing with gay abandon,' he said weakly.

'Well, *you* don't let yourself do anything with gay abandon.'

'I shall forget you said that.'

'Hey,' she said, her forehead furrowing like moist ploughed earth. '*I* know that when you tell everyone you're going on a cruise, you don't necessarily mean a big boat on water.'

'I wish I'd never told you.' He'd always known secrets were better kept to oneself. His own, at least.

'You didn't have to *tell* me, shithead.'

Only Framboise could have got away with that.

'When I say I want to get married – what I mean is, I have to get married.'

Sword boggled. He surveyed the wreckage of an inadvisable supper on the table as if it were somehow to blame for what he was hearing. 'You're not – ?' He could hardly bring himself to contemplate.

'Not what?' she played him along in that way she had, batting her false eyelashes in Southern Belle parody.

'You know – I mean, it sounded . . .'

For a moment she stopped the game and let her bulbous, surprisingly blue eyes rebuff the thought. 'It would be possible, y'know. I'm not that old.' Now he had offended her. 'Anyway,' she went on, 'What's it to you? I'm not even saying I want any of that ol' magic, though it's possible you should never have taken me to see *Four Weddings and a Funeral*.'

His brain cranked round. 'You weren't thinking of me?'

'Hell, no.'

'I see.'

'Hey – you're my best buddy.'

'Sure.' He felt crushed, suddenly.

When he looked at her he couldn't work out what she was thinking. She took his hand and looked into his eyes.

'Have you ever thought I might have to justify my happy stay in London? Like with a residency Visa?' she asked with devil moons in her eyes.

They left Puccini's and walked slowly arm-in-arm down to the light and shadows of Trafalgar Square. Amid the tourists and teenagers and out-of-towners saying romantic goodbyes before they caught trains home from Charing Cross, they stopped by a fountain.

Sword stared at the pool and saw it as bathwater disappearing down the plughole. 'Why not me?' he asked eventually.

'Bad idea.'

It occurred to him that he'd taken it for granted that they were a couple, in their way. I want you to say it, he pleaded with his eyes.

'Oh, c'mon,' she said.

He said nothing.

Framboise's voice was soft but immovable. 'Like I said.

I don't want to ruin anything between us. What we have is based on free spirits.'

'You sound like an old hippie, he grumped finally.

'Hardly. Nothing further than the truth, in fact. This marriage would be like a business arrangement. You know what it's like at the moment. Even Broadway stars can't get over here to work unless there are reciprocal arrangements for some of your people to go play back there. And besides . . .' She looked at him tenderly. 'Never mix business and pleasure and all that.'

'There are honourable exceptions,' riposted Sword. He was appalled at how much he minded.

Framboise hoisted a shrug up to her great round face. 'It wouldn't be a good idea,' she murmured gently.

A searing thought occurred to Sword. 'If you were married I'd hardly be able to see you as I do now – you'd be drinking champagne in the bath with someone else for a start.' He fell back on their old metaphor for companionship in order to twist the knife.

What galled him most was the way it seemed to cut him more than her.

He returned alone to his fortress house in Highgate. It was here, in his Gothic folly, above the tangerine light of the city, that he knew all things were possible. That dramatic effects could be wrought from ordinary beginnings, if one only possessed imagination and resolve.

Its rich colours, mysterious recesses and sensuous floor coverings were a testament to one man's dedication to the art of high pastiche. The marble pillars were painstakingly painted drainpipes. The *trompe-l'œil* bookcases were finished with chicken wire. The elaborate cornicing was dragged polystyrene.

Sword lumbered down the deep red corridor to the

kitchen, breathing in the scent of lilies, following his nose through the transitional trail of ersatz opium pot pourri, to the lingering aromas of fresh herbs and spices.

He sat at the refectory table, tracing knife cuts in the wood with a thumbnail.

8 | *The Nice Girl*

The features department was staffed by two distinct types of woman writer, each specialising in their separate prose styles: the Nice Girl and the Confrontational Bitch. Rosy was pretty sure she fell into the first category, yet she was worldly enough these days to know that some of the stories she had been sent on – and the subsequent grubbing necessary to make a piece attractive to those fabled ABC1 tabloid readers – proved that there was no such distinction under the skin.

Never mind that it seemed so much more respectable than working at Gossip HQ. It was still the same game.

The worst part of it all, as far as Rosy was concerned, was that the internal gossip among so many women toiling together on this section of the paper invariably turned to the beauteous deputy diary editor, Jamie Raj. The reporter's mantra *Who*, *What*, *Where*, *When* and *How* took on an entirely lecherous meaning in these conversations, leaving only the *Why* a matter of speculation.

Rosy saw him constantly around the editorial floor, loitering elegantly by the women's page office and the coffee-machine nearest the latest attractive newsroom secretary.

Naturally, her own two-month liaison with him was not up for discussion.

When he said hello to her in the corridor, she felt sure he was sending her up.

The features editor was a rodent called John Lunt. Appointed two months previously, the man was already setting records for panicky indecision. The blame and brutalisation of his staff which inevitably followed was the most telling indicator of the extent to which he was out of his depth.

The woman deputy who had appointed Rosy had soon departed.

At the other side of the room, John Lunt and the beauty writer were now coming to blows with the No. 4 on the paper over the Spring Clean spread. The blackhead correspondent's seasonal pamphlet on behalf of mineral water and celery versus female facial imperfections had run into trouble.

'Too many sebaceous glands, not enough sex,' snarled executive fourth-in-command, bringing his power to bear on the rat. 'We need well-filled leotards and knowing smiles, not a zit-*fucking*-masterclass.'

Rosy shuffled the mess on her desk and considered the prevailing attitude at the *Dispatch* to women. What shocked her now was how little she was shocked.

She stood up awkwardly. It was time to leave.

She allowed herself five minutes to tart up in the Ladies' before meeting the diary crew down in the Scribblers Club, the basement bar known to the newspaper's hacks as The Annexe.

Anthony Sword's pragmatic manner was largely based on the useful self-knowledge of a man who has concluded that he will never be a great writer because he has never forgotten to stop work for lunch. His greatest talent, as Rosy well knew, was for lunchtimes of sublime ingenuity.

At Scribblers, however, he was as near to being on uncomplicated home territory as most people ever saw. When he took up the seat favoured in 'his' corner, the effect was that of a king on his throne.

Rosy felt absurdly flattered when he lumbered to his feet as she approached, and kissed her on the hand.

There was one greeting that wasn't so easy though.

Despite the elaborate show of politeness between her and Jamie, awkwardness prevailed. It had got so bad recently it seemed to have finished off any remnant of their previous friendship.

'Hi,' she said, dismayed at how flat she sounded. Then, for something to fill the uneasy space as she looked around: 'How's Pearson – is he coming?'

Sword threw out his arms in mock despair. 'Pearson has discovered an actress, you will be unsurprised to learn – this time called Amy Burton. He is devoting what declining energies he has to bolstering yet another hopeful theatrical career. Just don't even mention Pearson,' sighed Sword. 'Man's a fool. If I think about the ass, I'll sack him. Should've done so years ago.'

Rosy grinned. When her former boss was in this kind of good mood, there was nobody more entertaining. Her thoughts wandered off for a moment as she re-ran a few happy memories of her improbable first job in Fleet Street.

'Any chance *you* could get Features off my back?' She realised he was talking to her. 'It's all your fault, Rosy Hope,' Sword thundered, but ebulliently enough.

'Er . . . it is?'

'How are you getting on with that appalling little rat John Lunt?'

She smiled, but – diplomatically – not as widely as she felt at finding out what Sword thought of the features editor.

'What is it with Features? Everyone else can comprehend the simple premise that when I say no, I mean no.'

Rosy certainly could. 'They're not still on about doing you for the Happy Families slot?'

Sword nodded, with a snarl. 'Fathers and Sons. They must be bloody desperate. I tell you. Has the man no one else to hound?'

'Lunt?'

'Lunt,' he said, investing the features editor's name with an expletive quality from the depths of his beard. 'Man's a foaming madman. Is he off his trolley?'

No one denied it.

'It's simple enough to understand, one would have thought,' grumbled Sword. 'I write about *other* people; I do not speak about myself. Far less submit to the dead pen of Lunt, a man with all the glamour and excitement of a week-old Wonderloaf. What I want to know, is who's put him up to it?'

'I don't know,' mumbled Rosy. 'Although . . . he did ask me if I could . . . you know, . . . help out . . .'

'And have you?' growled Sword.

'Have I asked?' said Rosy indignantly.

Mercifully, the star columnist dropped it there.

Pearson and the column's ace *paparazzo* Keith 'The Beast' Silver arrived at last, with the person Rosy least wanted to see in tow. 'Hi-eee, everyone! Not too late, am I?' cried Lulu Bisset.

Rosy's heart plummeted. Of course, she should have known that Lulu would come along.

Lulu gabbled away. 'Only I was just getting into the

cab to come back – the wedding was lovely by the way, red dress on the Town Hall steps, are we in colour tomorrow? – when who should I meet but David and Serena! *Had* to stop.'

Lulu knew everyone in London, it seemed, and let it be known as often as possible. And Daddy knew the proprietor of the *Dispatch*, which made it all possible. It should have been nothing to Rosy – but it wasn't.

'If only I'd known you were writing about Tatjana Raphael, Rosy!' cried Lulu, turning on her.

It never ceased to amaze Rosy how many patronising vowel sounds the word 'only' could accommodate, given practice. She decided to say nothing.

Lulu didn't even look her way as she plonked herself down uninvited on the battered Chesterfield between Rosy and Jamie. 'Since I found out she knows Charles and JoJo, we've all become *suuuch* good friends,' Lulu went on, clearly unwilling to let it drop after she'd made her point.

Rosy pursed her lips and wrestled with an instinctive scowl. Jamie smiled at the girl appreciatively. The indiscriminating Lothario, thought Rosy.

The other girl tossed back glossy conker-coloured hair, ostentatiously crossed her unfairly good legs and reached for the Beast's cigarettes without asking. 'She didn't tell you about the fling she's having with the producer, and the appalling pass the theatre boss made at her last week? What a shame . . . although I'm surprised you didn't know – I mean e-e-everyone was talking about it last week at The Groucho . . .!'

Bitch, thought Rosy. And then she realised that what upset her most of all was that none of the others seemed to see what Lulu was like. She sought momentary solace in drink.

'In my old age,' said Sword, majestically changing the

subject, 'I shall open a restaurant for people with healthy appetites, and call it Chompx, with an x.'

'What news of Framboise?' asked Rosy brightly. 'Talking of food.'

'Delicious, as always,' said Sword. 'She was asking after you the other day – apparently she saw you across a crowded garden centre, pestering an earl.'

Rosy laughed. 'Nothing much more incriminating than stocking my window-boxes, if it was last week, I'm afraid. Why?' She wasn't giving anything away while Lulu was around.

'We may be planning a surprise assault on that front.'

'Oh, yes?'

'We thought we'd send Lulu in – as a storm trooper. Brett Trent is free again,' interjected Jamie.

Pearson tutted. 'We can't have that.'

'Free – but not exactly easy,' drawled Lulu.

'Try,' said Jamie. 'Lie back and think of Sword.'

I bet she would too, thought Rosy.

'Can't it be Matt Pyne?' pouted Lulu. 'I met a man who knows a PR girl who says the buzz is he's the next big thing.'

'That may be,' said Sword. 'But are we talking about his career?'

'That TV advert he did, in the swimming pool – he's got to get a big film sooner or later.'

'I met him at Mirabeau's the other week,' weighed in Jamie. 'He was standing at the bar, so I went up and said, "Right, first one to get the barman's attention gets to buy the drinks" – and then I just stood there. He seemed really chuffed to have won.'

'Boy's a prat,' agreed Pearson. 'All those young women. Wasted on him.'

Lulu shook her head. 'Matt Pyne is An Event. You'll see.'

'Poor Pearson,' said Sword. 'He is in a constant state of being overtaken by events.'

Rosy caught a glance between Jamie and Lulu she would rather not have seen.

She began to imagine them strutting out to evening jobs together – and then forced herself to stop. Jamie enraptured by Lulu's hidden shallows was a torture of the imagination she could do without.

9 | *Sword's Office*

Some days in Anthony Sword's domain, his schemes and stories were whipped up with the lightness and delicacy of a champagne sorbet. Other days, the complaints grossly outnumbered the secrets to expose and the gossip had all the consistency of grandma's potato cakes.

Today he was working himself up for a classic display of temperament.

The rival press offices of the Prince and Princess of Wales had exhausted all possibilities in the domestic squabbling line. Which left only one way to proceed – a staged *rapprochement* which was too tedious to contemplate.

The ex-Home Secretary Sir Philip Hawty was trying to plug his latest publicity gambit: a volume of memoirs.

The Earl of Trent sent word that his box of amaryllis was ready for collection, but otherwise there was not a hint of high tattle.

Sword hadn't even the heart for a go at the idiot Pierce of the *Post*.

He had taken up a belligerent afternoon position on his cream *chaise-longue* in front of the window. Above him swayed an office potted palm. Below, he could see pleasure boats and tugs chugging down the Thames. The master gossip pinpointed the tips of his shoes over the bulge of his stomach, then raised his chin to the ceiling. 'RIGHT – what have we GOT?' he bawled.

'Interesting developments in the literary world,' suggested Pearson. 'Bill Fitzwalter's had to give back the £20,000 advance for his book on *The Homeless World* because all he can show for it is two scrappy chapters and some very well-fed ex-tramps living in his Camden front garden.'

Jesus wept, thought Sword. 'A funny paragraph, if that,' he sneered, fixing his second in command with a saturnine stare.

Jamie had been out for a spirited session at The Traveller's Club with some strategically-placed old Oxford chums. He reeled off the results with his customary languid confidence: 'Divorce for the Salcombes and the Tarquin Tates. Affair with the jewellery networker for Curlew Trussock – Darlene's bonking the man with the water purifiers. Contract-terminating furies with the director for half the cast of *Basic Instinct – The Musical.* And Lord Kelforth's public indecency is coming up at Snaresbrook next week – his wife's chucked him out and he's set up home in the cleaner's cupboard at the House of Lords to avoid the publicity.'

Jamie did this, now and then, when an eruption of temper was clearly imminent, to keep Sword aware of his admirable abilities. Nor did Sword need to give him the satisfaction of praise for a job well done.

The gossip columnist turned on the final member of his reporting staff.

'Lulu?'

'We-ell, I've been working for *days* on the Lottie Landor story . . .'

'Which is?'

'She's got a lovely part in a new film.'

'No need to ask where *that* story came from then.'

'I'm sorry?'

'You don't spend *days* on an actress-gets-acting-job story. It's a top right picture, end of story.'

Lulu pouted defiantly. 'Well, if that bloody woman Eva Coutts would only get everything straight before she called in with the information, it might just be that simple – '

'Ahem,' interrupted Jamie. 'The Beast took a new picture of little Lottie looking most beguiling last night leaving Chelsea Harbour. Definitely worth using, I'd say – only it would have to be in the form of an illustrated Pierce attack.'

What a gentleman he was. Either that or his amenability was by way of workplace foreplay, thought Sword. 'Fine,' he grunted. 'But what about the JoJo Spute row over the nicked diamonds and the furniture restorer?'

'Well, it's a bit *awkward,*' said Lulu. 'She's a really good friend of mine, and I kind of gave her my complete assurances that I wouldn't do anything about that story.'

'Hell's teeth.'

'I have my standards,' said Lulu.

'And you're proud of that are you?' roared Sword. 'It's no good knowing people if you can't fucking do anything with them!'

She flinched but stared back. He read this as insubordination.

This time, he thought, the proprietor had a lot to answer for.

Later that afternoon Sword came across his girl reporter in a rage of self-righteous indignation on a telephone in the newsroom.

'I know, I know . . . I mean, I just don't know who he

thinks he is,' Lulu was fuming. 'It's bad enough in the mornings, but after lunch, the man is *seriously* impossible. It's quite uncalled for. I can't see how any civilised person can stand for it. In fact, I'm going to say something to my father. I've given Sword his chances, and now, I have to say, this is *it*.'

Sword approached. His feet were light with menace.

Then he let rip.

Across the vast newsroom hands stopped on computer terminals. Conversation withered. Papers rustled. And the sun went in as the air turned blue.

10 | *Rosy at Home*

The upstairs flat at 24 Endymion Road was a mess as usual. Somehow, Rosy had never got quite sick enough of Emma's terminal untidiness to move out of the clothes-heap and book-dump they shared in Fulham.

'The glorious thing about not working on the Diary anymore is that I've got my evenings back,' said Rosy, kicking the door closed behind her. She tossed the *Evening Standard* to her flatmate on the sofa. 'Not to mention my waist. All those endless drink and chat and canapé parties I had to go to . . . it's been ages since I could get into this skirt.'

Emma puffed out her cheeks in fellow feeling. 'Know what you mean.'

'Well, I see you've been busy again today,' said Rosy tartly, righting the spilled waste-paper basket with her foot. She surveyed the open drawer spilling out bright clutter, the dirty plates and discarded wrapping and offcuts of a bunch of flowers. She plucked two browning apple cores from the carpet.

True to form, Emma stretched out and ignored her. Having made her point, Rosy didn't want an argument either. She wanted to talk about Sword. Or rather, Jamie.

'How was he?' asked Emma, meaning Sword.

'Two and a bit bottles of claret – the rest of us were on

white – and it was views of Vesuvius in the newsroom by five-thirty.'

'Eh?'

'Volcanic eruptions of temper,' explained Rosy. 'Which can be very entertaining when it's nothing to do with you.' She tossed aside some volumes of abandoned Milton and George Herbert, and sat on the arm of a chair.

There were still double-parked books up every wall space of their tiny flat, but Emma was at last able to put some away. She had almost nailed her man – the poet Marvell – in that she had finally (nearly) finished her thesis. It was yet to be seen whether she would become Dr Emma Blackett, PhD on the strength of it. Until then – and Emma said she'd never heard of anyone with a social life who'd actually finished a thesis – she was doing what all nicely brought-up young women do in London while waiting for the real thing. She was dabbling in service.

'Hope he's calmed down by tomorrow – got some snippets from a rather good lunch today myself.'

Since their college days together, Emma had always been the friend who understood. Now, through her legions of well-connected friends, she was working part-time for a firm of party planners, and knew that parties were not always social events. She had passed on more stories to the Sword's Secrets page in past weeks than Rosy.

'Oh, he was right as rain by six. He's like a hurricane: he blows himself out.'

But Emma was already engrossed in the front page of the evening paper. The headline raged hysterically about the possibility that more Cabinet memoirs could – probably – rock the Government once again. 'I've always wanted to know,' she murmured. 'What *exactly* does it mean, "It was revealed today"?'

Rosy grinned. 'It means "We've only just found out." '

Emma snorted.

'Or in this case,' went on Rosy, ' "Sir Philip Hawty's PR machine has just cranked into first gear." It's all pathetic, if you ask me.'

Her friend raised her eyebrows.

'I met him at a party in East Sheen,' said Rosy.

Emma looked sceptical.

'I told you, at the time! I'd only just started on Sword's column. Don't look at me like that . . . it was *work*.'

That had been the night Rosy had determined to come face to face with Anthony Sword's dotty theatrical tipster. The reporters on the column spoke to Eva Coutts up to a dozen times a day when she rang in with stories about actors and actresses for the column – and they also knew how much money she made out of it – but no one had ever met her, it seemed. When Rosy had arrived at the party she'd been shocked to the core by the procession of media men in fishnet tights, the games of strip musical bumps, and the blatant use being made of the casting couch. Not as shocked, though, as when, some months later, the gossip columnist had suddenly revealed that Eva Coutts was his mother.

'Not going out tonight, then?' asked Emma.

'Nope.'

'I thought Tom was ever ready.'

The mention of Tom Matthews momentarily sapped her good mood. 'Which leads inexorably to guilt,' mumbled Rosy.

'He is still on the scene?'

'Yeah, yeah.'

'He's . . . *nice*,' said Emma.

'Nice? Of course he's nice. He's the nicest guy in the *Dispatch* newsroom. He's the chap with the winning smile they send out to all the difficult doorsteps.'

'Aaah, the perfect career couple . . .'

Rosy hurled a cushion. 'My mother likes him.'

'Uh-oh.'

It went without saying that Mrs Hope had been less than full of enthusiasm about the previous *Dispatch* man. 'He looks like a roué, dear,' she'd pronounced after the statutory ordeal-by-introduction, giving one of the special *tsks* she generally reserved for disappointing Tory behaviour and the woman down the road who would persist in posting Vote Labour stickers in her bay window. Rosy had to give her mother credit for perception, although roué was probably putting it too mildly.

Irritatingly, Emma read her mind. 'Seen Jamie lately?'

'Jamie thinks I'm an idiot,' said Rosy. 'The sad thing is, that he's probably right.'

Emma didn't try to persuade her otherwise.

'I saw him at lunchtime today, as a matter of fact.'

Her flatmate's interest pricked up.

'Only that vile girl Lulu was there too. Oh, I'm sure she's not vile, it's only me being awful. She's so attractive – that skin which might once have seen off a blemish in 1988, and those legs – I expect it's only because she makes me feel so inadequate.'

A humph from Emma. 'No, what rankles is that she's a boaster and bragger – and she's the kind of girl who has seventy-five best friends, all of whom she met last week. I think I might even have been one of them once, for about a fortnight.'

'You know,' said Rosy indignantly, 'she *actually* told me that the only journalism she'd done before she arrived at the *Dispatch* was a fashion spread for a student magazine at Oxford – where, no doubt, she fancied herself as Zuleika Dobson, like all the others. She made it quite plain that, in her opinion, only losers like me have to graft on local papers first.'

'You cordially dislike her,' shrugged Emma, getting into her stride now. 'But then, *you* are a nice person. Most people loathe her.'

11 | *A Shining Example*

As far as Anthony Sword was concerned, all was quiet on the East Sheen front. Eva Coutts, Top Contact of the diary page, was currently a shining example of what a mother should be. She was holding off the sex, rage and sin, in other words – at least in her own front room.

What she got up to on the telephone was another matter.

'Teeth are still me own, but truth to tell,' rasped Eva down the blower, 'I am no stranger to decay. The crowning glory is not what it was, but I've not looked back since that first teasy-weasy hairpiece *circa* 1967. Now tell me all about you, dear. Lovely-looking young girl like you must have a stash of fellas, eh? What name shall we put to it, then? Don't be shy now . . ." Eva scribbled. 'Lovely dear, lovely. Ooh, I did enjoy that bit of telly you did with that handsome chap – what's his name again? There wasn't anything going on as shouldn't be, was there? And anything strange or startling in the past that we'd do best to have out in the open before someone less scrupulous comes along and starts asking awkward questions?'

She eased the switch of a tape recorder with a practised thumb.

'No secrets. Always best, when you start in this game, dear. That's right.'

'It's blooming hard work and it doesn't get easier,' said Eva when the interruption was over. 'Though at least she rang me back, unlike some I could mention. Don't know who some of them think they are these days. When you think of all I've done for them in the past.'

Sword raised his palms in acknowledgement. It was Tuesday night, and he was ensconced in a soggy velveteen sofa at No 2 Fairlawn Avenue. For, as every publicity-conscious hostess in London knew, Anthony Sword never accepted invitations for Tuesdays.

Viewed from outside the East Sheen semi was a standard pebbledashed box with a flash of stained glass window to one side of the door. Inside, the house was cluttered with the sentimental artefacts from Eva's theatrical past. It was a bursting repository of torn posters, tatters of costume, battered lacy hats, sun-toasted telegrams, a faded Japanese screen with more exhausted old clothes slumped over the top, bouquets of dusty silk flowers and dim tassled lamps, all dominated by a Vaseline'd mirror.

And those words again. *Just who do you think you are?*

They were beginning to play on Anthony Sword's mind like a gathering of pecking birds on an old rhino.

'No long-service medals for what I do though, is there – nor any sniff of a nice cash bonus?' she added hopefully, patting newly permed grey hair.

'Don't push it.'

'I know I don't get out as much as I once did, but I tend to do better this way. Occasionally I'll sally forth in the old warpaint to see some other old actress who's insensible or in a coma, which gives me great satisfaction. But generally it's just me and Mae West and the old blower. Though the day they bring in them videophones is the day I shut my books for good, eh?'

Eva tickled Mae West as the cat settled into her plump lap.

Sword settled deeper into the old couch. If it was Tuesday evening, it was Eva's night. He left the *beau monde* in peace, and went home to his mother. Not that it had ever been an easy relationship; even now, after years of *rapprochement*, his feelings for her ranged from abject frustration to love, usually in that order.

He let her ramble on as she got up to wet the gin glasses once more. Very often he got the best stories of the week here. Eva was still the most formidable theatrical tipster in the business.

'I haven't heard much from little Lottie whats-er-name – was in that film with . . . ooh, you know the one, you've written about him – '

The best stories, if he could decode them, that was. 'Landor. Lottie Landor,' he said. 'I don't think we need bother ourselves too much there. A case of odious clutches, I'm afraid.'

'Eh?'

'Benedict Pierce. He seems to have some bonk of convenience going there.'

'With our Lottie?' snorted Eva. 'She was always such a *nice* girl.'

Sword drained his gin. 'No such thing as an innocent party.'

As you should know, he might have added, but he was too wise to bring all that up again.

'How's Framboise?' Eva asked, later.

'Now there's a question.'

'I'll get the bottle, moisten the glasses again,' said Eva. She shuffled back again with the Gordon's.

Sword braced himself. 'She's decided she wants to get married.' He put up his hand to stop her from saying anything – 'Not to me.' He noted with grim satisfaction how the old woman's face dropped. 'So she can stay here, in London,' he added. 'She says they're on to her already.'

'They?'

'The authorities . . . whatever.'

Eva fiddled disapprovingly with the strings of beads around her neck. 'Well, you and she – '

'She doesn't want me to,' he said, anticipating her comment.

'Ah, well. Maybe she'll come round, love.'

'I didn't say I wanted her to.'

Mercifully his mother, for once in her life, left it at that.

A slight tremor as Sword held up his glass was – he hoped – the only physical manifestation of the tension he felt.

Here he was sitting, apparently cosily, with the woman who could unlock the mystery and still he said nothing. He had been working up to this for months. This week he had an ultimatum: broach the subject or Framboise would do it for him.

The biter had been bitten, Sword realised. At last he wanted to hear the one story she had never been willing to tell him. For thirty years he had sublimated his desire to know; indeed he had dismissed it as of no consequence to the successfully self-invented man.

At nineteen he had walked out of a long-defunct school of performing arts in north London, dismissive words ringing in his ears. A stage career of stock parts, *at best*, Miss Betty La Valle had predicted. Wearing a suit swiped from Wardrobe, which even then strained over his squat form, he set off. By the time he reached Soho, he had become the first incarnation of Anthony Sword.

Anthony Sword, pompous young *bon vivant* in an eccentrically old-fashioned suit, took his place at a restaurant table. Three days later the old *Evening News* printed his review, sent on spec, and he was a newspaper food critic.

He grew in confidence.

He ate for London and for free.

He grew.

He dogged the steps of the rich and famous to their favoured tables, and noted how they dined. And who dined with whom.

And so his life began.

For thirty years that had been enough. Now, as he agonised over how he could come out with the question, he realised how much he needed to know.

Who am I to think I am?

Who is my father?

For as long as he could remember, Eva had told him, in the same words, 'I lost your father during the war.'

For as long as he had been aware that Eva was a woman of charades and secrets, he had suspected those words had Wildean overtones.

12 | *Following Sword*

Under the heading *SEXUALITY AMBIVALENT* was an exhausted scribble that Crighton recognised as one of his 'night after' scrawls. The file was full of them.

This entry detailed Anthony Sword's trail from Puccini's Restaurant, WC1, to Trafalgar Square, where he spent thirty minutes talking with the singer Framboise Duprée, a black American national, before leaving her at 11.43 p.m. He had proceeded to the Soho Brasserie, W1, and then on again for a scenic tour through several of the pink pound establishments of that area until, finally, he bellied up out of a camp casino and made his way home to Highgate, alone.

As far as Crighton was aware, the gossip columnist had had the opportunity to do nothing more than talk to a couple of strangers in zips and leather.

Crighton had been with him throughout.

Sword had visited the men's room only once, and naturally he had followed him there too.

It was almost – and Crighton had had ample time to consider this over a stream of designer beers – as if Sword himself were searching for something.

It might have been love, but it sure as anything didn't look like it from the way the columnist locked eyes with his bottles of red wine and barely even glanced over their shoulders.

The telephone rang and he answered.

'Crighton.'

'Hello. My name is Padget.'

'Ah, yes.'

'I'm at Victoria Station.'

'Good.'

'Where shall we meet? Shall I come to your office?'

'That wouldn't be wise. How about the park?'

'St James's Park?'

'Check.'

'Check?'

'That's OK. Now, do you know where the bandstand is?'

'I do.'

'The bandstand in half an hour, then,' said Crighton.

'How will I recognise you?'

'I am wearing a grey suit with a military tie.'

'Ah. Won't there be quite a few other people similarly dressed in that location?'

'That is exactly the point.'

'I see. Then, perhaps I should tell you that I am in a green raincoat with sturdy shoes. In deference to the occasion, I shall be carrying a rolled copy of the *Daily Dispatch*. Isn't that what people do in these circumstances?

'You may have seen too many films.'

Crighton walked past the entrance to the Passport Office on Petty France and turned down Queen Anne's Gate. He crossed Birdcage Walk and entered the park. Ignoring the metaphorical possibilities of several skids in the black messes left on the paths by the great Canadian geese invasion, he strode purposefully to the appointed place. To his left, as he crossed the main bridge over the lake, was the grey mausoleum of Buckingham Palace, to his right the gracious surges and swoops of governmental buildings above the trees.

Soggy pieces of bread, smeared with dirt and scorned by the duck's and swans, were drowning in the brown water by the bank.

The empty bandstand was a great canary cage on the green.

What better place for his little bird to sing?

The sturdy brown shoes stopped in his downcast field of vision some feet away. As he appraised his informant from the shoes up, he saw a cottage loaf of a woman in a belted raincoat. The newspaper was squashed under her arm. Her thin slit of a mouth was pursed under curranty eyes which darted in the course of her own inquiries. Grey wispy hair escaped from a green knitted hat which matched the coat.

Around them the grass whispered with discarded food wrappings.

'Have you the time?' she asked, matter-of-fact.

'Mrs Padget?'

They acknowledged each other with a perfunctory handshake.

'Do you have it?' asked Crighton.

She gave him a crisp envelope. It was unsealed.

'May I?'

She nodded permission, and he slipped it open. The black and white photograph had worn to felt at each corner.

'It's them?'

'Yes. Taken during the war. Look at his uniform.'

'There is quite a resemblance.'

The woman sniffed a certain forced agreement.

'Is there anything else you have to tell me?'

She gazed past him towards a group of lunchtime picnickers. From the rear, the occupied deckchairs looked like bulging striped shopping bags. 'It is thought,' she said, carefully, 'that if . . . they . . . had known how long this would take, they might have taken more direct . . . action.'

'I am well aware of that.'

'I was told to tell you that you must try harder with the woman.'

Crighton sighed. 'I want to wait.'

'Meaning you have got no further.'

'It's not that simple. This is a matter which requires the utmost delicacy at all times – especially in view of the . . . public image. The publicity is not encouraging.'

'Mr Crighton, the point of this inquiry is that we are quite willing not to judge a book by its cover. In other words, we are talking about . . . the story behind the story. That is what we need,' she said, with a sniff. 'For good or bad.'

When he returned to his grey office, the voice on the answering machine gave him what he needed to know. On standard issue notepaper, Crighton scrawled the name Rosy Hope and made a note of the address: 24c Endymion Road, London SW6.

He reached for the A-Z, and checked.

He could walk it from Fulham Broadway.

13 | *Girls' Night Out*

Dark shadows under the eyes were caused by lack of oxygen to the skin, according to the beauty editor's special in the *Daily Dispatch* the next morning. Rosy peered into the mirror over the mantelpiece and breathed deeply. Again and again she filled her lungs with air and slowly let it out. No improvement. If anything, the bags were worse and her face was slightly redder.

'I can't see how anyone can keep breathing like this and still live a full life,' she said to Emma when her flatmate strolled into the sitting room in a dressing-gown, streaked with make-up.

'Sorry?' Emma swigged straight from a litre carton of orange juice.

'There's an article here by the Blackhead Correspondent: "Face Up To Life – Stimulate your facial muscles to glow with health and happiness." '

'Oh yeah?' retorted Emma, unimpressed.

'You have to breathe deeply and then pull faces to tighten up all the vital muscles.' Rosy gargoyled at the mirror.

'Dangerous,' said Emma. 'You'll never get him back like that.'

That evening Rosy returned from a fruitless day, spent

telephone-chasing a Hollywood-star-turned-Montana-recluse who emerged only every five years. To make up for his predictable lack of interest in an interview with one Rosy Hope of the *Daily Dispatch* of London, she bought three pounds of apples on Fulham Broadway on the way home, along with some caffeine-free blackcurrant and rose-hip tea, soya milk, evening primrose oil capsules, and unsweetened muesli.

This was definitely *it*. Time to lose pounds and get a life.

The worst turn Jamie Raj had done her, did he but know it – and Rosy agonised that he might – was that he had spoiled her for anyone else on the paper.

Under normal circumstances Nice Tom Matthews might have been just the guy to console her. He had arrived at the *Dispatch* via the *Yorkshire Post*, an altogether more impressive debut than Rosy's own start on a south London weekly. He was pleasant-looking, with light brown hair and alert brown eyes; medium tall, medium build, medium attractive. After the exotic extremes of Jamie Raj, that made three mediums distinctly in his favour. Other women didn't throw themselves indiscriminately at Tom's sculpted beauty – they actually had to talk to him to find out how nice he was.

Unlike during her brief time with Jamie, she found she didn't mind in the least when Tom told her he was working that night. For one thing she could trust him implicitly, and for another, she didn't want to spend every spare minute in his company. Dinners and films, when they could, were fine by her; yet she sensed his hurt doing battle with his patience.

They had met in the reference library. Didn't *that* just sum it up.

At nights sometimes she could still feel the floor-plummeting agony of walking into a party to find Jamie

Raj oblivious to everything in the crowded room but his passionate entanglement with a well-connected blonde. It wasn't the half-heartedness of his excuses afterwards that had been so mortifying.

It was that she'd been stupid enough to think she might be different.

'Sleeping with someone doesn't always count,' asserted Emma with her usual confidence as they got ready for a girls' night out.

'That's a new one on me,' said Rosy, summarily rejecting a pair of black leather jeans. Ditto a pair of flappy palazzo pants. Outside the window of their sitting room the darkening evening hung sticky and stagnant.

'There are all sorts of reasons to modify the total – depending on who wants to know, and why,' went on Emma.

And there were almost certainly those who wouldn't be able to give a precise total due to losing count, mused Rosy. Inevitably, Jamie Raj was on her mind.

She pulled herself together. 'OK, then. Give me examples of who wouldn't count.'

'A love scene on camera. A film producer to get the part. A kidnapper – '

'A *kidnapper*?'

'A war hero, then.'

Rosy cocked her head disbelievingly. 'You're not thinking about that chap in the Blues and Royals? As I recall, you saw him in Hyde Park and practically threw yourself under his horse.'

Emma was shaking her red curls. 'In retrospect,' she said, with dignity, 'that was patriotism.'

'That architecture student, then.'

'Strictly educational,' said Emma.

'The fitness instructor?'

'His . . . that was curiosity.'

Rosy laughed. 'So how many would you admit to?'

'As I say. Depends who's asking and why.'

'OK, let's say someone you think you could get serious about, but who doesn't know you well enough yet not to let it matter.'

'It always matters.'

Rosy acknowledged as much.

'To someone serious – five or six,' Emma went on. 'That's about right.'

'As few as that? *These* days?'

'Old attitudes die hard. Whatever men say, they still want a near-virgin. Why are you looking at me like that?'

Rosy shrugged, then smiled shamefaced, feeling herself redden. 'For once in my life, I could be the genuine article.'

After a few jars with the girls in the Slug and Lettuce, The Fridge was full. Heaving with acid jazz, bodies and sweat, the Brixton club was the inside of an ant hill. The dancers seemed so *workmanlike.*

'E' may have set the white man free, but he was everywhere in chains on the stage. Four half-naked bondage boys were offering baby oil to the dancers below – followed by their glistening muscles for massage.

Rosy aquaplaned across the wet floor.

'Aldooto watray,' yelled Emma.

'WHAT??' screamed Rosy. The beat was deafening. Much, much louder than when Rosy last went to a club.

'I told you to wear trainers!' shouted Emma, pulling her closer.

Emma was dressed for action in tiny shorts over thick tights, and a cropped tie top uncannily similar to the one Rosy could remember proudly parading as a six-year-old.

Rosy jiggled self-consciously on the feral dance-floor. Not only that, but she seemed to be expected to do it all on mineral water. Drugs, as far as she was concerned, had never been an option.

She felt about fifty-three.

At three in the morning Annie said, 'I'm getting tired of this.'

Rosy nodded her head in abject relief. She had made it.

'Let's liven up somewhere else,' said Emma.

Somewhere else turned out to be an all-night coffee bar in a side street off New Covent Garden market. Already it looked as if fruit and veg buyers and suppliers were gathering to start their day. Through the friendly fug, they lent an air of reassuring normality.

'So?' asked Emma.

'I thought it was bizarre,' said Rosy, stirring brown sludge in an Italian cup. 'All those glazed eyes and mindless jerks.'

'The dancing or the dancers?'

'Well, both frankly. I mean, when I was seventeen and having a good time, I was out of my box on Liebfraumilch and uncontrollable friendliness – not looming up at people with an other-worldly stare.'

Emma shrugged.

'I hadn't realised how long it's been since I was a student. How much *older* I feel,' said Rosy. And, she might have added, *wiser*, since her surprising metamorphosis into a Media Career Person.

Sophie raised her eyes. 'You're not old.'

'Obviously not, in years,' said Rosy.

'Ehem,' said Jane. 'At the risk of being controversial, I'll admit to thirty.'

'You know,' said Rosy, 'I'd wondered for ages who actually wore Lycra flares and tops like old bathmats and silver trainers. And there it all was. The reason for it all – and I feel no part of it.'

A frown from Emma. 'You've lost me.'

Rosy looked to Jane.

'Take platform shoes,' said Jane. 'To me, they'll never be anything but Be-It-On-Your-Own-Head shoes, said with a sharp intake of breath.'

'Sorry?'

'I begged and pleaded for a pair of platforms when I was ten years old – shoes of Elton John-like proportions. My mother gave in eventually after weeks of sulks and tantrums. They were quite appalling, but I wore them with pride. No, come to think of it, I wore them . . . with *Pop Sox*.'

'Original platforms!' breathed Emma, with mock-heroic emphasis.

'The original cringe,' said Jane. 'I can't look at the family photograph album for 1975, it's too galling.'

They dissolved into laughter.

'You see our point,' said Rosy.

Emma conceded, but sarcastically. 'It's been a Girls' Fright Out.'

14 | *Benedict Forks It Over*

Whenever anyone outside the business talked of the rivalry between Anthony Sword and Benedict Pierce, the *Daily Post*'s man-in-the-know (supposedly) habitually brushed it aside as a long-standing joke.

Now Benedict wasn't so sure.

He was beginning to take the cross-paper insults extremely seriously. Which was one of the reasons he had mixed feelings about the Marquis and Marchioness of Weedon's triangular affair with their estate gardener. He was nearly there with the confessions needed to write the story, but it had been common knowledge among certain circles for so long that it had probably become one of those revelations it was more dignified not to print.

Should he do so, he could fully expect the full ridicule of Sword.

If he didn't watch it, he would soon have the full round stomach of Sword too. Extracting information from anyone who might really have something to tell him invariably involved a large meal somewhere along the line.

He'd had breakfast with an American movie agent who was promising exclusive access to Robert Arden, the reclusive Hollywood actor who emerged from Montana once every five years to make a film and then to collect the subsequent Oscar.

Of course an interview with an idol was a big deal. But he knew he could do better. Benedict's devotional instincts had long veered from idolatry to a kind of homespun plutolatry. The worship of wealth, he found, was a much more reliable source of succour.

An Arden interview would get him to Cannes for the *Daily Post*. And once he was there, Benedict would be selling his own film project, built around all the important factors: Names, Fame and Blame. The only factors that mattered in a world obsessed with true revelations. It would be . . . the Chelsea Set meets *Four Weddings and a Funeral,* starring the subjects themselves. Their country estates. Their cars. Their friends. It would be *Ciao*! magazine in living, breathing pictures!

And it would bury Anthony Sword.

Why, he might even be tempted to include a highly unflattering portrait of the buffoon in his movie. Splice in real footage. Show the man up for what he was: a posturing nonentity. The exciting possibility of revealing some unsavoury detail of Sword's dubious provenance spurred Benedict towards his lunch with Sir Philip Hawty.

It was one of those occasions when Benedict was torn between wanting to be seen in an impressive venue and keeping the meeting relatively discreet. In the end he settled for Simpson's on the Strand.

He gave the former Home Secretary what he hoped was an obvious enough meaningful look. It had become a journalistic commonplace to say that Sir Philip Hawty's achievements – political and otherwise – had been glossed by disaster.

'If I'm going to give you any publicity for these

memoirs of yours, then I'm going to need something by way of additional information, Sir Philip. Off the record, naturally.'

'It's come to something when the hacks want something below the line,' said Hawty with good-natured pomposity.

Benedict stared him down.

'So what kind of information did you have in mind?'

Benedict opened fire as casually as he could. 'At least you haven't succumbed to the This is My Fabulous Life syndrome.'

'Meaning?'

'All unsightly mistakes and ex-lovers expunged.'

'Have to give you chaps something to get your teeth into.'

'Indeed,' said Benedict. 'I have a particular interest in your mention of a certain Eva Coutts.'

He studied the old Tory carefully for a reaction. There was not a silver hair unglued. Not a flitter on the fading-matinée-idol face.

Hawty shook out his napkin dismissively. 'I hardly mention her. She happened to be the hostess of a couple of parties where I met other people. Can't see what the interest is there.'

'I am *very* interested.'

His prey opened the menu with singular calm and gave a practised impression of a man more interested in choosing his food than discussing a mysterious past liaison with a Fleet Street gossip columnist.

'You still keep in touch with her, I take it.'

Hawty looked up blithely. 'I really can't recall when I last had anything to do with the woman.'

'Perhaps I could remind you, in that case,' said Benedict with a slow smile as he produced a brown envelope of party pictures from beneath the table.

* * *

His third restaurant meal of the day was at The Belvedere in Holland Park.

'Hair is relaxed, except on Saturdays,' *ES magazine* had decreed of this establishment. Benedict Pierce, a man who was never relaxed about his shining blond horns of hair under any circumstances, had finally managed to secure a coveted terrace table there.

Breakfast and lunch had been so successful, he was on a high. With any luck, his good run would hold for dinner.

Lord Holland's former stable block was a mecca for habitués of Tramp on a warm, unseasonably sultry night when only suburbanites who had planned their evening long in advance were in the capital's nightclubs. Outside, Ferraris and Bentleys jostled for space.

Benedict drove up smoothly to join them. He had wangled an extra few days with the new Aston Martin in exchange for writing an additional piece for the *Prattler* and wasn't going to waste it on a place where the cars didn't make an entrance. He took his time locking the Zagato, smoothed his hair once again and ambled in.

He acknowledged familiar faces as he made his way upstairs, and stood, just long enough to be noticed by everyone, on the entrance edge of the terrace.

'Now I know it's almost summer,' murmured Benedict to one of the nation's best-known glitz opera stars and her gleaming toyboy. He nodded down to the garden where George Hamilton was being served champagne while topping up his permatan with the last rays of UV.

He looked back from that reassuring scene just as a head-turning woman in an exceedingly short skirt wove her way through the tables. Benedict's guest had arrived.

'Lulu, darling!' he greeted her.

15 | *Sword's Day Out*

'So,' said Framboise, fixing him to the bathmat with the steel in her voice, 'what did you say to her?'

Sword let out a long, deflationary breath. Trickles of water wormed their way down his battleship of a body as he paused in the final stages of his morning ablutions to answer the bathroom telephone.

'You did do it, didn't you?'

Silence. And drips.

Of all the distinctive rooms in his opulently decorated house, this bathroom was the seat of his *folie de grandeur*. Extravagantly modelled on Mad King Ludwig of Bavaria's Linderhof grotto, its finest feature was a great gilded conch at the head of the vast bath. As the gossip columnist wallowed in his pool, he would soak to purposeful blasts of Wagner pumping through speakers sunk in two stone urns.

He raised his eyes to the midnight blue ceiling painted with gold stars. 'I tried.'

'I see,' said Framboise. 'I go away for two days and you think that lets you off the hook.'

He wasn't going to ask her where she'd been.

'It's not for *me* that I want you to do this,' she sighed. 'She's not the easiest person. Straight answers have never been Eva's forte.'

'Like mother, like son.' Another pause. 'You did talk about it, though? A little, at least?'

'I – as much as I could.'

'And?'

Sword gave a heartfelt sigh of anguish. 'Framboise, I don't think she knows herself who my father was!'

In a burst of the perceptive solicitude which made him love her so much, Framboise changed the subject and enticed him to spend the day with her. 'I gotta go out of London. To Kent – where *is* Kent?' she told him. She had been asked to lunch by Lord Spelbridge, a widower whose misty memories of love had been revived by her much-admired Cole Porter night at Puccini's. Or so she told Sword.

'I suppose I could come,' said Sword, without much conviction. 'Maybe a day in the country would do me good.' If he was honest, the prospect of the good Lord's well-regarded vineyards might have provided a spur.

'Great!' said Framboise, proving how business-like she could be when moved. 'Then, if you don't mind, you can drive Miss Daisy. If there's one thing I can't deal with in this country, apart from the lack of sun, it's your toy trains.'

An hour later, he purred down the spitting gravel driveway from his house in the vintage cream Bentley he used for special occasions and was soon picking her up outside her flat in one of Islington's better Georgian terraces.

'That's more like it,' she said, settling in next to him. 'Hey – I hope you don't think I only asked you along for the ride – '

Sword gave her a mock scowl. 'Yes, Milady,' he intoned.

'Aw, c'mon. I called His Lordship and he says he's

looking forward to meeting you. Let's go, let's have a good time, OK?' she urged. 'D'ya notice my dress, by the way?'

'One could hardly fail to,' he said, surveying the riot of red blooms and greenery which covered her.

'I thought it was kinda the thing. I bought it to go to the Chelsea Flower Show.'

'Framboise, in that dress, you *are* the Chelsea Flower Show.'

She swiped the air playfully at him. He failed to react. 'Hey – what's going on here? You do want to go, don't you?'

He paused a moment, then gave in to her. 'Ye-es. But afterwards, there's . . . somewhere I want to look in on.'

Acid green spring had frothed up like bubble bath after one of the wettest Aprils on record. Every plant strained towards the light and stone walls bled purple and pink with aubretia.

The Bentley sliced solidly through the fragrant lushness, grinding dubiously a few times as it crested a winding hill, then surging down the other side with audible relief.

'This car gives good grunt,' admired Framboise.

'What a disgusting phrase. Where on earth did you pick that one up?'

'Just heard someone say that – dontcha think it's a great line?'

Sword grunted.

'My, my, not just the car.'

'And what is that supposed to mean?'

'Have you got a hangover?' she countered.

'These days it's the only way I know it's morning.'

After that they lapsed into a relatively companionable

silence, Framboise seeming to sense that his evening with Eva was not up for discussion again for a while.

As they bowled down the final hill under candelabra of pink horse chestnut and wild mauve rhododendron thrusting rampantly over the hedgerows, one of the most idyllic pastoral scenes of Kent unfolded beneath them. The garden of England worked its old magic, luring them helplessly into its sensuous trap.

Framboise caught her breath as Spelbridge Place was suddenly revealed below them through a frame of leaves. The ancient grey stone manor was flanked by a lake and a dark maze. Behind it, strings of vines clung to the upward slope of the next hill.

'It's the most beautiful house I've ever seen!' she sighed.

Despite his best efforts, Sword found his better instincts powerless in the face of a sudden onset of the furies. Of course, he was still fuming with Eva. But these present blues, he feared, had been prompted by the gradual realisation that their host's chivalry was nothing more than a good old-fashioned crush on his best friend.

Lord Spelbridge – seventy-five if he was a day – looked positively skittish as he led Framboise to the table and plied her with oysters and his own pink *methode champagnoise*.

By the end of what could have been a delightful luncheon, the fermentation taking place in Lord S's oak barrels had nothing on that going on in Sword's mind.

They adjourned to the winery.

'Do you want to spit?' The baron asked him. He had ranged a row of bottles for tasting in a cool cellar lined with barrels.

'You noticed,' said Framboise sarcastically in Sword's direction.

'I'm sorry?' The jolly aristocrat was not with her.

'He's working himself up for a rage over something,' noted Framboise.

Sword stood, a little apart, rinsing his mouth with a perky little Müller-Thurgau. Framboise burbled her praise for the wine, for the gardens, for the house, for the landscape. 'It's so quiet here!'

'It *was*,' snorted Sword.

She turned to face him, forehead furrowed. 'What's eating you, honey*bunch*?

16 | *A Private Number*

Rosy gave a great yawn, as if she were limbering up to swallow a melon. Her reclusive Hollywood star was firmly staying that way, perfectly oblivious to the features editor's now-obsessive desperation for Rosy to prise him out.

'You're *who*, from *where*?' whined a nasal West Coast voice when she'd finally got past the flunkeys and managed to talk to his agent's assistant's secretary.

There was nothing for it but to mine a private number for the great loner from the Diary telephone book. If Anthony Sword didn't have a hot line to Robert Arden's hideaway, no one in England did.

Either that worked, or the features editor was putting her on the next flight to the South of France to start reconnaissance for an ambush operation. Word had been overheard at The Ivy that the greatest living Hollywood recluse was planning to jet into the Cannes Film Festival for a two-hour heavy-security visit.

The way Rosy felt after only three hours' sleep, she couldn't imagine how she would summon up the energy to make the journey back from EC4 to her own bed in Fulham, let alone anything more ambitious.

In Sword's office, Rosy was highly relieved to find that

lunch had started early – except for Lulu, that was. She was shrieking into her phone – on hands-off mode – as she paced around her desk rolling up the waistband of her skirt. Rosy couldn't help but take Lulu's great legs as a personal affront.

She gave the other girl a friendly smile, and tried to mean it.

Lulu flapped a hand at her for quiet, as if Rosy – if not the whole newspaper – couldn't hear she was in urgent discussion with a friend over who would be at Sarah and Daniel's on Friday.

'Hi, Tina!' mouthed Rosy as she rounded the corner where the secretary sat. She motioned to the red volumes by Sword's vast mahogany desk.

Tina gave her a friendly wave to help herself. Minutes later, she realised that the big voice was booming in her direction.

'What are *you* doing in here, Rosy?'

'Oh, er . . . hello, Lulu. Just checking a few numbers that I didn't seem to have quite right.'

'I see.' Lulu tossed her mane.

Rosy carried on with her mission.

'Actually, Rosy, your name came up in conversation last night.'

Rosy looked up but affected disinterest. No doubt Lulu was going to tell her anyway.

'About the time Jamie ordered you out to Mirabeau's to get some nightclub stories and the only person you could find there to talk to was Benedict Pierce! You poor thing – what a hoot, though!'

That would be right, thought Rosy grimly. Trust Lulu Bisset to get on to what was perhaps Rosy's most embarrassing episode *ever*. No doubt the girl knew everything. No doubt it had come straight from Jamie. Rosy shrugged as nonchalantly as she knew how.

'Of course, your problem working for Sword was always that you didn't know anyone, wasn't it Rosy?'

'On the contrary,' snapped Rosy. 'That was my big advantage.' A fleeting cloud passed over Lulu's face. Rosy wasn't going to explain it to her.

'Is it just me?' Rosy asked Tina when the other girl had swept off in the direction of the picture desk.

The secretary pulled a face.

'What's Sword up to? I saw him looking very intent in the library this morning. He never usually goes through cuttings himself.'

'This and that. More of the other most probably.'

Rosy grinned. 'How *is* Framboise?'

'Wouldn't know,' said Tina. 'He keeps very quiet about her these days. Though that's probably a good sign.'

'You may be right. If she's in the Confidential file with Eva, then this could be serious. She's practically family,' hammed Rosy.

There had never, as far as Rosy knew, been the slightest mention of a father.

'You're not listening, are you?' said Tom Matthews, putting a hand tentatively on Rosy's bare arm.

'I am, I am. Go on.'

He looked doubtful.

'You were saying . . .' Rosy said valiantly. 'About the picture desk – '

'That was five minutes ago.'

'Ah.'

They were standing in the corridor outside the reference library. Rosy was clutching Robert Arden (in the form of his cuttings for the past ten years, that was) and Nice Tom Matthews was getting ready, from the look in his eyes, to clutch at straws.

'You've lost me.' He gave in. '*You* said you were up to

here with Hollywood stars and had to work tonight. I was only trying to come up with some suggestions so you'd be free to come out to dinner with me tonight.'

'I can't,' said Rosy with an exhausted grimace. 'They're sending me off to Cannes. Not even Sword's best numbers could do the trick.'

'Cannes? Has all that started already?'

'Next week. But we want to steal a march.'

March? Rosy felt the best she could offer was a feeble stagger. On the way back to the desk she'd coveted for so long in Features, she wondered what would happen if she said she couldn't go to France. It would probably mean she'd be out the door anyway – with her P45. The new features editor had just pulled off a masterstroke of brutality by reminding her that her six-month contract in his department would soon be up for renewal.

The immediate employment alternatives were not inspiring.

Freelancing? She'd be too depressed after blowing the glory of a *Dispatch* staff job.

Temping? She'd have to learn how to type with all fingers first.

Waitressing? There was that little bistro round the corner from her in Fulham, but could she keep smiling for long enough to urge the unpalatable towards the unappetising?

There wasn't much alternative but to go home and pack.

She didn't escape the *Dispatch* building before one more upsetting scene, though.

'Hey, Rosy!'

She turned to see Jamie Raj sauntering up the corridor towards her.

'I hear you're off to take on the world of films.'

'News spreads fast,' said Rosy. It really wasn't the time to have to deal with those amber eyes. But here they were, sweeping over her with that disconcerting look of private amusement.

'If you want any help, while you're out there – '

'Funny,' said Rosy, dully. 'That's what someone else has just said.'

She couldn't read the change in his expression. 'I've been down there a couple of times to do a Cannes column,' he said. 'It's an absolute madhouse. All I'm saying is . . . if you need any contacts, or help this end, don't hesitate to call, all right?'

Since when had Jamie come over all solicitous about her? 'Thanks,' she managed to say, lamely.

'And Rosy – any stories or interviews you get that you can't use, you will pass them back here, won't you? Liz Hurley's supposed to be arriving there any day now, and I'm interested in – '

So that was Jamie's game. 'You would be,' sniped Rosy.

He looked surprised at her tone.

'Likely – I *don't* think – that I'm going to waste my time setting you up with the actress of the moment when I've got more than enough on my plate already!'

'You don't get it, do you, Rosy?'

A pause.

'If I had an interview lined up, I could come down and be there to give you a hand,' went on Jamie. 'No doubt I could knock off a film festival column without too much trouble.'

She stared, unsure what to make of that and stung by his smooth confidence.

'I fancy myself in director's breeches with a crop.' He grinned wickedly.

Rosy winced. 'You fancy yourself, full stop.'

17 | *Ale and Arty*

'My mother claims she entertained the troops,' said Sword. 'We are not, I fear, talking Vera Lynn here.'

'She's quite a woman,' agreed Framboise cautiously. She gave a wanton look in the direction of a cream tea shoppe called Quaintways as the Bentley bowled through a picture-postcard Kentish village.

The war, Sword had always suspected, had been used by millions as a convenient cover for rampant indiscretion. For years he himself had decided to leave it at that – if only to spare himself the turmoil.

Framboise, as he'd known she would, wanted all the details of his last conversation with Eva. There wasn't much he could tell her.

'My mother, the other night, was . . . *herself*,' said Sword. 'The Mistress of Discretion when it suits her.'

His companion sympathised by placing a warm doughy hand on his.

'I mean – ' he went on, 'Do you ever have a vision of someone making a film of your life? Well, the way I see it, if this were in the sixties, Eva would have been played by Bette Davis, you know what I mean?'

Framboise chortled, but gently. 'A cantankerous old biddy persecuting her only surviving son, that kinda thing?'

'Something like that.'

'Heck. I'm sorry, A. I shouldn't have gone on at you – '

'It needed to be said.'

She said nothing to that.

Caught by the charm of the slanting evening sun, they stopped at an ivy-covered country pub on the way back to the metropolis. It was called The Porcupine.

'Just the place for a prickly customer,' noted Sword.

'And I bet I can find exactly the right thing for you inside, too,' grinned Framboise, disappearing into the beamed darkness of the inn before he could stop her. She emerged minutes later to join him at a wooden garden table with two pints of beer. 'Old Codgers Ale,' she told him triumphantly. 'Could've been named for you. Cheers!'

He smiled weakly. That made him wonder again. 'So. What were you up to these last few days?'

'So that's what's been on your mind,' said Framboise.

'I only asked.'

'I haven't been anywhere near a register office, if that's what you think.'

'Huh.'

'Huh? What's that supposed to mean?'

'If you don't know, I can't tell you,' mumbled Sword.

'Oh, great. So we're going to do childish here. C'mon, A!'

He said nothing. It took several gulps of ale before he loosened the grip of the green-eyed monster enough to emit a strangled, 'Sorry'.

'Accepted,' said Framboise. 'Now tell me what you think about Lord S – and is there a Ladyship S anywhere around?'

'Lord Spelbridge?' started Sword before he could check

himself. 'He is a decent wine-making old widower, and you can't be thinking – ?'

'Can't you think about anything else?'

Sword appealed for pax.

'Thank you,' said Framboise. 'He wanted to talk about me doing a concert – in his garden this summer, OK? Nothing more personal than that.'

'One of your nightingale sorties?' He recalled, trying to ignore an unwelcome pang in his chest, how she had first sung for him outside in the garden of the Grasslands Hall health hydro.

'Sure. On a strictly professional basis. Any objections?'

There was nothing he could say to that.

Sword took a long time appraising the outside of the pub as they stood up reluctantly to leave.

'Watched any good pubs lately?' asked Framboise, after some minutes of his mute survey.

'Hmmm.'

'I was going to spare you my Inn crowd joke.'

'Might be best,' he answered distractedly.

A long moment passed as his stare fastened on the upstairs windows frilled with creeper and ivy and tried to determine their true shape under the greenery. Then he returned his gaze to the porticoed doorway which had first lured him to stop.

'A . . .?'

'Sorry?'

Framboise was interested now. 'This one of your old haunts?'

'I'm not sure.'

Then he decided, for now at least, he could confide in her. 'Take a look at this,' he said, drawing an old photograph out of his breast pocket.

She took it wordlessly.

A pause.

'It's Eva.'

'Thank you for that brilliant contribution,' said Sword, temper sparking.

'Who's the soldier?'

A leaden stare from Sword. 'Look at the building behind her.'

Framboise did. 'I think it could be,' she said slowly, staring at the pub, then back at the photo. 'The creeper covers a lot more now, but . . .' Then she seemed to realise. 'So this is the somewhere you said you might drop in on.'

'You're being far too English. This, according to the note,' he gestured at the picture he held, 'could lead me to my father.'

'Note? What note?'

'Someone – I don't know who – has been sending me notes and scraps . . . about fathers and sons.'

'But who would do that?'

'I don't know,' said Sword. 'I really don't know.'

18 | *Photographic Evidence*

Now Benedict Pierce had proof positive that something was wrong: Anthony Sword was smiling at him.

The quaff and trough crowd had descended on the Palm Club for its celebrity launch night. A famous cabaret spot back in the thirties, the Piccadilly venue had recently re-emerged as a smart meeting place for the nineties.

Or so its PR teams were hell-bent on proving.

The revitalised cream and chrome decor swooped and whirled around the rooms like Ginger Rogers and Fred Astaire in a Busby Berkeley production.

Benedict's partner, trussed up in a tiny boned black dress which might have seen service as a corset in a TV trollops-and-highwaymen drama, was Lottie Landor, glass in hand. Around them, the A and B-lists grazed: fashionable folk, their chroniclers, decorators and therapists.

It was bad enough being in such close proximity to Anthony Sword, hulking as he was like the Great Pyramid of Khufu over there with his cohorts. It was irritating beyond belief to see the shameless hordes of celebrity party-goers tripping over to chat to them. But his smile was far worse.

Benedict could afford to bare his teeth back.

Thanks to Lulu Bisset, parked as she was in her useful lay-by on the information highway, he knew the truth now about Eva Coutts and her monstrous son.

And he was a man with a plan.

The shimmering gold dress clung to Emily Strong with barely more success than the dimpled West End starlet had in hanging on to her precarious celebrity.

Now Benedict saw the extent of her desperation: she had come on the arm of the old political opportunist Sir Philip Hawty. He watched as the pair beamed a sickly smile for the photographer from *Ciao*! and scanned the room for a likely hack to make a story of their entirely bogus togetherness.

Sir Philip's face froze as he saw Benedict, but he gathered himself and came over alone.

'You're still talking to me, then,' said Benedict.

Sir Philip gave a twitch of a sunken cheek. 'I'm not sure exactly what you're trying to pin on me, old boy, but let me make the situation absolutely clear. I'm telling you again categorically that my intimate acquaintanceship with Eva Coutts lasted for two weeks in 1944. Only.'

'Not according to my sources – ' began Benedict slyly.

'Those photographs you produced were taken at that time – at a time during the war when all was danger and drama and confusion.'

'You were in your element then.'

Hawty ignored that. 'Normal standards of behaviour simply did not apply. Young men preparing to be sent overseas to fight for freedom and their lives took what comfort they could.'

Benedict conceded the point.

'This . . . *outrageous* flight of fancy you have that my friendship with a pretty young actress in the darkest days of this country's history could have resulted in what you suggested is quite *unthinkable* . . .'

'The other photographs, however, were taken at a party last year,' said Benedict. 'At a secret venue in East Sheen.'

The senior Tory was perspiring under his thinning silver hair. His butterscotch complexion, so admired by the shire ladies, was quickly paling.

'So you cannot deny, Sir Philip, that you have had recent contact with the woman.'

'This is quite outrageous!'

'It would appear so,' said Benedict, feeling on top form. 'But so is the idea that you could have systematically lied since you entered Parliament thirty years ago . . . and then been so careless with the subsequent calculations when you came to write a volume of memoirs as to alert the enquiring reader.'

'Lied? About what, precisely?'

Benedict took longer than he needed to extract a cigarette from a silver case. 'Your age, Sir Philip. Like any sensitive actress, you lied about your age.'

'I, er – '

'You cannot tell me I am wrong,' observed Benedict, casually flicking open his cigarette lighter.

Hawty apparently could not. 'Besides,' he said, switching smoothly back now to the more dangerous subject, albeit with a murderous narrowing of the eyes, 'if your absurd theory were true, why would Eva Coutts never have told me there was a child?'

Benedict had never been one to ignore the obvious. 'She is waiting until the time is right,' he said. 'For *him*.'

Not much later, his rotund rival Sword raised his glass in mock-greeting as he passed them *en route* to a tray of more drinks and a plate of food. 'Do I hear the sweet cascade of beans being spilled?' he asked derisively.

'Louder than *you'll* wish,' smirked Benedict.

Sword was unbearably smug. 'Thirsty work, good gossip,' he said.

'It's good to see,' retorted Benedict, 'that you're still a glutton before punishment.'

'What *is* he up to?' Jamie followed Sword's gaze over the Palm Club crowd to Benedict Pierce and his tightly squeezed actress companion.

Sword hurled another devilish smile over at the party pair. Then he puffed a huge, disdainful breath. 'Let me tell you, his readers are suffering.'

'I hear he's off to Cannes next week with Lottie and her new dubious film,' said Jamie. 'European co-production – we all know what that means. Kit off in all languages and unlikely dubbing . . . and the lead's played by a large, silent Croat.'

But Sword was barely listening. He was too busy keeping tabs on Framboise as she worked her way around the pillared party room, constantly waylaid by her many new fans. She was roaring with laughter over something with the composer Curlew Trussock – far too eagerly for Sword's liking. According to the story in his own column that very morning, the much-married composer was dangerously near to being free from matrimony again.

Being a cold-blooded pragmatist himself, Sword found it hard to imagine the lack of those qualities in anyone else.

'I was thinking,' said Jamie casually. 'We haven't done a Cannes column for years.'

'Now there's a thought,' said Pearson, joining them with a Terry-Thomas leer.

Jamie silenced him with a firm look. 'A Cannes column. Shall we show Benedict how it's done?'

'Whatever,' said Sword.

From his vantage point, he could see Framboise – who tonight was a beacon in a glossy tomato-coloured wig – nodding enthusiastically to the millionaire musical man.

Several cocktails down the line, and with Framboise nowhere in sight, wasn't the best time for the Palm Club's chief public relations woman to accost him with her offer. Naturally, he sent her packing.

But the damage to Sword's equilibrium had been done.

He fulminated over her possession of the facts, and the pushy lateral thinking which had inspired her to do something with the date. He should never have allowed his name and details (such as he gave out) to appear in *Who's Who*.

'It was only an offer,' said Jamie, with merry puzzlement at the brooding reaction he had just witnessed.

'Bloody good offer,' chimed in Pearson, still incredulous. 'A huge staggering party awash with free drinks and promises. Mark the great occasion in style.'

Sword snarled. He had always hated birthdays.

There was no reason to suppose his fiftieth was any cause at all for celebration.

19 | *No Cannes Do*

Rosy's quest to find the current whereabouts of the reclusive film star Robert Arden had reached an impasse after a day and a half on the Côte D'Azur. Well, actually, *impasse* was a little optimistic. It implied she'd once had some good idea of the route to take.

As it was, she bowled along La Croisette under blue skies at Cannes knowing that this was the life. Or that it would be, if she could only bring off the impossible. Slumping down to earth under the realisation, she had the feeling she would rather be anywhere else than here. She hated herself for being so wet.

She was a seasoned professional now. Surely.

At noon she went into a Tabac and paid what seemed an extortionate number of francs for a copy of the *Daily Dispatch*. Banner headlines on the local newspapers screamed of a grisly bungled kidnap by gun-toting youths. Over a double espresso in a café down a side street, she searched for inspiration.

The Sword's Secrets page was a reassuring constant. Among the tales of high and low life, it carried the following piece of nonsense:

Is the party over – yet again – for embarrassing

> one-time top Tory Sir Philip Hawty? The champagne abruptly stopped flowing in the early hours of yesterday morning, when his unlikely date Emily Strong flounced out of a bash at the new Palm Club.
>
> Sometime West End success Emily, 25, daughter of Liberal peer Lord Strong, screamed at her elderly 'paramour': 'You snog like an old sheep!' before her gold Versace dress abandoned the unequal struggle to stay up.
>
> Jettisoning the creation for the cameras, she exited the revitalised Piccadilly venue into the night, pursued by a posse of over-excited publicists.
>
> As astonished guests rallied round a pallid Sir Philip he stuttered for a moment but recovered his wits in time to hijack the limelight to mention his pathetic memoirs.

Rosy could just imagine. At least it made her crack a smile. Since her arrival on the French Riviera there hadn't been much cause for that.

Her room in the Hotel du Jardin was a cramped garret. What had looked like a promising three-star exterior disintegrated inside into a grudge match of brown carpeting and creaking boards. By the time the unfortunate traveller reached the top floor, it was like being in another country.

The single bed would have been comfortable enough, if it hadn't been for the massive spring which surged up from the mattress into the small of her back. She could probably live with the wobbly leg on the scratched wooden table she was using as a desk – when she managed to find something less vital than her contacts book to use as a prop. And as for the rattling window, stuck closed with paint in all the wrong places . . .

There were chambermaids and kitchen staff in Cannes with better accommodation, of that she was certain.

She pondered morosely whether she could have upset the features secretary who had made the travel arrangements, or whether this was the editor's cunning plan to keep her out and about.

The guilty recollection that the *Daily Dispatch* was paying her a not insubstantial salary to lie on her wretched bed reading *Paris Match* in the middle of the afternoon sent Rosy scurrying out.

Either that, or the unending saga of Johnny et Sylvie *et maintenant tous les autres* in the magazine had worked its old magic on her powers of endurance.

The May sun was hotter than it was in London. Rosy's arms and face were already beginning to burn as she walked the smart white streets. There was no sense in retracing her steps that morning round all the huge palace hotels – the Carlton, the Majestic, the Martinez, the Gray d'Albion – searching for a lead.

The film set weren't due for days. There were conventions of dental technicians, and even a UFO-spotting group from Toulouse, but barely a sign yet of the movie industry's movers and shakers on their annual pilgrimage.

She had more coffee in a bar near a billboard where a poster was going up. She hung out long enough to see it revealed as an advertisement for an improbable film called *Surf Nazis Take A Bride*.

Rosy trudged on. In the boutiques the clothes were a rebuke to her sticky lack of chic, or so she felt in her creased blazer and chinos. From all directions, it seemed, perfectly groomed French women assailed her self-consciousness. They strolled confidently into the swankiest shops, walked tiny dogs, swayed along wrapped in those gilt chain belts you needed a twenty-inch waist to bring off.

Rosy melted a bit further into the pavement. The rue d'Antibes made her feel hot and sweaty and swollen with . . . *Englishness*.

20 | *Benedict and the Name-Droppers*

'It's a dangerous game, socialising,' said Benedict, rubbing his bruised skin, 'and I blame the blue-eyed blonde for starting this whole Thai kick boxing craze.'

He had sustained the blow during the course of a delicate line of questioning. The MP's mistress and charity ball organiser had claimed her foot slipped.

Lottie grinned. 'This film project you've got involved with . . . it's not going to turn into a martial arts film is it?' she asked, with a sly chop of the hand. 'Brett Trent *is* Bruce Lee . . .'

He raised his hands as if to say, *Who knows*?

They could hear Big Ben tolling nine o'clock as they arrived back at his red brick mansion flat in the locational limbo between Westminster and Victoria – although it was never Victoria in Benedict's mind. He shared his address, he liked to think, with a former Prime Minister and any number of high-ranking politicians and judges – although so far, it had to be said, they had proved less than free and frank, let alone neighbourly, about their private lives.

Lottie curled up on his sofa. 'You're definitely going to do it, then?'

He fussed with the mood lighting. 'No. I'm thinking about it. The book is due to be published next week.'

'Benedict . . . what do you know about the film industry?'

'I don't think that matters. My involvement would be more as a consultant. An orchestrator. The people who know about films are the ones who make films.'

'That's what I'm worried about,' said Lottie. 'That you might think that.'

He drew the curtains and did not reply.

'I think it would be a good idea for you to meet some people,' she said.

'Now?'

'No time like the present.'

Benedict sighed. It had been years since he'd acted on that sentiment.

Sure enough, it was film fun for beginners.

When they arrived, the low, functional room in a pub on Wardour Street was heaving with young-ish people in flying jackets and large boots. The uniform was black, with denim shirts, flying jackets and big boots. The conversation was name-swapping on a scale Benedict had not witnessed since a royal briefcase had gone missing, with the hack pack in hot pursuit.

'Second sound man. Timmy Mount.'

'Head gaffer. Denis Jones.'

'OK. *Rig Driver*. Pete Morland.'

'The film was a disaster anyway, mate. I mean, the sound was pretty good . . . but the lighting!'

'And the story!'

'I don't actually recall the story.'

'Hugo, can I introduce Benedict Pierce?' said Lottie. 'Benedict, Hugo is one of our up and coming directors.'

Benedict had never heard of either of the films she named.

They shook hands.

Lottie explained their mission.

'I have rarely heard such shameless name-dropping,' said Benedict drily. 'Which is saying something.'

Hugo flicked shoulder-length hair from his forehead. 'You gotta show you really know films. There is also the symbiotic relationship between fake friends and an intimate knowledge of the closing credits of *Withnail and I*.'

'I see.'

'Of course there are a lot of phonies who only know the obvious names. Like the Powell and Pressburger opus.'

'Oh?'

'You must know Powell and Pressburger. If you want to be in films, you have to think that they're the great forgotten English genii. Personally, I know the title and chronology of every Powell and Pressburger film, even though I found *The Red Shoes* ground-breaking but ultimately unconvincing and I've only seen half an hour of *Peeping Tom* which I thought was boring, primary and nostalgic.'

'I see,' said Benedict again, this time with even less conviction.

'The point of the deification is that everybody comes to respect how difficult it is to make films now, and that this is the essential lot of the artist.'

'The Zeitgeist,' interjected Lottie.

'Yeah,' said Hugo. 'In the fifties, you made stirring class-conscious stuff full of the most "Gor blimey" characters you ever heard, going into ironing boards and sinks and angry young men. Then, in the sixties, you came to Wardour Street to hang out and make the tea and zippy little optimism trips. The seventies – that was horror and exploitation. And since the eighties, you've come to make TV documentaries about the demise of the film industry.'

It all sounded, to Benedict, as if the time was ripe for a social revolution. 'Interesting,' he said, in a way that implied they shouldn't take his personal interest for granted.

'So,' said Hugo. 'Your project is . . . exactly?'

Benedict was blasé. 'I'm in Cannes next week,' he said. 'Exclusive interview with Robert Arden – ' He enjoyed the jaw drop that produced – 'and then, you know, I may hang out a while. Shoot the breeze . . .'

'I should introduce you to some people.'

'You should.'

Sure enough, by midnight Benedict had been introduced to some of the biggest names in the business. Whoever once said that the son also rises had surely failed to take into account the legions of daughters, nephews, nieces and grandchildren. All around, he felt, he was pressed by disconcertingly familiar smiles, eerily reminiscent eyes and voices which struck a chord. Why, the perpetuation of a showbusiness name was practically an industry in itself!

'Why shouldn't we be pursuing our own needs? It's in the blood,' argued one son-of.

'But there are so many of you!'

Naturally, though, Benedict took all their names and numbers.

21 | *A Message for Rosy*

Rosy had no doubt that Jamie's motives were as pure as the driven sludge. That didn't stop her feeling a huge sense of relief when she found a message from him – her only message – waiting for her when she returned to the Hotel du Jardin.

Someone had remembered she was here.

From her current predicament in the jaws of the dragon, Rosy knew that any communication would be a step forward. A returned call from the features editor would have been nice, and failing that, a sliver of elusive information from the *Dispatch*'s reference library.

Needless to say, her quarry Robert Arden remained as unreachable as the man in the moon. The Montana numbers she had were now unobtainable, according to the international operator.

When she read the message from Jamie, she didn't know whether to laugh or cry:

> Beast and I arriving tonight.
> The party starts 11.30 a.m. on Carlton Terrace.

Rosy suppressed the galling thought that he had wangled the trip to continue baiting her. Standing at the reception desk, she found her legs shaking as annoyance and desperation battled for her better judgement.

'Is everything all right?' asked the man on the desk.

'Yes, fine,' she replied. The hotel staff spoke and wrote such immaculate English there was no question of any misunderstanding over the message.

It would have been easy enough, she supposed, for Jamie Raj to ask her colleagues where she was staying. It was typical of him that he should assume she'd come running wherever he decreed and not bother to let her know which hotel he'd be in if she couldn't make it.

That evening she hated herself for spending ages getting her long hair dried just so, and indulging in some not-so-basic body maintenance with some hideously expensive French lotions. Then she begged an extra pillow from the maid, positioned it over the offending bedspring, and settled for as much beauty sleep as she could manage in the circumstances.

According to *Paris Match,* Gérard Depardieu was heading for the film festival, so she tried to dream of happy chance meetings. The problem was, great bear-like French film stars didn't do that much for her.

The next morning Rosy's heart flipped around like a salmon returning to breed. Whatever happened, she promised herself, she was not going to let Jamie Raj upset her hard-won equilibrium again. She had to remind herself of that several times.

The promenade – La Croisette – was filling with tourists and celebrity-spotters now that the festival had begun in earnest. Rosy wove her way through them to the white palace hotel. At the entrance to the Carlton was a towering cut-out poster of the latest James Bond brandishing a revolver.

Jamie was sitting on the terrace when she arrived. His jacket hung artfully on the chair behind him. In his Ray-Bans he looked more film star-ish than any of the stubbled tiddlers being hyped around town. Several wealthy-looking women at nearby tables were blatantly giving him the eye.

He stood up and kissed her lightly on both cheeks. 'What would you like?' he asked.

It was a pointless gallantry. A bottle of Mâcon Lugny was already cooling in an ice-bucket on the table. He hadn't touched a drop, she noticed. Jamie never needed Dutch courage – at least where *she* was concerned. 'Oh . . . I think I'll have a white wine.'

Jamie poured. 'I remembered, you see,' he said, raising his glass. 'You like this wine.'

Rosy was glad he kept his shades on. Those havoc-making amber eyes slew her every time. 'So, how's it going?' She fell back on the old standby.

'Fine. Ish.' He paused. 'No, actually – dreadful. To tell the truth – '

'I doubt it, but go on.'

His look was impenetrable. 'I'd forgotten what a nightmare this place can be. You know how it is.'

'Tell me about it.'

'I mean, do you go to lunch on Soraya's yacht or do your duty on the BAFTA boat? Does one accept drinks at the Majestic when there's an unofficial arrival at the Gray d'Albion beach? And what about the screenings over the unreliable talk at Le Petit Carlton?'

'Sure,' said Rosy.

'Then there's the hotel – '

'Yours too?'

'Tina's put me in some ridiculously social place. The Beast and I were up till dawn drinking with Rob Lowe.'

Rosy gagged. It was hard to tell which Jamie was

enjoying more: his elaborate tease or his obvious pleasure at her discomforting failure.

'Still, I expect you've got Cannes all sewn up already?'

'I'm getting there,' Rosy assured him.

Jamie took a drink. 'Only that's not what I heard.'

'Oh?'

'Rosy. No press accreditation, no invitations, no introductions to the right people . . .' He flipped over his own laminated press pass.

A fit of the shakes seized Rosy as her fury boiled over. Histrionics were not her style. Without saying a word, she stood up abruptly and left.

It was only afterwards that she realised she must have left her notebook behind, with its sorry account of her progress so far, and that she still had no idea where Jamie was staying.

22 | *Sex Without Shopping*

However slippery Benedict Pierce's grasp on his career as a social columnist has been on occasion, he prided himself on rarely making a mistake with the important names.

His shirts were Harvie and Hudson.

His shoes were Lobb.

Even his groceries were signed Justin de Blank and Boucherie Lamartine.

Off-duty, though, he was total-look Boden man. He wore the moleskin trousers and poacher's jacket with all the confidence of the Knightsbridge-to-Country set who modelled the clothes in the catalogue.

For those in the know, the Boden brochure – with all its chummy familiarity – was the Bluff Yourself Sloane Ranger manual of the 1990s, choc-a-bloc with the Harrys and Charlottes of the moment showing off the wares. It also provided an invaluable guide to the seamless acquisition of that certain style should one require it.

Followed to the last silk knot cufflink, it was a guarantee of authenticity.

For those of a certain mind set, in other words, it was nothing less than mail order monotheism.

The last person Benedict wanted to see staring out at

him from the glossy pages of the latest edition – he was making a close examination, with notebook – was one 'Jamie Raj, 29, a social columnist' wearing a blue double-cuff shirt and a charming hand-blocked silk tie.

But there again, it was heartening to see so many of the well-bred names he had encountered on his fact-finding tour of Wardour Street. He gazed at Lottie with a renewed affection.

Under the covers with Lottie, in the assiduously restored bedroom of his flat, Benedict had no such sartorial props. He traced the outline of her lithe body as she lay (a little actressy touch, this) swirled round with sheet on her side like a fallen classical statue.

The relationship, he sensed, was foundering on the twin mud banks of flimsy opportunism and miscalculation.

She no longer clung to him and stroked his neck that way she had.

The flattery had mostly dried up.

She teased him much more, although not in a particularly humorous way.

The hazy afternoon sunshine lit her plump face and highlighted a startling red eruption near the nose which would, undoubtedly, become the focus of much distress as soon as she was up and about. Benedict stared at it, and then past her.

This flat represented the remnants of his worth after two divorces which had bought his ex-wives – and probably their lawyers, too – fine properties in Hampstead and Notting Hill.

For a while, he had thought he could detect that heart-stopping quality about Lottie that had got him into so much trouble with the others, but then, gradually, he had relaxed. Benedict had no doubt that Lottie had a ruinous shopping streak in her somewhere, but she had never cast covetous looks at his credit cards. For that, he was profoundly grateful.

His two young daughters were already being schooled in the same expensive tastes as their mothers. Other journalists developed RSI from working too hard at a keyboard; Benedict had found his hand forced so often in the direction of his bank account that he was in danger of flying in the face of his entire profession and developing repetitive strain injury from writing cheques.

Lottie stirred and opened her eyes as he drew his hand back up to her waist. She smiled sleepily and said, 'You've got your lonely face on again.'

She left after a croissant brunch and a fond-enough farewell. As he crammed what he would need for the coming weeks into two Louis Vuitton bags provided as freebies by a PR – one was delightful, two a masterly triumph – the telephone shrilled.

It was Sir Philip Hawty, wanting positive reaction to a ploy to interest his publishers in a surprise blitz of bookshops for maximum impact. The dogged old politico was always on the look-out for a new trick.

'Leave me out of it,' said Benedict. 'I'm not here. I'm on my way to Heathrow. Plane leaves at three.'

'Off anywhere nice?'

'Cannes.' Benedict snatched up the scented candles from his bedside table in case Lottie decided to share his hotel room, and grabbed the essential peach oil, which she hated, in case he got lucky.

'Lucky sod.'

'This is *work*, Sir Philip. I have the interview of the year there, as well as . . . a project I am developing.'

'Of course, of course!'

'So if you don't mind . . .'

'Perhaps I should come along too?'

'I'm sorry?' Benedict had a sudden vision of a drooling fox let loose in a chicken coop. In terms of political history and achievement, Sir Philip Hawty ranked somewhere alongside the house cat at 10 Downing Street. As a man who had embodied the word sleaze long before the term became current, however, he was right up there with Nixon and Mao.

'I've . . . er, heard on the grapevine that the Project, as you call it, is based on a certain . . . book.'

Benedict wasn't sure how he should respond. *Not your book, you twerp!* would surely not be advisable at this stage. The grapevine was certainly in tip-top working condition – just as he was about to leave the country. 'Your task is here, Philip,' he said firmly.

'Yes, but I'm sure I could – '

'It really wouldn't be a good idea.' Benedict shuddered. The prospect of Sir Philip Hawty in Cannes lent a whole new dimension to greasing up to cross the Channel.

'It is to do with my book though,' persisted the ex-Cabinet minister.

'Ye-es, yes . . . as you know, your book is uppermost in my mind, Sir Philip . . . and . . .' he swallowed his words here, ' . . . another one.'

The other man didn't pick up on that. 'You will keep me fully posted?' he said.

'Of course.'

'Only, I've always had the highest regard for your version of events, Benedict. And I'll say now, how very much I've appreciated being sixty in the *Daily Post* for the past three years.'

'The project is not off the ground yet. It's still in the air,' flapped Benedict, with all the precision for which his column was known. 'But, as I made clear to you the other evening, your first performance is coming up soon.'

'Jolly good.'

'Think of it . . . as a kind of audition.'

'I . . . that means I'm not a definite yet?'

'Right here,' said Benedict, in a tone which brooked no dissent and made what he was about to say sound as important as could be. 'Your place is here, for the present. *You* make your debut in London.'

'I understand.'

'I hope you do, Sir Philip.'

Benedict hung up, then swung his feet onto his bed. Hands behind his head, he lay back, tycoon-like.

23 | *Intimacy and its Aftermath*

There was lipstick on two of the cigarette butts in the ashtray in front of Jamie. Naturally that was the first thing Rosy noticed when she slunk back to the Carlton Terrace for her notebook.

It had only taken her half an hour to steel herself to return.

'You don't waste any time,' he said. Jamie Raj was grinning irritatingly as she reached, silently, for the book.

'It wouldn't be any use to you,' said Rosy, zipping it ferociously in her bag.

'Oh, I don't know. After what's just happened, it might well be useful to track down Robert Arden and his extremely protective agent and personal manager.'

Rosy sighed. Of course he would have flipped through it.

He nonchalantly reached for his wine glass and flashed his eyes over the rim, amusement at her feeble jottings glittering amber to make the point. *The way he always used to for a private joke.*

Rosy got a grip. 'You're going to tell me anyway, so could you get on with it because I really have things to do.'

'I hope I won't have to remind you of this rather

grudging conversation in years to come when you're sent off to interview me in my jacuzzi on set.'

'Oh, yeah . . .'

'I may just have been discovered.'

'Found out, more like.'

'Rosy, *Rosy,* so cutting. In your absence, a very smart woman has intimated that she can make me a star.'

'In your dreams, Jamie.'

He raised his palms in a gesture of irresistibility and hammed: 'She said she could put me in movies!'

'Hmm,' said Rosy. '*Snuff* movies, with any luck. Although there's one that sounds quite promising, about Surf Nazis.'

'You should watch yourself, Rosy. Bitterness shrivels the soul.'

A loaded silence.

'Look,' said Jamie at last, 'This is quite ridiculous.'

The silence lasted almost as long as the first.

Rosy swallowed. 'You're right. I suppose.'

He gave her another of his private looks, and poured her a drink.

Rosy tested the awkwardness between them like a Victorian bride perched on the side of a honeymoon bed. Or so it felt, away from the comparative safety of their workplace back in London. 'It isn't too soon for a civilised conversation, then?'

'Probably not. But maybe you need to air a few grievances first.' Jamie was always more astute than he looked.

Rosy hesitated. 'If I start, I may not stop for a while,' she said, straightfaced. But she was infinitely relieved to see that the corners of his mouth twitched upwards.

'Why not just go for the "we should never have tried to be anything more than friends" line, and leave it at that?'

'Why? Can't you take criticism?'

There was an awkward moment.

'OK, it was my fault,' said Rosy. 'I made a mistake, for goodness sake. I was young, I was innocent."

'It was only a year ago.' He was mocking her now.

'Feels like a lifetime on the *Dispatch*.'

'Not that innocent, either."

'Naïve. Very easily impressed,' she added hastily.

Jamie said nothing, but looked her straight in the eye.

'Can we just leave it?' sighed Rosy. 'I feel nervous enough in this . . . maelstrom, without you making me feel worse, OK? I mean, if I'd thought that having a drink with a colleague would upset me even more, I'd have gone to my horrible hotel room and wept inconsolably when I had the chance.'

Jamie didn't smile. 'I don't suppose you'd believe me if I told you why it happened,' he said.

The *it* to which he referred so glibly was the time she caught him two-timing her with a blonde débutante model whatever. As Rosy recalled, it was one of the worst nights of her life.

She fixed her gaze on the purpling sea and cursed his technique. There was never much option, in a Jamie Raj interview, as to whether you carried on talking when you'd already said too much. 'But you're going to try me anyway.'

'I was scared. I really liked you a lot – '

'*Liked*?'

'Like. Present tense.'

Rosy stopped short of reminding him that wasn't the verb he had used at the time.

'You're not making this easy for me.'

Nor should I, thought Rosy, unable quite to discern her own emotion. She was high as a kite on two sips of wine. 'Go on then,' she said.

'It was trip wire, going out with that girl. To prove I

still could, that I didn't care so much that I couldn't see other women, play around a bit – '

'Be yourself, in other words.'

'Not exactly.'

Rosy could still feel the moment she found him. She could see him now, and feel the stab in her stomach. 'As luck would have it, I missed the moment you saw a blonde across a crowded room,' she shrugged now. 'But I did arrive in time to see the look on your face as you watched the room across a crowded blonde.'

He didn't reply.

'It might have been easier to keep my dignity if you hadn't been introducing her as your new woman to everyone in sight,' went on Rosy, exaggerating quite considerably here. Or so she thought.

Jamie did not contradict her.

'And quite apart from the fact that you – '

But she stopped in mid-flow as he rested a warm hand lightly over hers. Rosy looked up, uncertainly.

The Beast was heading their way, with a catch of lissom blondes. Their pearly publicity smiles blazed at the sight of Jamie Raj. For his part, he raked his hand through his dark floppy curls and ostentatiously made a show of sitting up straighter.

It was the inevitability of it all that got Rosy.

24 | *Sword's Dark Questions*

Anthony Sword stood glowering like a traffic light stuck on red. He was in the middle of a sumptuous private room at the Ritz, a glass of champagne in his fist. The publishers' hype for the latest execrable outpourings about the Princess of Wales had ensnared him against his better judgement.

He had vented his spleen on a publicity girl.

He had cringed forcibly enough to pop a button at the turnout of rent-a-quote backbenchers.

And he had got the joke that the party to launch the book was being held in the Marie Antoinette suite.

Now he was waiting with everyone else for the answer to the riddle: who was the author *this* time?

Cruel rumour had it that the Prince of Wales had sent a message of support, or that was the line the book people were assiduously promoting. In the absence of any other stunt left to pull in the vainglorious field of royal literature, this time the identity of the gusher – and his or her scribe – had been a stage-managed mystery, first detonated in the more hysterical Sunday newspapers.

He waved away approaches like so much flatulence.

Dark questions on the nature of contemporary British taste crowded Sword's mind. His inevitable conclusions made him feel, more than ever, the lure of a spacious oast conversion in Kent, or a Norfolk rectory. Anywhere quiet, in fact, where he could ignore with impunity this brand of nonsense.

Yet another young person was scuttling around with sealed press packs. She hovered close to him for a moment, as if uncertain whether to risk a full approach.

'Can you keep a secret?' asked Sword, steeling himself for his task.

The girl nodded.

'Well, you're no good to me then,' he griped.

The relief photographer – in the absence of the Beast – approached with what Sword chose to read as an irritating lack of respect. He was bearing a full glass of champagne only for himself, and a smug little list of guests he had recognised and persuaded to pose.

'I am not in the best of moods,' warned Sword, who found himself also taking exception to the young man's baggy dark suit and fashionable goatee beard, 'due to an administrative contretemps.'

'Doesn't sound good.'

'It most certainly is not. And until the editor of the *Daily Dispatch* understands that the most famous gossip columnist in the world does not selflessly craft his finest stories for the newspaper, only to have them cut for display around advertisements for drain-busters and treatments for piles, there will continue to be trouble.' Sword let his discontent linger between them.

'So, who's the writer of this book, then?' asked the photographer pleasantly.

Sword's throat growled. 'If I fucking knew that, would I be here?'

'Sorry, I thought you'd – ' The other man was wise enough to leave it there.

'Ladies and gentlemen, your attention please!'

Conversation stuttered and faded. Eyes and camera lenses swivelled in formation to the double doors where a short, balding man stood. Beyond him was another part of the suite.

'Ladies and gentlemen,' he reprised. 'Parade Publishing gives you . . .'

There was a drum roll.

Oh, for God's sake, thought Sword.

'. . . *Princess Laid Bare*!'

A collective gasp signalled horror and hilarity. A damask curtain was pulled back and – after a stunned few seconds – there was a stampede forward as a table piled high with copies of the book was revealed in the next room.

Anthony Sword stood his ground. The chronicler of our times ruminated like an old warrior bull in a field of grass. He sipped a little at his drink, and watched from what was soon a clearing. Then, keeping his sharp eyes on the Harrods' sale scene in front of him – all grabbing arms and life-and-death snatching – he wandered over to a tray to deposit his glass, and turned to leave.

A familiar figure in dusty black barred his way, lounging against the door-frame of his exit. Sword slowed as the Earl of Trent lit a Marlboro, then contemptuously flicked the spent match on to the marble floor. A hotel flunkey returned the contempt, glassy-eyed, as he retrieved it.

The Earl might have missed the big moment, as so many moments in his fashionably disastrous life, thought Sword, but the man was a study in disregard as he studied the end of his cigarette. His crushed insect face intimated heroic indifference.

Sword toyed with a smirk. 'Evening, Brett. We seem to be the only two with breeding enough to rise above this appalling free for all, this brainless brouhaha, this graceless gutter-licking.'

'Traffic in the King's Road was bloody terrible,' said the Earl. 'Couldn't get here any quicker.'

Sword laughed.

'Aren't you interested?' asked Trent, inhaling deeply. His thin white fingers trembled characteristically, their nicotine stains lately embellished with stubborn traces of potting compost.

'Sure,' said the gossip columnist, but wearily.

He received a reptile glance from the other man.

'I'm interested in who Rat of the Year is. That's the story, dear boy.'

'Put a name to Anon. A Non Person.'

'I should imagine he or she will be, this time,' said Sword.

'It's not that bad,' said Trent. 'I can assure you.'

Realisation took longer to dawn than it should have.

Inside the Marie Antoinette Suite, there were shrieks and derisive hoots. Half the gathering had their heads in a book, the others in their mobile phones.

Sword suppressed a belly laugh to produce a more dignified roar of disapproval. 'YOU?'

Trent's admission came with a disdainful shrug of his bony shoulders. 'Along with a selection of other consultants . . .'

'Consultants,' grimaced Sword.

'Isn't everyone nowadays?'

'But . . . you wrote it?' It was hardly a question. More a rhetorical prod to assess the extent of the madness.

'Wrote . . . is probably a bit strong,' admitted the earl. 'We took it in turns to sit on a desk and tell tales.'

'Don't tell me,' hissed Sword, 'More tales too beautiful to remain untold.'

'Nah,' said Trent. 'Money talks.'

25 | *Dish of the Day*

The dazzling white of the palace hotels dominating the seafront made Rosy even more aware of the workaday grubbiness of her shirt, and even perhaps, of her person too. On apartment blocks, neat rows of orange blinds were pulled down against the midday sun.

'Don't they do clouds, in the South of France,' she asked as she and Keith Silver trundled along under the relentless blue.

The ace paparazzo shrugged. 'Not much call for 'em.' He pushed a pair of aviator sunglasses up onto his head and jutted his face into the sun. His brow was studded with perspiration under his unruly dark hairline. He was still wearing unrelieved black. 'This is the life. Fancy a bully baisse?'

'A what?'

'My favourite – can't do a Cannes without it. A drop of that French fish stew whatsit,' he urged, when it was clear she hadn't a clue.

'Ah,' nodded Rosy, laughing. 'I thought you meant something rude. For one horrible moment it sounded like you intended to force yourself on some poor Frenchwoman.'

'Eh?'

'*Bouillabaisse*,' pronounced Rosy carefully. 'Don't you

think it might be too hot for that kind of lunch? I've never *been* so hot – I think I'm going to melt.'

'Brought yer bikini?' The Beast turned on a mock leer.

She gave him a look. 'I may have – strictly for private moments between me and a few grains of quiet, unpopulated beach.'

The photographer grinned. 'There's nothing like that here,' he observed, squinting in the direction of a teenager in Ursula Andress mode below them on the sand surrounded by ravening hordes of lensmen. 'Strip off and say you know Monsieur Pacino, and you'll have half the newspapers in Europe running your pic tomorrow morning.'

It was Rosy's turn to grin. She surreptitiously pinched rather more than an inch over her waistband. 'That may be more of a compliment than you know,' she said.

Halfway down a bottle of wine, Rosy could no longer stop herself mentioning Jamie.

'I can see he's in his element,' she asserted over the clatter of the photographer's cutlery as he loaded bread rafts of rouille and cheese, then paddled through a tureen of soup.

'He knows how to have a good time, if that's what you mean.'

I'll bet, thought Rosy, then wondered how much of a dig at *her* that was. 'So he's got everything all sewn up already then?' The envy was tangible in her voice, especially to herself.

The Beast waved a spade of a spoon and scrutinised her until she had to look away. 'Pigs fly?' he asked, returning to his own task in hand.

Rosy digested that. 'You mean, it's all a front – he's no further with his brief than I am?'

The photographer gave her a slow broad grin, garnished with the remains of a large langoustine.

'Then I know who the biggest show-off in town is,' huffed Rosy, 'and it isn't any of the actress pouting down on the beach.'

The subject, awkwardly, was changed. They talked aimlessly, until the Beast had dealt with his soup and could be urged on about past film festivals and the exploits of the paparazzi pack.

But Rosy's mood was kamikazi. 'How's Lulu Bisset getting on?' she asked.

'OK,' shrugged the Beast.

'Just OK?'

'She knows a lot of people. She's very confident.' He reached out for a toothpick, and began a thorough excavation of the remains of his lunch.

Rosy sighed. 'That's it, isn't it. The people with all the front are always the ones who succeed.'

The Beast sucked his teeth. 'I didn't say that.'

You didn't have to, she thought. Beyond the restaurant canopy, the old harbour bobbed with the chrome and white cruisers bought by some of the best front on the world. He followed her gaze and they were silent for a moment.

Occasionally, a confident well-dressed figure would cause the gawping tourists thronging the promenades to stop and stare. The object of interest this time slowed his languid stride, as if ensuring that his own was indeed the most prominent and magnificent of all the boats.

'Talk of the devil . . .' said the Beast, as they watched him.

Jamie was swinging his way towards them, backlit by the dazzling sun.

Of course he made out she was doing all right, that there

was little more anyone could have done so far, in the circumstances. Rosy felt the dead weight of his patronising manner. A snail trail of condensation trickled down the glass of cold rosé wine he ordered for her. Any moment, the tears welling behind her eyes would do the same.

She dug her nails deeply into the palms of her hands.

Then she summoned a surge of determination. *Front*, she intoned mentally.

Jamie was airily recounting his morning. 'The whole point of coming here, is to enjoy ourselves. The *Dispatch* wants glam, we give 'em glam . . .' Out in the bay, a million miles away from Rosy, speedboats cut diamonds in the blue water. In the sky, a tiny plane buzzed over, trawling a banner she couldn't read. 'I could take you somewhere, if you'd like.'

She realised Jamie was talking to her.

'There's a restaurant,' he said. 'A very discreet eaterie – '

'A discreeterie,' said Rosy automatically, but with no sense of fun.

'Dish of the Day,' he said. He looked at her intently and waited a second. 'We are not talking food here.'

'I got it,' said Rosy, irritated.

'So, do you want to come?'

She shrugged, a childish gesture she regretted even as she did it.

'Suit yourself. I am trying to be pleasant to you.'

'And I'm wondering why you're bothering,' she said. The words were out before she could stop herself.

Jamie got up and pushed back his hair. His golden skin was rich against his white shirt. The shade under the canopy seemed to deepen as she stared at him. 'Would you like me to get you another drink before I go?'

'I'm feeling no pain,' said Rosy.

It was his turn to shrug. Her arms goose-pimpled as he turned to go. As he began to walk away, she opened her mouth to say –

He didn't look back.

26 | *Benedict's Party Plans*

As a man who was more than usually dependent on the steam and puff of the public relations machine, Benedict Pierce made it his business to understand its internal combustion at all times. He knew exactly when to raise or lower the level of his performance, on the merest casual inquiry.

'Ah! The party person!' he lizarded from his lounger when he became aware that Kitten O'Shea, Practitioner in Public Relations, had been standing over his suntanning session for some time and was not, in fact, an obstinate cloud above, as he had at first imagined.

The pool was on the roof of his hotel. Far above the petty horse-trading of the Cannes carousel, Benedict had the interview of the festival in his pocket, and a screamer of a project in hand.

He could afford to take it easy.

He reached down by his side for fruit and foliage and hauled up a substantial drink that was less a cocktail than a package holiday in liquid form. 'The passport to a successful party,' he said, barely able to rouse himself for a consultation on the soirée he would host for his *Daily Post* column, 'is organisation, and meticulous attention to detail. Choice of drink. Lighting. Decor. Sumptuous food. Service. Atmosphere. Flowers. Colour.'

'Guests,' said Kitten.

'Guests, *naturally,*' confirmed Benedict.

'I'm afraid,' said Kitten, 'That was what I wanted to see you about. We're in celeb crisis.'

Benedict half-raised an eyelid. 'Yah?'

'Yah. Pretty desperate, actually.'

'Hit me with it,' said Benedict.

The public relations girl prepared to recite. 'We've had No-o-o from Spielberg, No-o-o from Sean Connery, No-o-o from Dustin Hoffman, No-o-o from the Duke of Northumberland, and No-o-o from Roger Moore. Yes, from Lottie Landor.' She stared at him with a mixture of bafflement and contempt. 'Who *is* Lottie Landor?'

Benedict sighed. 'We do have acceptances, though?'

'We-e-ll, yes. Joan Collins. And Christopher Biggins. But frankly if *they* don't say yes . . .'

'Yes, all right. Point taken,' said Benedict hastily. The warmth on his face, he feared, was no longer solely that of the Riviera sun.

'I'm *sure* everything will be fine. Absolutely fine. In the end,' said Kitten, fiddling nervously with a sheaf of devotionally thumbed address lists. 'We'll just need to work a little harder at it. I'm sure we'll get there.'

'Your confidence is truly inspiring,' said Benedict.

He was aghast to note that she took it as a compliment.

They moved on to discuss food and drink. It was just as well that the bill for the party would be picked up by the *Daily Post*, so long as he could eke out enough names to write half a column.

Especially as he could then write it all off against his other iron in the fire.

Kitten's parting shot was to the effect that if the Pierce name couldn't prove more of a draw, then not even Screen International and the freeloaders from the wing-and-a-prayer production companies would be there.

Benedict, she intimated, would be enjoying the party on his own, with barely a limp potato crisp between him and the ever-reliable Mr Biggins.

Any more of this kind of treatment, Benedict felt, and he would have to take drastic steps at this film festival. He might even have to take the bull by the horns for once and slink unseen into a screening session, a course of action he had always considered strictly for the sad and lonely.

He might end up having to go to the cinema alone.

Since his arrival at Hollywood-sur-Mer – ahead of Lottie – Benedict knew all about the pressures on film folk. Why, he was practically one himself, or so he rationalised as he faced another Tinsel-Towny hitch involving the door of the mini-bar in his hotel suite. He jemmied it open with a steel comb and took out a chilled beer.

The columnist had found the perfect image for his new venture in Paris *Vogue*, where a style prophet had decreed that high fashion for the summer was Le Look Scott Fitzgerald. It was suitably good news for his gleaming horns of blond hair and the collection of period flannels he had recently acquired.

He sported them when out meeting people.

For people, read women. One had been a dead ringer for Michelle Pfieffer. She wasn't Michelle, of course. And even less so when they had emerged out of the casino into the bright foyer. But he could dream, when he had to.

He dialled a number, and walked out on to the balcony carrying the telephone. Positioned as he was at the western end of the broad blue bay, his panoramic view was like having a box at a vast amphitheatre where the stage was made of icing sugar against blue back-lighting.

'Merv?"

'Uh?'

'Merv. Benedict Pierce here.'

'Uh-huh.'

'I'm in Cannes. I arrived last night, so let's make a firm time to do the Arden interview.'

'Uhhh . . . sure. We'll get back to you.'

'I'd rather get this firmed up now.'

'Yuh-uh. Listen, man, you know how it is.'

'As a matter of fact I do.'

'Soon as I know, I'll call ya.'

'I'll give you the number.'

'Uh . . . yeah, OK.'

Benedict hung up with a twinge of misgiving. A feeling that his cupboard was a little barer than he'd anticipated. Or would have been, had he not had his other interest. Benedict Pierce was not a man who would ever fire off a stone with only one bird to kill.

His second call was more of a hit.

'Bernie?'

'Yuh.'

'Benedict Pierce here.'

'He-e-y! The royal exposure man!'

That was more like it.

27 | *Rosy Alone*

Another call to the *Daily Dispatch* only served to underline what Rosy had suspected for days.

'Until you have a positive lever on Arden,' growled John Lunt in his most unforgiving Bad-Day-in-Features tone, 'I don't want to hear from you again.'

Through gritted teeth, she said: 'According to my sources, Arden hasn't arrived yet – he's still in London.'

'I don't care if he's on the top deck of a London-*fucking*-sightseeing bus, you have been sent out for the story and I want the story!' screamed the features editor.

Which was par for the course, given that normal powers of reasoning had never been a prerequisite for anyone getting a features editor's job on the *Dispatch*. Which was undoubtedly why the man got results. Usually.

Not only that: Rosy suspected that if she had been in favour he might have given her the job of following the Princess of Wales to all her soothing therapies for a few days, instead of which, that prime task had gone to the newest freelancer in the department.

She was also beginning to suspect that famous recluses were absolutely right in avoiding the whole wretched madhouse.

Meanwhile, she was part of the insanity. 'I'll, I'll keep trying then,' she continued feebly. 'Er . . . hello?'

But the features editor had gone.

It was clear that all she could count on from that quarter was a display of antipathy until such time as she could prove that the newspaper's funds had not been wasted on her plane ticket. And, not for the first time, she wondered whether her trip out here was all that it seemed.

When she allowed it to, the dark possibility that her six-month contract on features would not be renewed ate away at her confidence.

Cast out from home and excluded from life in Cannes by the lack of gilt on her clothes and shoes, not to mention brass in her attitude, she found a suitably shady hole.

'Un sandwich, s'il vous plaît,' she ordered, in a back street cafe.

The waiter nodded. 'Jambon? Fromage? Salade?'

'Valium, si vous l'avez.'

'Eh, quoi?'

'Salade,' said Rosy.

She munched it over the copy of *Le Figaro* from the hooks by the bar, rapt in the tale of two sixteen-year-old girls from an uneventful village south of the Massif Central who had stolen a car and set off on a bloodthirsty rampage with a hunting rifle. They killed two people – a policeman and a shopkeeper – before being stopped.

'They were such quiet girls,' one of the stunned mothers was quoted as saying.

'They were happy to stay at home, watching television and videos.'

'Hey, Rosy!'

Barely before she could swallow the piece of lettuce she

was dealing with, Jamie Raj had arrived at her table. 'Mmmff,' she contributed.

'The Beast said you were looking for me,' he said.

'I wouldn't have put it quite like that.'

Jamie grinned widely, then helpfully plucked a ribbon of tomato from her chin.

Oh great, thought Rosy. *Accessories by* Légumes de Paris.

'Mind if I join you?'

'I can't stop you.'

A hard stare. 'Be my guest, is the usual response.'

'Sure.' She pushed away the remains of lunch with leaden hands.

'I've left the Beast with a Romanian version of Demi Moore and about six pouting PR girls. He's run out of film, but it doesn't look like anyone's concerned with small details.' He was trying to raise a smile from her.

'I think I've seen them.'

Jamie ordered espresso and let a practised expression of concern ride the waves of a Phil Collins song on the record system. Rosy knew better now than to fall for that. He reached out for a strand of her hair that had escaped her makeshift pony-tail. 'It's not an admission of defeat, if you tell me what's wrong.'

Despite herself, Rosy felt a sting of gratitude behind her eyes. She grimaced. 'Life, justice and the *Daily Dispatch*,' she said, 'would probably cover it. That, and the eternal dichotomy between Theory and Practice, not to mention Appearance and Reality, and anything else man has failed to resolve since Aristotle set the ball rolling.'

'Ah,' nodded Jamie. 'In that case, central to my hypothesis would be one John Lunt.'

'More or less. There's definitely a letter wrong in his name.'

Jamie laughed. 'That's more like it. It was pretty mean of them to send you out with no accreditation. There's no way you'll get in anywhere without it.'

Rosy raised her eyebrows to admit as much. 'Give me Sword any day.'

'The old prizefighter.'

'Exactly. At least . . . I can cope with his strain of madness. Whereas this . . .'

'You wouldn't necessarily say that if you were in my position,' warned Jamie. 'Like the Glorious Twelfth, Sword has become a revered but somewhat outdated institution, and, as you know, he is at his most dangerous when he senses uncertainty.'

'Meaning, as far as you're concerned?' Not that there was likely to be any other kind of meaning for Jamie.

'Oh, a range of objectives. Blow Benedict Pierce out of the water, for one.'

Rosy gagged on her coffee. 'Benedict's here?' That was all she needed.

'I caught him my first morning, in a new Ralph Lauren blazer, coming out of the hairdressers. You've never *seen* such a sheen on a man's coiffure.'

'I can imagine.'

'Then, I have to produce two columns, for Friday and Monday, because Sword has some top secret operation on over the weekend. He dumped that on me yesterday. I don't suppose you've got any stories I could use?'

Rosy shook her head.

'So,' said Jamie amiably, 'the way I see it is that we could both use some friendly co-operation.' She couldn't argue with that. 'Want to come to a party or three with me this evening? Strictly business,' he added when he saw the look on her face.

'I don't – '

'I need someone to help fill the columns. You need to get into the thick of it to get a lead on Robert Arden.'

Rosy still hesitated. 'I don't really have any choice, do I?'

'Well, not exactly. But, Rosy, we're only going to a press party. Listen to Phil.' As he nodded towards a speaker in the corner, there was an ironic twist in the corner of his mouth. The words of the song implied that she would not find it *that* easy to get back together with him.

'Oh, for God's sake,' groaned Rosy.

But as she said it, she found she was smiling.

28 | *Sword's Dark Shadow*

In London, Anthony Sword received the news about Sir Philip Hawty with more *sang froid* than might be expected of a man who sun-dried his own tomatoes.

'He's given me a full and frank statement – on a story we're not even doing!' said Pearson. 'Yet.'

Not for the first time, Sword lamented the tragic decline in standards of public life. Once national scandals were great blockbusters which brought down governments and economies, ruining careers. Now they were squalid little fiascos which positively *made* careers.

This ex-Cabinet minister's claims now stretched to a fumble with an alleged 'key member of staff' at Buckingham Palace.

Sword drummed his fingers, and regarded his tweedy colleague stonily. 'You're sure it was him? Telephones can be tricky beasts. Only takes a half-decent impersonator to . . . I am thinking, Pearson, of the case of the Bogus Buck House Life Guard, 1977 . . .'

The other man had the grace to acknowledge his unfortunate part in a previous débâcle by dropping his watery eyes. 'I know, I know. But I've been most careful. In fact, he left a message. I called him. Same number we've always used.'

'Even so – '

'It's a pre-emptive strike.'

'Served on a silver salver, as it were?' snorted Sword.

'He thinks we can be relied upon in his hour of need – in view of our, er, previous diplomatic handling of his affairs.'

'No pun intended.'

'He's come clean first,' said Pearson.

'He's jumped headlong into the shit wagon in the hope he can stop it running out of control,' hypothesised Sword mercilessly.

The elder hack grinned. 'Phrased with your customary delicacy.'

Together they played back the telephone recording. The unmistakable plummy voice gave an account that was indeed full and frank. In high serious mode, Sir Philip intoned the nitty-gritty: 'And I here confirm that physical relations were . . . joined – '

'*Joined*?' Sword rolled his eyes.

'Sshhh!'

'. . . and I can also confirm that my wife – at the time – Mary, was fully appraised of these unfortunate . . . circumstances. During the course of this . . . liaison . . . I was party to a great deal of information concerning . . . the highest in the land . . . which will provide a true insight and form an integral part of the film . . .'

'Film?' grunted Sword.

Pearson grimaced a don't-know.

There was much more of the same. Sword flicked the switch.

'Perhaps never in the history of gossip have such fine carnal revelations been obtained by such blameless means,' said Pearson, proudly.

'Hmm.'

'I wonder about the girl, though.'

'In a hotel with a nice man from the News of the

Screws, I would have to imagine – if she's what has brought this on.'

'What do you want to do?'

'Let the asshole hang himself,' said Sword.

He was stung into the kind of blind resolution which occasionally sent him wandering incognito across Hampstead Heath, by the stubborn resurgence of a scrunched ball of paper. The eye-catching red envelope bounced over the rim of his waste bin as the office cleaner made her first round. She retrieved it, but the damage was done.

That morning it had contained another note.

Or rather, not a note this time.

There was nothing written on the back of the postcard. The picture on the front was a reproduction of the painting titled, When Did You Last See Your Father?

That evening, Sword found himself at the Soho Brasserie.

'Nellie, I *am* Heathcliff!'

'Who are you calling Nellie, you butch bastard?'

'It's my *line*, dearie. Are you following this script, or not?'

As if the luvvy conversation at the bar stools were not enough, Sword also had the sound of Elton John warbling '*I Feel Pretty*', to contend with.

Amid the art decor splendour of possibly the most non-threatening gay meeting place in London, he fidgeted. Straight couples and tourists wandered into the Soho Brasserie and happily ate and drank, pretty much oblivious to the more colourful traffic. It suited him. But this evening Anthony Sword was feeling more uncomfortable by the minute.

There had been nights lately when Sword felt the conflict between self-knowledge and hope like a dark shadow on his trail. It lurked in the recesses of Green's and Wilton's, beneath the olive tree at Daphne's, and in the lulls in conversation in less mainstream establishments.

As he had explained to Framboise in the first weeks of their friendship at the health hydro at Grasslands Hall, he was not interested in romantic relationships of any kind. But that wasn't how he felt now. Framboise had been the catalyst and star witness to his conversion.

His night excursions, post whichever restaurant, to this bar and that hangout, had only served to confirm what he had first felt and chosen to ignore. He could look at anyone else but her, and feel nothing.

The only antidote – as ever – was to work. If he could only concentrate on what the waiter was telling him.

'So I got up centre stage . . . and the director's getting impatient . . . and the accompanist hits the wrong key. First audition I've had for weeks, and that really sets me up, so I open my mouth and shut it again . . . and like the darkness is *humming* with disapproval. I'm that fuckin' desperate . . . but I've suddenly remembered that I *don't sing*!'

The gossip columnist laboured a smile. 'Not many donkeys around here still got their hind legs, Marty.' The guy could talk the wood off a door.

'Interested in Ken and Em?' asked the waiter, tray on hip.

Sword made a balancing motion with one flat hand.

'You might like this. Some of his ex-Frankenstein crew at Shepperton came in the other day. *Hot* rumour about the great Robert Arden.'

'Yeah?'

Marty leaned in. '*Transvestite*.'

Sword rolled his eyes heavenwards. 'Never . . .'

'Closet.'

'From?'

'Contact.'

'Where?'

'Madame Jo Jo's.'

'Maybe,' said Sword, 'Maybe not.'

The waiter flicked a pressed white cloth over his shoulder. 'By the way – I think you have an admirer. Over by the door.'

'Eh?'

'Not bad-looking, if you go for the super-straight effect. Charcoal suit, tie. He was looking at you the other night, too.'

'What?' Sword craned round but saw only a blur of crowd. 'You know him?'

'Only that he's been asking about you.'

'He's still there?'

'Er . . . can't see.'

None of the clientele gave him more than the customary glance of recognition as he passed them on the way out to Old Compton Street.

He went home.

When he reached his house it was to find his burglar alarm wailing to the night.

29 | *Aristocratic Pretensions*

It was a fair indication of her state of mind, Rosy supposed, that the shaggy palms lining the seafront looked so much like up-ended loo brushes.

Her bright new career was going down the pan.

She pushed her hands deep into the pockets of her jeans, and kicked along with nowhere left to go. What hidden agenda could there be, anyway, in sending her out to find a man who made a whole persona by keeping out of sight, if not to ensure her failure and the non-renewal of her contract?

For once the sun had gone in and rain threatened. She shuddered as she passed the Palais, hurrying on around the Place de General de Gaulle and beyond the port on the Allés de la Liberté, a tree-shaded area where flowers were sold in the morning. Scuffed leaves and petals on the ground were the only evidence of that now.

When she eventually stopped and sat down on a verge under a tree, it was for a long time.

The gangling, white-faced guy in black could have been any one of the film industry pretenders she had run into in the past week. She watched, utterly detached, as he sauntered across the road towards her. He was even toting the regulation black canvas rucksack – no doubt bulging with the treatment that really was on the brink of a hot deal.

He was only feet away when she did a double take.

'Brett?'

The Earl of Trent staggered back. For a second, his inbred cockroach features registered alarm, then he bared little sharp teeth in a distracted greeting. 'Rosy Hope! What are you doing here?'

'I could ask you the same question!'

Fidgeting with a strand of black frizz that had escaped his pony tail, Brett Trent leant close enough for her to smell the Marlboros on his breath as he kissed the air above her cheeks, then sat down beside her before replying with his usual candour. 'Thought I'd come out with some mates, do some deals.'

Rosy looked sceptical.

'And then . . . I was advised to make a quick getaway to the Costa del Sol.'

'Brett . . . you're in France.'

He gave her a scornful glare. 'I *know*. I just didn't fancy Italy, that's all.'

Rosy let that go. 'So. Why the getaway?'

'Ah, that. The Chelsea Greenhouse got busted.'

'*Busted*? For what?'

His beady black eyes glittered, but he said nothing. He didn't have to. She clocked on in a rush of embarrassment at her own naïvety – knowing as the pieces slipped into place that she was possibly the last person in south-west London to realise.

'Those funny, frothy plants that you keep in the back of the conservatory by your office – and the new rainforest exotics . . .?'

The Earl shrugged in a dopey way.

'Marijuana? Cocaine?' Rosy felt her grin spreading, despite her personal mortification.

'Only marijuana plants,' he said. 'All good natural stuff. I tried cocoa leaves, but there's not much you can do but chew on them for altitude sickness.'

Rosy shook her head silently, then suggested, 'Give them to social climbers?'

He may have misunderstood her reticence. 'As seen in all the best drawing rooms, my greenery supplies,' he insisted. 'Practically anyone who's anyone has got one.'

'Oh, very likely . . . I don't think.'

'I'm serious.' He looked genuinely offended. 'Belgravia's a saturation market. There are several elderly Eaton Square countesses, for example, who came to me for pot plants – as recommended by knowledgeable junior members of their families, naturally. Everyone knows how fashionable gardening has become.'

'The green movement repackaged as a touch of the Vita Sackville-Wests,' said Rosy cynically. 'And what about all these grand old ladies fencing the stuff?'

'The effect on the number of visits they get now has been dramatic. Some are even flying high, ripped to the tits with Harry and Henrietta, pre-SW1 Club. Gives a whole new meaning to family trips,' said the earl with satisfaction.

'Or high society,' sighed Rosy.

'So what *are* you doing in Cannes?' she asked as they walked slowly back into the crawling streets of the town centre. 'Or is it as simple and undramatic as being on the run from the drugs squad?'

One good point arose from her ambiguous status at the *Dispatch*. It had solved any conflict of interest involved in sitting on the hot tabloid story of the latest hiccup in her aristocratic companion's well-documented life of serial disasters.

Not that the earl's demeanour suggested any undue worry on that score.

Maybe it wasn't even true. Or, more likely, he wanted her to write about him. There was always so much that was misleading, thought Rosy.

There was also something in Brett Trent's sudden vivacity. He struck a pose which was, at best, Tarantino manic. At least she assumed it was his best side he was giving her.

'Don't tell me. Let me guess,' said Rosy, sarcasm corroding her pretence of good humour. 'You're going to be in the movies.'

'How did you know?'

Rosy could only laugh. 'And introducing . . . from the G-Plan school of wooden acting . . .'

'It's going to be big,' he said, unabashed. 'I just gotta get my shot.'

'Oh, I'll bet. They just have to put the final seal on the financing package, but it's already sold to Bulgaria and Poland. They're looking to Kinshasa for the video rights.'

The earl had apparently mugged up his new interest enough to say: 'You can be very wounding when you're in the mood.'

'It's been my speciality of late.'

'Not having a good time?'

'You could say.'

'You here for the *Dispatch*?'

'Well, they *sent* me. As of this morning, though, I'm not sure what exactly I'm doing here.'

He was evidently confused.

'I'm here while I'm deciding what to do next.'

That situation seemed fair enough to him. 'Look, I'm expected . . .' He consulted a large plastic tangerine Swatch. 'I should have been somewhere ten minutes ago but – '

'You have people to see, movers to shake . . .'

He scratched his head. 'Not really. Only a small blonde gossip columnist with an obsession. Want to join us?'

'Count me out,' shuddered Rosy.

30 | *Canned Party*

On the catwalks of Paris and Milan that season, the screen sirens of cinematic history glided again in draped chiffon.

Linda Evangelista was Veronica Lake.

Claudia Schiffer was Anita Ekberg.

Glamour had supplanted grunge, except, that was, in Rosy's film festival wardrobe. On the walkway to the Wolf Pictures party boat, Rosy Hope was Forrest Gump at C&A.

Or so she felt.

'And you are?'

Rosy was faced down by a baseball cap and a chin. The brown linen dress crumpled a bit more against her skin. 'Er, Rosy Hope,' she stuttered. The words which wouldn't come were: *And what's it to you*?

'Of?' The only good mark in this guy's favour was that at least his cap was on the right way. From the bagginess of his clothes and the way acne and sunshine had textured his face into a peanut shell, she suspected that had been a recent decision.

'Of?' repeated Rosy, taking her cue from his truculence. 'Which organisation? Why are you here?'

She stood a little straighter. 'The *Daily Dispatch*.'

'Of?'

'Oh, really . . .'

'Which city ya based in?'

'London.'

'And the Daily Despot is a newspaper?'

'You're quick.'

'Right.'

'And, er, aren't you forgetting something?'

He stared at her blankly.

'Who are *you*?'

A moment elapsed, after which he walked abruptly away, leaving her feet corroded to the deck by the acid of his sneer.

'Who was *that*?' she asked a passing waiter who could not have been much older than Peanut Features. Even he shot her a look of abject pity.

Rosy shrugged, and plucked a glass from his tray. Three gulps later, she was ready to face the party. Her options, she quickly deduced, were currently limited to Benedict Pierce and his unlikely actress consort.

Dignity is all, she reminded herself as she set her course over to them. It was too late to change direction when she saw the rude youth offer Benedict a curiously stilted high five in passing.

'Who *was* that?' asked Rosy, after her own awkward greeting of the rival gossip columnist had been saved by Lottie's high spirits. 'I was standing there, minding my own business, when he barged up and started interrogating me as if he owned the boat!'

There was no mistaking the sneer on Benedict's lips. 'Well, darling, actually he does.'

The sight of a skinny Manhattan millionairess across the deck acted on Rosy's conscience like a picture of Yasmin le Bon taped to the fridge door. Rosy chewed guiltily on her positively last canapé.

'Don't tell me, Nan Purchase is moving into the film industry now?' she asked Jamie as he materialised, to her great relief, at her side.

'She made half of Hollywood's finest who they are.'

'Oh?"

'You don't seriously think that actors over forty-five look like Warren Beatty and Harrison Ford – or Robert Arden, come to that – without some pretty expensive help, do you?'

'What – they all go to Nan's health centres? It figures, I suppose. If the miracle she worked on Sword last year is anything to go by.'

'Nan Purchase and Sword have much in common,' said Jamie. 'He looks at the people he writes about and says: "Who are all these people? I have INVENTED them." Nan has the satisfaction of looking at famous faces and bodies and thinking exactly the same.'

'Or maybe not different *people*,' mused Rosy. 'They love themselves far too much for that. More like an invented timescale. You know, someone like Warren Beatty probably books in and says, "Gimme back 1975".'

Jamie laughed. 'They must take in their best films for surgical reference.'

'Hmm,' said Rosy. 'I'm afraid that's what's worrying me. About Robert Arden.'

He gave her a tender look. 'Rosy, the day you're *not* worried . . .'

'No, but, don't you see? Some actors always play themselves, no matter which film they're in. But this guy really is an actor. Every time Robert Arden comes back and makes a movie, he looks utterly different. Five years go by, and on-screen he's completely different. I mean, he won his Oscar last time for playing an autistic vagabond.

Somehow though, I can't see him still hanging out by the soup kitchens with old string round his waist and a ZZ Top hairstyle.'

Jamie looked thoughtful.

'It's not even as if recognising people is my strong point,' frowned Rosy. 'Don't you remember, when we went to that political book launch and I asked Norma Major if she'd ever seen inside Number Ten. She was terribly nice about it, which made it all worse somehow.'

'Robert Arden's agents don't have a current stock photo?'

Rosy shook her head. 'No, that's the whole idea.'

'You've got on to all the US news picture agencies?'

'I've tried everything.'

'Well, then, this is your lucky night,' said Jamie.

'That would make a change,' said Rosy.

'As the lady says, she's a People Person,' whispered Jamie, staring over at the perfectly-moulded millionairess. 'Come on. Nan Purchase would love news of Sword and Framboise.'

31 | *Benedict and the Queen*

In this make-believe world, Nan Purchase was the cat that had the virtually fat-free cream. The Liposuction Queen was talking to a scion of one of Hollywood's royal families.

'I've remodelled your mom,' she was saying as Benedict approached gingerly and hovered.

'Was that the blonde, brunette, or faintly oriental mom?' asked the kid with third generation photogenic cheekbones.

'All of them, honey. She's one of my most devoted clients – although I warned her that another lift so soon after her Miss Saigon phase was not a good idea . . .'

They both laughed, the Manhattan millionairess keeping her tiny head preternaturally still and her smile frozen.

When Benedict moved into her gunsight, her mouth snapped shut as tightly as the clasp on her Hermes Kelly bag. It had been a while since Benedict had wined and dined her in an attempt to win her alliance in his war against Anthony Sword, but it did not appear that she had forgotten.

Nan Purchase had been told at a gathering of Sacred

Significance that the feather was the connection between people and the spirit.

Thus, the mauve boa, she explained to Benedict. The feathery toy explosion around her skinny shoulders was the most darling item on the sainted Calvin's catwalk.

The gossip columnist had to weigh up his chances of running into her at a more intimate gathering before he made his pitch.

He seized his chance.

As a foreign socialite who often spent the Season in London, apparently oblivious to the social implications, Nan Purchase regarded the royals as one of her specialist subjects. Back on home territory at the Russian Tea Room, it guaranteed her a prime table with kindly light.

He leaned heavily on that angle. The film, he said, was the truth behind the fairy tale, a corruscating exposé of the hypocrisy of modern Britain, from politics up.

'The man who wrote the latest book about the Prince of Wales justified his work by saying that he was a seasoned journalist who had travelled the world reporting on the latest catastrophes,' said Benedict. 'That would seem a fair assessment of the royal situation.'

'Go on.'

'The public wants a monarchy that's full of magic – but they also demand to go behind the bedroom door.'

'A fairy tale, you say. Like the Emperor's New Bedclothes?' Nan's horse face was dead-pan.

Benedict remembered now how quickly their conversations had veered into cross-purposes in the past. Still, he was doing this for one of the world's least original reasons: he wanted her money.

'It's a microwave movie?' she asked.

'A what?'

'A quick fix, fast turnaround.'

'Absolutely not. This will be a ground-breaker, and

crafted by the finest British . . . er, craftsmen. And women.'

'So what's different about this one?'

'I'm glad you asked that. That is the *crux*. The great cast that is Society.'

'Eh?'

'The cast will play themselves.'

Nan did a double-take. 'Sword's theory, you mean.'

'I think we'll leave Desperate Dan out of this,' said Benedict – then, as a reflex, 'What theory?'

'He refers to all the people he writes about as his cast list.'

'Yes, well . . . exactly. That's exactly the point of my satire based on two explosive tell-all books.'

Nan tweaked a dubious frown at him. 'How far along are you?'

'All we need are a few more backers.'

'You and the rest of town.'

'I was hoping you might . . . in view of your special expertise . . .'

'Who do you have on board already?'

It was with a measure of pride that he said: 'Bernie Ziegler. As of this afternoon.'

'Bernie *Zeeee*gler!'

'Good, eh?'

'You, a project, and Bernie Ziegler. This I must see.'

'So I can -?'

'Never underestimate Bernie Ziegler,' said Nan with a cryptic smile.

Benedict's subsequent query was interrupted by the unwelcome appearance of his rivals from the *Daily Dispatch*, Jamie Raj and Rosy Hope.

32 | *Idol Pleasures*

The film PR was evidently getting desperate as the party grew more frenetic.

'Did you hear about Burt Ward?' she asked.

'Who?' countered Rosy, wondering whether this was the essence of Cannes: the place where half the throng asked that succinct question of the other half, with varying degrees of offence taken.

The woman did Bambi with her eyes. 'He was Robin. The guy who played Batman's sidekick in the old TV series.'

'That Burt.'

'Well, Rosy – may I call you Rosy? – he's offering an exclusive on his tights.'

'Pardon me?'

'His tights. Apparently they gave him hell all through the famous TV series. They itched like crazy. Do you want the story?'

'Is there one?'

The PR's expression changed. 'You're not from *Cult Hero Monthly*?'

Rosy indicated not.

'Shit,' hissed the woman. 'Someone said you were. And now I just gave the story away.'

'I shouldn't worry,' grinned Rosy.

But the PR wasn't laughing. 'To the right people,' she said sternly, 'those tights were seminal.'

Rosy left the party with Jamie. They were barely off the gangplank and on dry land before she was berating herself.

'How was I to know that was Judd Macauley?' she wailed. 'Since when did I go to a teen white rap movie?'

Jamie shook his head. 'Don't you read the papers, Rosy?'

'I shall ignore that.'

'Only teasing,' he said. He quickly put a finger on his tongue and dabbed it at her cheek. 'Tssst! My, my, your face is burning.'

'I told you I never recognise anybody,' mumbled Rosy.

'Forget it! The guy's a nothing.' He assessed her embarrassment for a second. 'OK, he's a rich prat-of-the-moment nothing – but next year? Think of it this way: you're just way in front of the pack to say "Judd who?" '

She allowed herself to smile at that.

She then found herself telling him about being mistaken for a reporter from *Cult Hero Monthly*. 'I mean, do I look like my life is not complete without the inside story on Robin's tights? When you see me, do you sense the aura of anorak and Dr Who memorabilia?'

Jamie bit his bottom lip. 'Rosy, I have something to tell you, and there's no easy way of breaking it.'

'What?"

'You're a sweetheart.'

That startled her. 'What's that supposed to mean?'

'What it usually does.'

'Great. So you're saying I'm a silly idiot who gives the impression that she could get gushy about some old underwear on behalf of a sad and sentimental readership,' she sulked.

'Did I say that?'

'Not in so many words.'

There was a leaden silence during which they reached the edge of the marina. 'Don't jump,' said Jamie, at last.

She couldn't think of a reply.

'I can't say anything to you these days, Rosy.'

Rosy felt a sulk was a real possibility, mainly because her reaction had nothing to do with whatever he was saying tonight. The problem was entirely rooted in what had gone before, and had never been spoken about.

She opened her mouth to reply, crushingly, if she could manage it.

But he had crept up on her from behind, put his hands on her shoulders and turned her round into a soft, deep kiss.

'You always did have this effect on me,' said Jamie.

'I was going to say that,' murmured Rosy. She resolutely ignored a stray note of cynicism.

The mellow moment was playing out against a backdrop of Hollywood's most enduring clichés: the beach, the moonlight on the sea, a crescent of twinkly lights. What you only got in reality, thought Rosy with a sudden vision of a fat woman at the seaside by Beryl Cook, was a lumpy mosaic effect on your bottom from sitting on the pebbly shore.

It was largely with this in mind that she evaded his offer of a nightcap at his hotel.

'Dinner, then. Tomorrow night,' said Jamie. He nuzzled at her neck, then stroked her shoulder.

Rosy teased him with a *faux-Bardot* pout.

'Not even for dish of the day?' He nibbled her ear.

The velvet tickle was charged with unfinished business. 'Oh, all right then,' she said as the effect eroded her hardest resolutions. 'If it's business . . .'

* * *

When Rosy succumbed to a bout of romantic fatalism – and she was fully aware that she was doing so now, sitting on the bed staring into space in her seedy hotel room – her thoughts veered dangerously towards the conclusion that the gods had looked down less benevolently than they might have done in the past.

But sometimes there was a rhyme and a reason.

Kicking over the traces of her ridiculous obsession with Jamie would clearly involve some painful reassessments. But, hell, maybe she would have to steel herself to do it.

When she had been with Jamie she had felt sure of herself, of her value. Without him (and his certainty of his own value) she felt once more undefined.

And yet, she had never really had any illusions about who or what Jamie was. At the time, she'd thought that said something positive about the relationship. With hindsight, she could see it for what it was.

The monstrous delusion that love conquers all.

Perhaps it was time to lay the ghost. As it were.

33 | *Sword on Wardour Street*

Trendy restaurants like Le Dingo Café, an establishment for real and mock Sydney-siders, and the Ultimate New York Deli Place came and went, but the French House pub stayed where it was in Dean Street, a stone's throw from the sad, grimy bunkers of the British film industry. Its gloom and Truite aux Amandes were a testament to the way it was.

Anthony Sword clung to that.

He had a restorative solo lunch and walked down the street to the screening cinema, where he fervently hoped he had missed the film. If his information was correct, then this was the place he would find what he needed. He followed his nose to the sandwiches and drinks laid on after the preview of the latest US bloodbuster.

'Ah . . . *Freed* Willy!' sniped the *Dispatch*'s diminutive critic when he lumbered through the door. 'What are you doing here?'

Sword made an appropriately whale-like noise.

'Checking up on the littlest fish in the sea, thank you, Zack.'

Sword was gratified to find that the knowledge he'd acquired of the capital's trust-fund media babes since Lulu Bisset's employment on the column would at last come in useful. He approached a male of the species, who had been featured in the Sword's Secrets page after too many painful rewrites.

'It's Hugo, isn't it?'

'Yah?' said the young guy in a flying jacket and boots that could plough a field.

Anthony Sword needlessly introduced himself. 'What are you up to these days then, Hugo?'

'A couple of things in development. Possible documentary for Channel Four. The usual, you know . . .' Sword indicated that he was aware of the difficulties. 'No money . . .'

Apart from the trust fund, thought Sword. 'Apart from the money,' said the gossip columnist, 'which can be raised by those who want to make films based on stories which can be marketed to the tabloid newspapers?'

The would-be young director perked up.

Sword shook his head. 'I'm not in the market. Not in the sense you'd want. But you've heard all about this . . . wonderfully ludicrous film that half of London wants to lose their shirts on?'

'I have my ear to the ground . . .'

'The word is, Sir Philip Hawty, Lottie Landor . . . Benedict Pierce are involved. The basis is one of those appalling royal books.'

Hugo scratched his head through his floppy long hair.

'Ya-ah . . . I have heard,' said Hugo. 'Benedict Pierce is the executive producer, right?'

'News to me,' said Sword. 'This is a man who could not produce a belch after a vindaloo.'

'And . . . Tom Weedon, and Minky Winkworth, and Pooks Tribley, Tara Huntly-Worsley . . . Brett Trent and all that lot?'

'Heaven preserve us.'

'They say it will be *Ciao!* magazine in living technicolor.'

'Outrageous,' grinned Sword. 'I am relishing the comic possibilities already.'

'Rank amateurs,' said Hugo dismissively.

'My point precisely.'

'Anyone can call themselves a producer now. They'll never get it together – and then they have to find the finance.'

'But such a project does exist?'

A shrug. 'Everyone has a project. Not nearly everyone will have a film.'

'So what are the chances then, for this one?'

His informant smiled. 'From what I hear . . . they may have a gimmick which swings it.'

'Oh, yes . . .?'

'All the peripheral characters are playing themselves.'

'WHAT?'

'It would be entirely in keeping with the Zeitgeist. A metaphor for what is happening to the art in this country, in fact.'

Sword was still working that one out – and much more precious pontification – when he caught a cab back to the *Daily Dispatch*.

Back in his office, the files he needed from the reference library had gone walkabout, as had Lulu, and Pearson McKnight had managed to produce only one meagre paragraph on his current fantasy woman.

The elder hack had been far too busy consoling the girl after the latest tragedy to strike her uncertain progress.

'Poor little Amy,' said Pearson. 'She would have been absolutely perfect for a part in this film. Her agent put her up, and everything was going fine . . . they were all most well-to-do and well-connected names involved, apparently . . . all was well until they asked her where they had seen her before. So she gave them her CV – and you know what?'

Sword raised a weary brow.

'They said there had been a terrible mistake and there was no way she could do the part because . . . have you ever heard anything so ridiculous? . . . because she was an actress!'

34 | *A Rosy Glow of Optimism*

When the sun came up the next morning, Rosy was ready for action. The features editor might not have wanted to hear from her, but she could have kissed the receptionist when she gave her a message from the *Dispatch* anyway: *Call Tina*.

'Tina? It's Rosy. How's things?'

'Fine! Found any nice film stars yet?'

'Don't ask.'

'Well, I don't know whether this will help at all, but I have a mysterious communication for you.' Rosy's heart leapt before she could wonder why Tina should have it. 'It's only a telephone number, but you never know, it could be the great breakthrough.'

'Hold on, let me get my pen,' said Rosy, scrabbling in her bag with one hand. She took it down. 'No name?'

'Uh-uh,' said Tina.

'Oh, well, it'll be a surprise. It's probably a double glazing salesman, knowing my luck, but thanks. How's Sword?'

'Oh . . . so-so.'

'Oh?'

'He's in one of his moods when he can't find anything and goes completely off at the deep end when no one else can find what he wants either. Then . . . he didn't go out for lunch a couple of days ago – '

'Sounds ominous.'

'I came back into the room with my Mexican tuna bap from the canteen, and he had his head in his hands on his desk, holding a leaflet from Families Need Fathers. He was really embarrassed to see me, and – honestly, Rosy – I'm sure he had tears in his eyes.'

'Crumbs. Do you know what it was about?'

'Dunno,' said Tina. 'But it made me go all goosebumply. He can be ever so sensitive, you know. They don't half wring the heartstrings, some of those charity appeals, you know.'

'Yeah, I suppose so. All the same . . .'

'But – you have to admire him – he got straight back to work. He did a really vicious job on Mark Thatcher, slated poor old Denis, then had a right go at Benedict Pierce and that Hawty bloke. Then when Pearson said that he might have gone a bit too far, he started stamping his feet and *screaming* that there was going to be a ruthless expenses clampdown and that Pearson's would be the first to be scrutinised by the fraud squad!'

'Tina's practising stress relief,' said Rosy that evening. 'She's keeping out of Sword's way.'

Jamie smiled. They were on the road to St Paul de Vence. Jamie had managed to hire a red open-top Peugeot 205, which he was flogging smoothly along the Nice autoroute. The radio played acid jazz and a tuneful French verbal burble.

Rosy's afternoon had not proved as fruitful as the morning had promised. The mysterious telephone number had been answered by a dull voice at somewhere called Crighton, where no one seemed to know who Robert Arden was, let alone where. At a press conference at the Hotel Majestic – Jamie had generously let her cover it for him – there was not the tiniest lead on the Arden case.

After a while they drove on in a dusky, scented, road-rushing silence. Red and pink and orange flowers bloomed profusely on the central reservation of the six-lane road. Rolling, rounded hillocks on either side blocked all sense of nearness to the sea.

'You're quiet,' observed Jamie, turning slightly. In a navy polo shirt and cream chinos, he was a modern-day Cary Grant.

Rosy felt a dangerous shiver of anticipation, then got a grip. 'So are you,' she shrugged.

They turned off and curved along a purpling track up into the hills, through a landscape of rocky soil and gorse and lavender and gnarled stubby trees. The sky was slashed with vermilion and chrome yellow. The Peugeot climbed steeper and steeper until they could see the medieval village of St Paul de Vence clinging to a cliff in front of them.

Rosy had been certain that Jamie would take her to the Colombe D'Or. The restaurant was a mecca for the hack pack in Cannes – if their expenses were up to it. They would come back, wallets as empty as their stomachs were replete, and force back beers at Le Petit Carlton where they talked the less fortunate through their gourmandise.

But Jamie parked the car and led her past the entrance to the Colombe D'Or. They walked on past a huge fountain and crumbling arches, and through narrow, cobbled streets. Chi-chi galleries and gift shops jostled for attention even in the calm of evening. He led her down a tiny stepped alley, on which the street sign read 'Montée de Casse-Cou'.

Breakneck climb, thought Rosy. She opened her mouth to point out the similarities with Jamie's driving, then thought again. She didn't want anything to spoil what could be a perfect evening.

From the outside, the Bar-Restaurant Xavier where Jamie stopped had the air of a locals-only hangout. In contrast to most of the other stone buildings in the village, it was in a sorry state. Its façade was worn and patched, and Rosy wasn't sure at all about the cracked menu board which boasted: '*Cervelles* de la maison'.

'Come on,' said Jamie.

'Um, there's no way I'm eating brains,' Rosy warned him.

'Don't worry – it's code.' He took her hand and led her in before she had a chance to ask him what he meant.

Inside, Jamie was greeted as an old friend.

'Armand, this is my very good friend Rosy,' he said, when a bear of a middle-aged Frenchman in a chef's apron had released him from a hearty, soup-stained clasp.

Rosy stuck out her hand, partly in self-defence.

Chuckling, Armand and Jamie exchanged rapid-fire French, which set Rosy's ears alight with compliments. The proprietor led them to a corner alcove where the white walls were roughly finished. The table benefited from the twin clichés of dancing candle and red tablecloth. They had barely sat down when a *pichet* of red wine and a bowl of black olives were placed in front of them.

Rosy let Jamie order for both of them. For once, food was the last thing on her mind. She didn't realise how nervous she was until it became apparent that she'd nearly drained her glass of wine in two, and that she was discussing a film she hadn't actually seen.

'What bothers me is how every mass-market American film seems to be about coming out a winner, personally and professionally, through some transformation,' she was blathering. 'It's implied that we are all learning some great moral truth, when all we are really thinking is that if Julia Roberts is supposed to be a top crimebuster, why does her top lip quiver so much and why does she need so many simple explanations of every plot twist?' Whether she'd seen it or not, all those films were the same and she didn't buy Julia Roberts as a special agent for the FBI under any circumstances.

She was unable, however, to call on the same critical faculties when Jamie said ingenuously, a little later: 'I've changed, you know.' She gazed at him, wordlessly. 'I mean, take today. I was set up this afternoon by a French PR with three platinum blondes, and they didn't do a thing for me.'

He was impossibly gorgeous in the candlelight.

A rogue voice in her head hissed: *so that's where he was.*

But for once she ignored the fret, preferring to wonder whether she should reach out for one of his lovely golden hands, then settling for willing him to make the first move, and soon.

35 | *Sword's Soul Dinner*

With a lascivious leer for the audience, Sword sent the tassels on his 54DD breasts twirling.

'Have mercy, Lord!' cried Framboise. 'It don't mean a thang, if it ain't got that swang!'

Sword attempted a feeble bump and grind, and curled his tongue. There was sweat on his brow, but he'd finally got the knack. The flying parts of his revolting plastic apron – which depicted a nearly naked woman – were whirring like a twin-prop engine. The kitchen was marginally less messy than the closing scene of *Full Metal Jacket*.

Framboise wiped a mirthful tear from one brimming eye. 'OK, Tallulah, the cabaret comes later. First you're the cook, so git yer butt over here to deal with this marinade.'

'Yes, Ma'am.'

Their dinner-party for eight – he resolutely considered it *their* dinner party – was the closest Sword was getting to a birthday celebration.

No matter who had what great event in mind.

He had finally come round to a Fantastic Feast, mainly because it was his own idea.

They were having Champagne and his favourite St Emilion. And soul food.

'You'll love it,' Framboise assured him.

'That's what I'm afraid of. I am ever mindful of what happened to Mr Presley,' said Sword, when she returned from the Portobello market with a wagon-load of cornmeal, pork, yam and the gluey ingredients for what she described elegaically as 'one big, bad, *dee*vine mammy of a dessert'.

They were having a blow-out, in other words. Although, still residually aware of his waistline, Sword was resorting, against his better judgement, to using crème fraîche instead of double cream.

He was also going easy on the simmering bone of contention between him and his *confidante*. A pact had been made that no mention at all would be made of Framboise's husband-hunting activities. That had been an absolute prerequisite.

As far as the masquerade in hand was concerned, though, Sword's sense of theatricality had prevailed: the table was set in the garden, under a striped and swagged bedouin tent, where scented candles and gilded fruit nestled opulently in a centrepiece of roses and lilies. The final touch would be a scattering of petals on the ground.

Inside the kitchen, at four o'clock in the afternoon, the scene was more prosaic. Framboise, crashing at one of his prize pottery bowls, was making spoonbread. She wore one of his old shirts and a chef's apron, a concept he found that he liked, very much indeed. As they worked side-by-side, humming to the radio, she shared the kitchen secrets of her grandmothers, embellished by proud tales handed down from the slave quarters of the great plantations of the Deep South.

'Hey, hon, you sure stepped in those sweet potatoes!' she said, when he offered his handiwork for approval.

'I beg your pardon?'

She gurgled with laughter in that way she had. 'It's a compliment. Umm, umm, umm! Your pot-burnin' makes me want to slap my grandmamma!'

'I take it that's good news.'

'The best.' They gave their progress a serious, silent tasting. 'Mmm. It brings it all back, you know. I can hear my own grandmamma's voice saying those things. I'm telling you . . . it's bad.'

Her expression was so beatific that Sword laughed. 'What you're saying is that if Proust had been black, he'd have got all sentimental over a bite of chit'lins.'

'Something like that. But this is food, not picky little French biscuits,' sniffed Framboise.

'You're right there,' said Sword.

'And we didn't talk like that the whole time, either.' She studied his face, then said. 'It was always kinda conscious . . . this opposite-meaning language. My God – black slaves discovered *irony!*' Her palms were spread as wide as her eyes in hammed horror.

'All right, all right,' said Sword uncomfortably.

'You don't have to think about it everyday, but it's all there inside.'

'History, you mean?'

'History, A. What we are. Think about it.'

Eva was the first to arrive. She stepped out of the minicab Sword had laid on, resplendent in bronze crêpe and surprisingly tasteful onyx beads. He ushered her inside. Being a mother, she made straight for the kitchen.

The scent of deep-fried chicken and sweet molasses was as pungent as incense.

Eva greeted Framboise with a kiss and took a critical look at her son's decor. 'This is new,' she said, nodding at the banks of fitted cupboards. Sword had painted the wood himself, using the rubbed wax of a candle to achieve distressed effects in driftwood grey. He had skilfully added the same crud-of-ages finish to the display shelves. 'And what are these?' She picked up one of his deep blue bottles.

'Poison bottle,' said Sword portentously, recognising the familiar note of disapproval in her voice. 'Victorian.'

'Hmm,' said Eva, taking in the scene. 'It's the Old Curiosity Shop!'

'Thanks very much.'

'Now if you'd gone for a nice bit of Formica, it would all wipe clean in a trice, none of this – '

'Yes, thank you, Mother. Champagne?'

The advance party gathered by the high Gothic window which looked out to the garden. Between artfully faded curtains clipped to a wrought iron rail, they could see his fantasy banqueting scene on the dusky lawn. Sword noted with satisfaction the alluring glow of his faerie bower inside the drapes.

'Oooh!' gasped Eva. 'A touch of the Rudolph Valentinos! The Sheik's seduction tent!'

It hadn't occurred to Sword before then, but that was exactly what his subconscious had wanted it to be.

With immaculate timing, the rest of their guests all arrived during the first magnum of Krug: his old drama school friend Stella Winsome, now an apple-cheeked TV cook, and her husband Alan, God's accountant and her business manager; Mary Hawty, the rejuvenated ex-therapy ex-wife of the ex-Home Secretary Sir Philip, and her solicitor *beau* Johnny Tatton; and Simon Garner, known as Grunter, the proprietor of Sword's favourite Highgate restaurant.

These seven guests were the nearest Sword had to an inner circle, and he welcomed them heartily. The only jag of doubt to score his smooth enjoyment of the evening's beginning came as he busied himself with a bottle.

'I hear you're about to be announced as the lead in the new Trussock musical,' Sword caught Grunter gushing to Framboise as he refilled glasses.

'Oh, we're talking. Y'know,' she replied coyly.

She did not elaborate further, and he tortured himself, as he went to check on the Aga, that it was not musicals that she and Trussock were discussing at all.

36 | *Le Grand Dish*

Rosy stared critically enough at her reflection in the mirror. But she was reassured to see that her face was matt smooth and her cheeks were only a little flushed. The ripples of her hair had already caught streaks of sun. She fumbled on some more lipstick, regardless of whether that was too obvious a sign of her intentions.

It hardly mattered.

The way her eyes were shining was a dead giveaway.

She walked back out to the dining room to find Armand and a bottle of cognac had moved in on their romantic twosome.

Then she remembered. 'Don't tell me, it's time for dish of the day,' she smiled valiantly. A glass was waiting for her and she gave it her best shot. The brandy burned its way down to the disappointed butterflies in her chest.

Armand resumed a story he was serving up with some gusto. 'An' then, you 'ave Patsy Kensit who play Mia Farrow, *non?* And Shirley Maclaine who play Debbie Reynolds, and a Natasha who will be Patty 'Earst – and so it is no wonder that our *pauvre* French actresses they are confused, *non?* So Arielle, she go up to Patty 'Earst and say 'oo are you, I 'ave never seen one of your films?'

Rosy smiled politely as the two men roared with laughter.

'You haven't had any word from Robert Arden?' asked Jamie. Armand's great gallic shrug took in everything from the Gitane burning in his fingers to the roll of his bottom lip. 'Oh, well,' said Jamie, turning to Rosy. 'I'd say that makes it pretty certain he's not in Cannes yet.'

More affirmative gestures from the Frenchman were accompanied by a broad smile. '*Aaah, mon père!*'

Sure enough, the other man who rolled up was unmistakeably an older version of the restaurateur.

'May I introduce my father, Xavier.'

He greeted them with hearty handshakes and sat down. 'An' now I too shall make us think of some more sex, rage an' sin that is good for Mademoiselle Rosy . . .'

A distant bell tolled in her mind. But her head was already singing with the wine and the way Jamie was pressing his leg against hers under the table.

'I thought they were never going to stop,' giggled Rosy, when at last they were on their own and meandering hand-in-hand back to the car.

'Don't knock it. He's just written my first column.' Jamie turned her gently towards him. 'Which means I have all the more time to spend doing what I came here for. You.' His kiss was a toe-trembler.

They drove back to Cannes with the roof down, INXS hammering at the stereo speakers. There was no question about where they were going.

As she'd fully expected, his hotel room was a hundred times nicer than hers. The window was not only adult-sized with a view of the bay, it had a balcony and silk curtains. Jamie opened the balcony door.

Most importantly, in contrast to the torture rack provided for her as a single bed, the sleeping arrangements for Jamie were king-size. Not for the first time, she pondered on the relationship between travel accommodation and personal standing back at Dispatch House. Then she let such worries dissolve as Jamie emerged from the bathroom.

'Do you want a drink?'

She didn't.

'I, er . . .' There again . . . but no. She was dry-mouthed, not thirsty.

'Yes?' The spell of the night ride had been broken, thought Rosy, and with it her conviction that she was doing the right thing. Awkwardness was a stone in her throat.

'I never stopped thinking about you, Rosy. You have no idea what you put me through.'

She wanted to believe it.

He put his arms around her waist and held her tightly. 'You must know how much I care about you.'

They kissed long and hard, and when he began to discard her clothes she was feeling all the elation she'd worked up when she'd gone over and over this scene in her imagination.

On the bed, she said. 'Hang on a moment.'

'Mmm?'

She clicked off the lamp on her side of the bed, so that the glow deepened into peachy and flattering, as opposed to discomforting searchlights.

Jamie ran his hand over her shoulder and smiled knowingly. 'You *are* still the same old Rosy.'

There was an intonation in his voice she couldn't let pass. 'Meaning what?'

'Oh . . . You've changed.'

She was still the same old pushover as far as he was concerned, thought Rosy.

'I thought . . . I couldn't get through to you any more,'

went on Jamie softly. 'You were always rushing around, collecting your big names and by-lines, off doing so well for yourself . . . sweet Rosy who knew no one a year ago . . .'

'Jamie . . .'

He laughed, but in a rather strained way. 'Why did you treat me like that – as if you were moving further and further away . . .?'

It wasn't the time to say: *The way I treated* you?

'I suppose,' said Jamie, 'I couldn't bear you changing . . . and not caring about me any longer.'

Rosy put aside the rogue thought that here he was telling her she'd changed, when the reason they had parted was precisely because he hadn't. 'Believe me,' she said, reaching out for him. 'I wasn't ignoring you – not with my mind.'

'There were times when I thought you hated me.'

'As if . . .'

He continued whispering endearments but she had no need of them. When all was said, and she was undone, she was becoming accomplished at putting doubts behind her.

How often had she wondered whether she was irredeemably in love with him? As she came for the third time, she knew she hated him for making her feel so good.

37 | *A Spectre at the Feast*

'The way excess comes upon me,' said Anthony Sword, flourishing a gambo drumstick like a latter day Henry VIII, 'is that the brain shrieks "no", the stomach sighs "YES!", and the mouth does what comes naturally.' They all raised their glasses to that.

'What worries me, is how self-conscious everyone has become,' said Grunter, with some seriousness. 'Present company excepted, of course.' He swept a grand gesture around the gathering in the fluttering marquee set in the grounds of the Graceland of gossip.

'Hear, hear!' called Eva, joined by Framboise.

The candlelight played on the faces of his guests as the bibbed bistro owner expounded his theory. 'Did you know, for instance, that there is a hostess-turned-foodie-fashion-victim who has been distraught since her speciality Sea Breezes were adopted as the signature cocktail at the Atlantic bar? Or the current situation where one simply daren't even mention Steak Diane or Lobster Thermidor outside the inverted commas of a seventies dinner party . . .'

'Fondue!' tossed in Stella, with a wince.

'You'd need "fancy dress" on the invitations for fondue, darling,' said Grunter.

Framboise led the laughter with her rich brew of bass and blues.

'Yet, I'll give you another example which shows the complete opposite,' continued Grunter. 'I dined with a certain restaurant press relations lady last week, and she told me that a Very Smart Person Who Ought To Know . . . has been serving Campbell's soup sauces as part of her intimate suppers.'

Raucous gasps of mock-Gothic horror.

'I said to her . . . I said, "Don't you think that a Campbell's soup sauce is an absolute abomination which flies in the face of all that we have been fighting for on these shores over the past years?" And you know what she said? "This is a *post-ironic* Campbell's soup sauce"!'

'I think I know who you mean,' chipped in Lady Hawty, with the grimace of one who might well have been obliged to dispose of such a nonsense using napkin and handbag under the table.

'Full-time job keeping up,' frowned Sword.

'Where I went the other night, it was all terribly English,' said Framboise, camping up the accent. 'This chap turned to me after pudding and said: "Tickle more goat?" '

'What?' asked Eva. 'The dirty old devil!'

'It was quite a relief, let me tell you, when it turned out to be a cheese, from the depth of Devon somewhere.'

After further proof of Anthony Sword's decadent attitude toward his wine cellar, the ceremonials began.

Eva's gift was a new CD recording of *La Bohème*.

Framboise gave him a pair of antique opera-glasses inlaid with mother of pearl.

Stella and Alan produced a glorious chrome olive oil dispenser.

Mary and Johnny and Grunter between them had come

up with a set of framed cuttings from old movie magazines signed by the stars. They had made a perfect choice: Vivien Leigh, Barbara Stanwyck, and, on a yellowing page headed Melody Master, the autograph of Ella Fitzgerald. They had tracked them down via a man who knew a dealer who knew an old couple who had once worked in the hospitality suite of a theatre in San Francisco.

He was infinitely touched. 'Always judge a man by his presents,' he grinned.

Conversation mellowed over coffee. To Sword's great pleasure in his own good judgement, the night remained balmy enough to stay in his chosen setting. 'Helped no end by this crackling pair of braziers,' said Sword proudly.

Grunter and Alan sniggered.

'Sounds like a Carry On film,' said Eva. 'Talking of which . . . you've heard about this film?'

'Film?' said Sword, absently, feigning ignorance.

'Ooh . . . all those . . . people you write about . . . you know . . .'

Sword raised his eyebrows, but indulgently. When his mother's information could be unravelled, it was always deadly accurate.

'Ah . . . I may have had a few sherbets this evening . . . but . . . everyone's talking about it, the people in it . . .'

'Do I sense an Actor-In-Acting-Job-Drama in the offing for the column?'

'At one time, it was aristos in rock bands – now they're all into films.'

'Don't tell me – a production from the crazed imagination of 007 Lord Diplock deep in his Shepherd Market penthouse.'

'No stoned earl unturned,' laughed Grunter.

'That's the one!' said Eva. 'He's in it . . . and ooh, loads of others. I'd do it myself, only . . . it's been a while, you know . . . there's that young one, with the hair, you always write about, and the tall one with the bits on the side . . . and they're all playing *themselves!'*

'Don't they always?' asked Sword.

Eva had left, East Sheen-bound, in her mini-cab by the time they got to the bottom of that one. Sword swung a fork into the remains of the Mississippi mud pie with a lumberjack's vigour.

'What was that?' asked Stella.

'What?'

'Isn't that the doorbell?' she said.

'At this hour?' Sword dismissed the suggestion.

'Go and see.'

'I'll come too,' volunteered Framboise.

At the door was a man in a chauffeur's uniform, holding a peaked cap. 'Anthony Sword?' Sword nodded. 'I have a message for you.' A white envelope was proffered.

Sword flicked on an outside light, and ripped into the envelope. The message this time was succinct. 'Meet your father.'

Silence.

'What is this?' scowled Sword, handing it instinctively to Framboise. 'Who sent this?'

'I'm sorry. I cannot tell you, sir.'

Framboise's reaction hardly did justice to the gravity of the situation. 'Well, whaddaya know?' she whistled.

'Meet him?' barked Sword, slapping the note.

'He's waiting in the car, sir.'

'This. . . I don't think . . .'

The crunch of footsteps on gravel confirmed that he was right in that one respect.

Seconds later, the gossip columnist found himself staring into some sickeningly familiar features.

And behind him, suddenly, another man appeared out of the darkness. Sword recognised him immediately as the photographer who worked for the Onlooker column in the *Daily Post*.

38 | *Chasing Merv*

'Merv?'

'No.'

'Is Merv there?'

'No. This is Marv. Who's calling?'

Benedict ignored the infinite possibilities for confusion he had dialled into, and enunciated as clearly as he could after three bottles of Côtes du Rhône and as many joints the night before. 'Would you know where Merv is, Marv?'

'Listen jerk, I don't even know who *Merv* is.'

A pause. 'He's not you, then?'

'Who *is* this?'

'Tell him . . . tell him this is Pierce.'

'Pierce *Brosnan?*' Benedict detected a twinge of respect in the West Coast vowels. 'Sure I'll tell Merv. You sound pretty rough, man.'

'Just tell him,' snapped Benedict.

He congratulated himself on remembering to leave his number.

On his way out of the hotel, he picked up a message from his secretary back at the Post. Sir Philip Hawty, it said, had been in touch to say 'Mission Accomplished'.

Benedict caught up with his next quarry on the steps of the Palais des Festivals at around lunchtime. 'James!'

Jamie Raj swept a made-for-TV smile over a gaggle of schoolgirls on the concourse who had snatched his photograph with a Canon Automatic. They were failing to agree which film he had made, or who the stunning girl was on his arm.

Benedict, on the other hand, was enviously aware that the blonde was a Côte d'Azur heiress for whom he personally would have swum to Tangier, or walked to Monaco, should the chance ever have arisen.

As it was, he greeted them nonchalantly and said, 'I may have a proposition for you, dear boy.'

'I am incorruptible, Benedict. There is no way I will be bought by the opposition. Except for a great deal of money, that is.'

Benedict laughed. 'I'm not talking newspapers.'

'Not another pathetic attempt to meet a decent woman through my good offices.'

'If that's a reference to the lovely Rosy Hope, you can – '

Jamie held up his hand.

The *Post*'s man wondered for a moment whether his rival's deputy editor really would turn out to possess the overriding vanity he had always ascribed to him. 'I'm wondering whether you might fancy this for real?' He swept his arm around to encompass the palm trees, the star-spotters, the garish pre-publicity posters.

'This . . . what?'

The amber eyes were interested now, Benedict was sure. 'Jamie, I could make you a star.'

Of course, he was rather cosmopolitan, but Jamie Raj had always had the *Look*. That misleadingly foppish, Ralph Lauren model about ancient university town way about him.

Long before Hugh Grant came on the scene.

The putative star smiled raffishly. 'How reassuring it is, Benedict, to see that in life, as in your tedious column, you've bought every last hackneyed phrase.'

Benedict had taken that as a holding no. Back in his hotel room he was soon revitalised by a passionate siesta with Lottie. After the small dissatisfactions of the morning, he was more than pleased to find that it was only his spirits that were sagging.

He rolled off her, and pulled her gently into the crook of his arm. Her hair was soft and coconut scented against his chest. He sighed contentedly. 'Are you having a nice time, little Lottie?'

'Mmm . . .'

'This could be the big one, you know . . . if it comes off.'

'Sorry . . . what?'

He chose his words carefully, in the event that the walls were bugged while the big cheeses were in town. 'The *Bernie Ziegler* project, of course.'

'IF is a very big word. Especially here,' she murmured.

'Have faith. Feel the excitement,' he urged, wondering whether round two might be on the cards.

She sat up sharply. 'Spare me the fantasies, Benedict – either before or afterwards.'

'Eh?'

Lottie was already half way to the bathroom. Her buttocks were pert pearls below the slim stem of her back. 'Thinking of Bernie Ziegler may do it for you, but I can assure you he does nothing for me.'

She was wrong in that.

Benedict had been thinking – hard – about the blonde Côte d'Azur heiress.

39 | *Many Happy Returns*

The morning after his birthday party, he had many happy returns of spicy jambalaya and hopelessness. Sword sank deeper into his garden seat. Momentarily, a shaft of panic bubbled up from his stomach, but he fought it back with a determined draught of wine.

The telephone rang, yet he wallowed incommunicado, a depressed whale contemplating oblivion.

His caller was persistent but, in the end, not as strong-willed as he was. By the time she appeared in person – a water-melon pink blur breasting the corner of the side of his grey Frankenstein's house – he suspected he might have had one too many. Already.

'Why aren't you answering your calls?' demanded Framboise. 'I have to come over in a cab every time I want to talk?' She stood in front of him, as four square as ever a round person could stand, hands on hips.

Sword said nothing.

'Very clever,' she retorted.

He squinted out over the plump rolling lawn. There were red roses in bud, and a brave show of petunias trumpeting over his half barrel tubs.

'And what's this?'

He swiped up his glass of Barolo before she got there, and up-ended it. A childish gesture, he knew. But then, wasn't that what this was all about? 'That, my dear Framboise, was a beaker full of the warm south.'

'And you,' she responded, quick as anything, 'are left, a blushful *hypocrite*.'

'Mmm . . . how poetic we are this morning.'

'We're talking here about taking control of your life,' said Framboise. 'Your *real* life.'

'Ah . . . in that case, perhaps you should join me in another bottle.'

She ignored the provocation. 'What's the first rule of gossip?'

He grunted irritably.

'How about . . . never believe a word until you check for yourself?'

Silence.

'Or, nothing is ever quite what it seems?'

'Spare me the truisms. If I'd wanted cod philosophy, I'd have switched on Richard and Judy.'

'I can't believe you! The way you're acting, it seems you might actually *believe* this!'

'Time generally throws out the chancier conclusions.'

She shook her head, not understanding.

'It has taken so long to come out,' explained Sword. 'There's more chance that it's true. Been hidden for a good reason.'

Framboise let out a frustrated sigh. 'Then . . . there's only one way to find out.'

He poured more wine and remained sullen.

'The taxi's out front waiting.'

'Eh?'

'We're going to see what Eva has to say.'

The world of truth spun on strange axles, Sword knew. He had long been wary of digging too deeply for it at 2, Fairlawn Avenue.

His feeling of unreality was compounded when his mother showed no surprise at their arrival at her house almost an hour later.

Sword came straight to the point. 'Sir Philip Hawty turned up last night. After you left.'

He noted the glance between the elderly good-time girl and Framboise. 'So I hear,' said Eva.

'You know what I have to say, then?' He should have known these women were accomplices.

Eva sniffed. 'I got the gist.'

Refusing to sit, Sword studied his mother intently. She was wearing more face powder than he'd ever seen. The effect – allied with the red rims of her eyes and the elaborate lacquer screen against which she sat – was disconcertingly Japanese. He had no idea why he should be the one who felt like Lieutenant Pinkerton about to betray Madam Butterfly. 'Well?' he said flatly.

Framboise had rattled in from the kitchen with coffees on a tray. He accepted a cup. He needed to be sober when he heard this.

'I – I'm not sure, dear.'

'Not *sure?*' He was pacing the Axminster.

'It's . . . possible,' said Eva querulously.

'Dear God!'

Receiving this news was like putting on diving boots. He was yanked powerlessly down to the depths of despair. He slumped backwards into a seat, provoking an angry crack from the ageing wood.

'It was a long time ago . . .'

'Well, that makes it all right then. Fifty years and approximately nine months enough time to make it all right!' gasped Sword, eyes rolling. '*Don't* treat me like an idiot.'

Eva was downcast.

'I think the time has come,' said Framboise, soft but firm. 'Enough with the idle chatter. What we need is some straight talking.'

40 | *Party Games*

Lottie Landor wasn't the greatest actress in the world, but Rosy had always liked her. When Rosy first started on the Sword's Secrets column, she had been kept fully briefed on all aspects of Lottie's life by the doyenne of the theatrical tipsters. Lottie was one of Eva Coutts' girls – or she had been.

'You seem to feature an awful lot in the *Daily Post* these days,' Rosy said to her disingenuously. 'What *can* it all mean?' The truth glowed in the actress's pretty cheeks. 'Don't go all coy,' teased Rosy.

'Benedict's been very good to me.'

'Lottie, I don't work for Sword any more. I hold no brief. If you're having a good time with Benedict Pierce, and you like him, well . . . that's great.'

The female lead of Chicken and Chips licked her lips. 'Let's say that we both get what we want out of it.' A pause. 'Why are *you* blushing, Rosy?'

'Am I? Must be the heat.'

Rosy's night – about a year ago – with Benedict Pierce was still bones-to-water on the cringe scale. She wondered whether Benedict had passed that juicy snippet to Lottie, then judged that the gossip columnist's sauve gentleman image was too important to him for that. The incident hardly spoke volumes about *his* irresistibility.

Lottie carried on regardless. 'Will you come to the screening? There's a BAFTA dinner after at the Palais. I made sure you were on the list.'

Rosy smiled. 'I got my invitation. Thanks, I'd love to.'

'Jamie's on the list too.'

'And why should that -?'

'You two were spotted on the beach the other night.'

Rosy rolled her eyes. 'The gossip in this town – '

'You're blushing again, Rosy.'

She was also hugging a far more satisfying bedroom memory. 'Have you seen Jamie here yet?' she asked, craning round.

'Uh-uh,' said Lottie. Then she added cautiously. 'You're not the only one looking for him.'

'Oh.'

'There's a very persistent French girl over there. By the door, in black – no, don't look round now, Rosy . . .'

It was involuntary. Rosy stared across the room. 'A very-blonde? With a silver Chanel rucksack?'

'Mmm,' confirmed Lottie.

'Who is she?'

Lottie bit her lip. 'Look, Rosy . . . I'm telling you this as a friend, right?'

Rosy's heart plummeted like a rock into a deep dank well. Fixing Lottie with a steady look, she said lightly, 'We all know what Jamie's like.'

'Her name's Minette, her father owns half the Riviera, and Jamie's been with her most nights since he got here. They had a furious argument over lunch on the Blass yacht this lunchtime and made up all afternoon at the Sofitel Méditerranée . . .'

'H-How do you know all this?'

'I was at the lunch with Matt and my producer,' said

Lottie gently. 'And . . . Benedict is staying at the Sofitel. You don't think he'd let a girl like that go by without tracking her every move, do you?'

Rosy tried to tell herself that it might not be true. She made a brave grab at blithe worldliness. 'Men, eh . . .?' she ventured, a wobble in her voice.

'Yeah,' agreed Lottie. There was a tiny gasp of a pause before she said. 'Now, *really* don't look now, Rosy . . .'

But it was too late.

It would have been hard to miss Jamie under any circumstances. The night after the night before, her every cell had been on the look-out.

There wasn't much room for misinterpretation in the way he kissed the girl hello.

Half an hour later, they had cut loose from the party. By a seemingly mutual need they found a bar and hit the Heinekens. Jamie and the blonde had disappeared together straight away.

'God, this is a relief,' said Lottie, exhaling cigarette smoke at the ceiling.

'You're telling me,' groaned Rosy.

A fan slogged round above them, while the decor was dedicated mainly to sporting memorabilia. Any declarations of passion here were clearly heartfelt, concerning as they did their devotion to the football field. At present those were the only male vows Rosy was prepared to believe.

'I mean, Benedict's great and everything.'

'I'm not on duty now, Lottie.'

'OK, he can be a real wanker.'

'Oh, I can't imagine *that* . . .'

As Lottie detailed Benedict's many shortcomings, Rosy's thoughts continually strayed back to Jamie. This time only *last night*, she fulminated, we were driving down the coast road and I was lying back luxuriously in my seat, and he was . . .

'Rosy?'

'Umm?'

'You were miles away.'

'I was . . . are you absolutely sure, Lottie, that Jamie didn't see us?'

'Didn't seem that he could have.'

'And they were together this afternoon – how can you be sure about that?'

Lottie paused, as if working out a diplomatic response. 'The same way I can be sure that . . . you went back to Jamie's room at about midnight last night, and you stood on the balcony for a while . . . and you left after breakfast this morning.'

'Wha-a-t? Are you MI6 or something?' Rosy massaged her temples. She couldn't believe how everything was crumbling around her so fast.

'I was with Benedict . . . in the room next door. It shares a balcony, and . . . I don't quite know how to tell you this . . . but when the balcony door – which is glass, right? – is open at night . . .'

She hardly dared listen now.

'Because of the lights, what's going on in the room . . . is kind of reflected on the door . . . like a screen . . .'

In other words then, she had done a nude scene, with not even a closed set.

Rosy steeled herself to give a measured reply, and then promptly burst into tears.

41 | *The Village of the Damned*

Rosy woke with a start. It was freezing. The window of her hotel room was wide open and rattling. Through it she could see the sky, grey and sullen, brewing up for worse.

For a moment she was disorientated. The curtains filled with air like sails, bounced slowly off the wall, and then deflated. Goosepimples pinched her arms. She was still wearing the black lawn dress she'd gone to the party in the night before. She had slept where she'd fallen.

She had a raging thirst. Her head was a block of stone when she tried to raise it from the bed, and her queasiness was far worse than it had been the previous night.

The previous night. The . . . party.

Jamie. Minette.

Rosy made it to the bathroom just in time.

Swaying back to her room on spaghetti legs, she fell on the window to close it, then slumped down on the bed.

Under the door, that morning's copy of *Screen International* lay unread.

Rosy lay back, undead.

As soon as she was strong enough to pick up the telephone, she placed the call to the only possible person.

'Emma!'

'Rosy?'

'More or less. How's things?'

'Fine. How's Cannes, more to the point?'

'It's the pits,' said Rosy.

Emma laughed. 'Same old film stars, same old glitz, same old Rosy!'

'Put it this way, Emma, in film terms it's less Harry met Sally than Village of the Damned.'

'I get the picture.'

Groans.

'Starring Jamie Raj,' pinpointed Emma, with unerring accuracy.

'How did you -?'

'The gorgeous Jamie is being sorely missed on the party circuit here. There was nearly a debutantes' revolt the other night at the Grosvenor House when he didn't turn up. There was an official inquiry, as a result of which several parties have been postponed by lovesick debs, but the terrifying mothers will regroup at the barricades for his return.'

'Very funny,' snarled Rosy.

'And not too far from the truth, either. So what's the story?'

Rosy told her, stepping up the narrative when she reached the beach scene. 'I mean, can you believe it, the guy was giving me lines from *Phil Collins* songs!' she groaned as shame crept up her neck.

'I can believe it all too well,' said Emma. 'And I suspect you did at the time.'

'God, I'm such an idiot.'

'I wasn't going to say it.'

'I mean, the bullshit register was going ape, but did I want to know? And you know what the irony is?'

'Uh-uh.'

'I sometimes think that I *am* the only one who ever knew him at all,' said Rosy.

'Oh, please . . .'

But Rosy was expounding her theory. 'So why does my self-esteem get all wrapped up in what he thinks of me? I can see where the idiocy begins – '

'Love as a reflection theory,' noted Emma.

Rosy gulped. 'Well, you're right there as far as Jamie's concerned. His greatest love is right there in his mirror.' She wasn't going to mention the other reflection, to anyone.

'At least you realise.'

'Emma, I've always known. That never stopped me before.'

'This is true.'

'In fact, that probably made it worse. The reasoning went: He reckons, he's so marvellous that he could have any woman he wanted, so anyone he chooses to have a relationship with will be right up there with the best he can find. Therefore, much flattery and confidence in oneself. He would never have a relationship with anyone who would not reflect well on him.'

'Mmm,' said Emma.

'Mmm? What do you mean, Mmm?'

'You're right in one sense. About reflecting well on him. The problem is, you don't seem to realise that your confidence was never much to do with him in the first place, but with you.'

'I wish I could go back to what I was before.'

'Before?'

'Prelapsarian, before the Fall. Before Jamie.'

42 *Sword's Vision in Purple*

'What I want to tell you is that I love you,' said Sword to Framboise.

She was a vision in purple, and as he said it her lagoon eyes softened. She smiled, directly at him, and his heart expanded to fill the world.

'I don't know what to say,' she said tentatively.

'Don't say anything,' he urged her, coming as close as he could while keeping his focus on her dear face. 'Just let me tell you what I've wanted to say for months but never dared.'

Framboise laughed, her round cheeks expanding to a curious fuzzy flatness.

'You're most kind, but I'm jus' me, doing my thing like I always have. I don't see myself as this cult figure you talk about.'

The camera cut to the interviewer. 'And, on that note, would you sing for us here? Ladies and gentlemen – Miss Framboise Duprée!'

Framboise raised herself from the studio sofa, and walked over to her band.

Anthony Sword, alone in his gothic sitting room, stared numbly at her on the television screen.

The sweet notes of her song pierced his soul.

He tried once again, with the usual result.

Whenever he had called Framboise over the past four days, he had heard the same chatty exhortation to leave a message. She hadn't got back to him.

Another call to Puccini's confirmed – worryingly – that she would not be appearing in her cabaret spot for at least another week.

The television jabbered to itself. Sword investigated his immediate options for an evening's entertainment. Whenever he saw the word *mini-series* written down in a TV listings guide, he misread it as 'miseries'. Usually, it turned out not to be a misreading after all, if he ever found himself watching the thing. He let the *Radio Times* drop from his hands as he slumped in his seat.

He let his eyes travel over the regency striped covers he had made for his junk shop chairs, his latest discovery in the Goldhawk Road. His housekeeper had done him proud with elbow grease on the tarnished tin pails that had been transformed into vases of Japanese-style blossom. Then there were his newest additions to the eclectic decor: the old shop window dummies, dressed in antique clothes.

On a night like this, it was like sharing a house with a motley collection of ghosts through the ages. He could still hear Framboise's shriek: 'Jeez! Madame Tus-swords!'

It was party night, as always, back in the centre of the metropolis. Sword clearly had time to get down to some social work there, but with his rival, Pierce, running limp bulletins on Lottie Landor and other obscure Europeans in Cannes, there was no need. The edge had gone from the contest.

Not that that made Sword feel the slightest bit better about his own predicament.

For the lack of one person, he was immeasurably

lonely. He had rung and rung her since they had gone to East Sheen together but she hadn't answered.

He regained his equilibrium in the only effective way. He sank a bottle of St Emilion.

Then he picked a fight.

He called Sir Philip Hawty's club and asked for him.

'Who's calling please?'

'Tell him . . . his *son*.'

An agitated silence, and the patter of large traditional shoes. 'Hawty here. Who is this?'

Sword produced a blood-curdling, cutlass-wiping laugh. 'Don't tell me you have forgotten already . . .'

'Sword? Is that you . . .?'

'Don't expect me to call you . . . *Daddy*.'

'Are you drunk, man?'

'Not nearly, yet. I want to talk to you.'

'Not here. I can't talk here, at my club. Er, how did you find me here, anyway?'

Sword cackled. 'It's in the book. Under Massage Parlours.'

'Ah.'

'I do hope I'm interrupting something?'

'Let me make my position perfectly clear . . .'

'What a ghastly proposition. No, let *me*,' said Sword. 'I don't know what the fuck you thought you were up to the other night, but I am not a man who takes kindly to having his parties disrupted by an incompetent and pathological publicity seeker.'

'I suppose that apologies are out of the question?'

'By a mile.'

'Ah, well, anyway . . .'

'It was Pierce who put you up to it, I imagine?'

'I . . . well . . .'

'Anything to do with a certain book, and the worst film idea ever mooted, even in these desperate times?'

'Ah . . . this is a little tricky . . . don't want to say too much . . . before contracts are signed . . .'

'Listen to me carefully, Hawty, and I will tell you what you will have to do to lessen the prospects of an uncontrollable scandal breaking in the most famous gossip column in the world.'

'And if I can't?'

'In that case,' said Sword equably. 'I destroy you.'

43 | *Through the Portals*

The moment had come.

On the other side of the road, the regular square shapes of the houses made pebbledashed battlements of Fairlawn Avenue as he cut across, striving self-consciously for nonchalance. Moments before, on the high street, he had caught sight of himself in a shop window and been thrown by the unexpected glimpse of a greying man in a nondescript raincoat. The impression, to his horror, was of a middle-aged boy. Someone whose twenties and thirties had washed suddenly away.

He rang the doorbell.

The elderly woman opened the door slowly and peeped round the edge.

'Yes?' she asked.

'Eva Coutts?'

'Who wants her?'

'My name is Crighton,' he said. 'John Crighton.'

'Of?'

'Uh, I'm from . . . your son, Mrs Coutts.'

'The *Sun*. I don't speak to *Sun* reporters.'

'No – not the *Sun*. Your son,' he said.

'What about him?' She had barely opened the door more than five inches.

He attempted a winning smile. 'Could I come in, do you think?'

She seemed to consider this for a few seconds. Then, to his astonishment, she did what few elderly ladies on their own should ever do.

Eva opened the door.

She was a bulky woman in a deep red dress covered with an old fashioned floral apron. Her hair was grey, styled after the Queen. When she smiled, her teeth were yellow against too much startlingly red lipstick.

'You should know,' said Eva, still smiling, 'that in my hand, which is inside my apron pocket, I have a large and lethal hat-pin that was once used to kill a man.' She paused. 'Should you be tempted to try anything.'

Crighton humoured her as he passed into the hall of 2, Fairlawn Avenue, the unlikely scene (he now knew) of legendary party gatherings of the great and the not-so-good. In his mind, it had been a shrine to suburban kitsch, but the reality was disappointing. A waxed rubber plant stood by a plush pink upholstered telephone seat by a small stained glass window, but otherwise the house was remarkably restrained.

She led him into a rear sitting room so crammed-to-bursting with theatrical memorabilia that it reminded him uncomfortably of his last asthma attack. The dusty atmosphere began to seize his chest.

'A cup of tea?' asked Eva, her manner friendly enough.

A piece of cake, thought Crighton. 'That – that would be nice. Please.'

'Sit down, then.'

He did so, on a gold velveteen sofa from which vantage point he had a view of the garden through open French windows and considerable drapery. Outside, lupins nodded and busy lizzies ran riot.

She was back within minutes. It was almost as if she had been expecting him. 'Now,' she said, setting down the tray and handing him a workmanlike mug. 'You can tell me what this is all about, Mr . . .?'

'Well,' began Crighton. He had rehearsed this moment so often during the past few months, it now seemed unreal. 'Your son, Anthony Sword – '

'I know who he is, thank you, Mr . . . er?'

'It was revealed last year that – '

'Are you *sure* that you're not from the *Sun?*'

'I am not a *Sun* reporter, Mrs Coutts.'

'Only, I've had no end of trouble with them, in the past. Never get anyone's name right, for a start . . .'

He sipped his tea. He could see her clenched hand through her apron pocket. 'I have . . . an interest . . .'

'Now just you hang on a minute. I've seen you before, haven't I?'

He regretted immediately that he had walked past the house on several occasions prior to taking this plunge. 'I wouldn't have thought so . . .'

'I can't for the life of me think where. It'll come to me . . .' She cocked her made-up face, and he noticed properly for the first time how her vermilion lipstick had seeped into the crevices around her mouth, giving a grotesque clown effect. 'You're not one of those celebrity stalkers are you? Only I've had me day, I'll tell you that now. But I've read about your sort – that woman . . . ooh, you know the one, she was in that film, with the man who . . . ah! m'poor ol' mind's gone . . .'

'I'm afraid I don't, and I'm not a st– '

'That woman . . . ah! you must know her – you'd know her if you saw her! You've probably stalked her, in fact!'

'Mrs Coutts . . .!'

Eva went on.

He stared in agony at her, perched on a seat under a

yellowing poster which bore the legend: THE BALLYHOO GIRLS . . . Mitcham Empire. 'Mrs Coutts! I am *not* a stalker.'

'Bet they all say that,' she mumbled.

'Could we perhaps . . .?'

'All right then . . . who are you?'

He sighed with exasperation with the woman, anxious to channel this stream of garrulity. 'You could say, I am a researcher.'

'Telly? A television researcher? Ooh, no, I don't do that. And I don't talk to anyone about my son. Never have, and that's that. Ask anyone, they'll all say it.' She made a zipping action across her seeping lips.

'History,' he said.

'You're a historian?'

'Of sorts, Mrs Coutts. Or should I say, Miss Banks?'

Silence.

'What do the names Evelyn le Chêne, Jean Moulin and Gardener mean to you?' he asked stealthily.

That rocked her, he could see. 'You know then?'

He nodded.

Eva was looking at him intently and quizzically. 'How?'

'The department . . .' he said, trailing off almost apologetically.

'Ah.'

'So you can see why I want to talk to you about the man they called L'Honorable.'

Silence.

'We may need some more tea,' said Eva eventually.

A fresh pot appeared and they began again, hindered at every turn by her recollections – or lack of them.

'You see . . . the man – you know the one, the one who

went to the place first and met the girl . . . ah! I can see her clear as a bell . . .'

He was getting nowhere. He could not decide whether these were well-worn tactics, or a serious personality defect.

'So you see . . .'

He did not see. He was wearying fast.

He cursed the realisation that the old dear had lost it. Her remaining marbles were straining simultaneously to drink tea and fail to remember.

She was dribbling now.

Crighton yawned. His eyes were heavy, but he made a concerted effort to heave them open and keep them pointing in the direction of her confusion, now he had her in disarray.

'Tell me . . . all about L'Honorable,' he said.

44 | *A Woman in Red*

Close up, the few truly familiar facets of Benedict Pierce were the ones Rosy had forgotten:

The way he almost always talked about himself.

His self-confident actorish drawl.

The way he weighed up his gold cigarette lighter and made sure the designer name was still there, as if it signified all he held dear in the world.

But since when had he held his knife like a pen?

Far from bothering to hide the fact that he had a line to the great Robert Arden, all he had done when she ran into him on La Croisette was boast about his connections.

She wouldn't have agreed to have a drink with him otherwise.

They were sitting in the American pavilion, a great tented structure on the sea front with a bouncy temporary floor and, no matter what disguises were effected, the unmistakeable air of trade fair.

Rosy lined up a pile of press releases she had collected from the Palais des Festivals, adjusting the edges until they were precision-engineered. The battle lines were drawn.

'You're not going to read those things?' sneered Benedict.

'Well, I – '

She wanted to say: 'Look, Benedict, could we get this over and done with? Let's agree that we're not going to mention a certain embarrassing incident after a night at Mirabeau's last year, and then you can cut the crap and tell me where I can find Robert Arden.'

Impossible.

She settled for disingenuousness. 'I was feeling guilty. Better do some work at some stage this week. Stage one: carry press releases back to hotel.'

Benedict might have noticed her cheeks flush if he hadn't been looking over her shoulder for someone more important. 'So, are you down here to help Jamie?' he asked, when it appeared he couldn't spot anyone. 'I thought you'd stopped working for Sword?'

'Well . . . sort of.' She didn't want to give anything away. If that meant he took her for an idiot, then so much the better.

'Lulu Bisset is with him now on the Diary, as I understood,' said Benedict. A questing wrinkle appeared on his smooth brow.

Rosy stifled a grunt of annoyance at the mention of that name again. Then she took the chance to get something straight that had irked her for months. 'She says she used to work for you, but you've never had a reporter called Lulu, have you?'

'No,' said Benedict. 'She was my secretary. For about two weeks.'

Rosy was taken aback, for the three seconds it took to realise how much that explained.

'She's ambitious,' went on Benedict, insinuatingly. 'As hell.'

'Hell would be right,' said Rosy before she could stop herself.

She couldn't quite read the gossip columnist's buttery

expression. 'I see. I gather she hasn't been that pleasant to you, has she?'

'To *me?*' frowned Rosy. 'What d'you mean? I don't really have anything to do with her.'

Benedict turned his baby blues on her. 'It's none of my business now, but to hear her talk, I'd say she was jealous of you in some way.'

'That's ridiculous.'

'Not what I heard.'

'I've learned to be very wary of the word jealousy in work situations,' said Rosy, feeling nervous tremors in her legs. 'It usually means something quite different. Like, *about to be done over.*' She resolutely was not going to ask what the perfidious Lulu had been saying about her.

Benedict arched an immaculately groomed eyebrow as this became clear. 'No one believes her when she says that Sword doesn't rate you, I can assure you of that.'

'I really don't want to know, Benedict.'

'You're a sweet girl, and very wise,' he said. 'There's nothing more vicious than Fleet Street gossipmongering when they turn on their own.'

Rosy went through the motions but Benedict's Arden contacts remained a firmly closed book. The gossip columnist was playing games with her now, knowing full well she was out of her depth.

She cursed herself for letting herself be suckered in so easily.

For never anticipating unprovoked nastiness.

Nor how big a grudge a man like Benedict might harbour over a burnt bedroom and spurned advances, even if it had all been a terrible accident and misunderstanding after a drunken night at Mirabeau's.

His spiked revelations about Lulu's unpleasantness lay

in the pit of her stomach like bitter iron filings. Rosy opened her mouth to make her excuses and leave.

'Aaagh!'

'Hey – watch it!'

'Uh-umph!' cried Rosy, as a hand swiped against their table and sent the glasses and stack of press releases flying into her lap.

A woman had landed on Benedict.

From the back, Rosy noted, she was the archetypal Benedict woman – a vision in couture red tailoring, with light spun sugar hair.

'Sorry! I'm so sorry!' she was repeating in a soft American accent. 'Please forgive me – this carpeting . . .'

'You can start by letting me breathe again,' snapped the gossip columnist in a tone that implied – correctly, it soon transpired – that this was no delicious young woman.

She stood up, painfully.

'Are you all right?' asked Rosy, shovelling the cascade of papers on to the floor.

'I guess I tripped.'

'That was quite a fall. Are you sure you're OK?' persisted Rosy, labouring her companion's lack of gallantry.

The woman tested an ankle. She was absolutely no slip of a girl, and in her late forties, possibly.

Benedict grumbled forcefully until she left in a welter of apologies. A red wine stain was spreading over the front of his cream suit.

'Oh, Benedict,' laughed Rosy. 'I don't believe a word of what people say about you – that you're never going to be another Anthony Sword!'

He stared furiously, mouth in a rictus of rage.

'With that finishing touch,' she pointed at the dripping wine – 'and the glower on your face, you're Sword to the life!'

45 | *Evening in East Sheen*

The red carpet – as rolled out by Eva Coutts – consisted of cheese and pineapple on sticks and a vat of Gordon's.

The view of Cannes spread out before them.

Against a vivid technicolor backdrop, bright teeth sparkled as unrealistically as the postcard Mediterranean sea.

The film festival was brought to No 2, Fairlawn Avenue courtesy of *Ciao!* magazine, while the inside information was provided between the lines in the gossip columns of the *Daily Dispatch* and the *Daily Post*.

'That little girl . . . ooh, you know the one . . . Lottie whatsername . . . She could use a kick in the pants, 'scuse my French,' said Eva, offering her guest a stumpy dead hedgehog of cocktail fayre.

'I'm afraid she's been getting something not dissimilar,' replied Framboise ruefully. 'There's something about that Benedict's eyes . . .'

'Know what you mean, dear . . . look at that picture there. Lottie almost wearing a dress, and him for all the world like a smarmy little ram.'

'It's the hair. Those horrid horns . . . there's so much lacquer there, a good musician could blow a novelty set on them.'

Eva tossed back another gin, and said mischievously, 'I probably shouldn't tell . . . but as it's you. I have been corresponding with Mr Benedict Pierce. I send him helpful cuttings.'

'Oh, yeah?'

'Have you noticed how many *hair loss* advertisements there are in the papers? *Evening Standard*'s lousy with them. They have lovely lines . . . Premature thinning? Almost indistinguishable pre-baldness? Hidden scalp ailments? I send them to him, now and then, from a concerned reader with an eye on his crowning glory!'

Framboise hooted.

'Oh dear . . . well, you have to have a bit o' fun in these dull times. Not nearly so much sex, rage and sin as there was, not that anyone's admitting to at any rate.' Eva flipped the paper over with a dismissive gesture. 'I keep my hand in with the acting, too, you know. For the past six months I've been a Swedish ex-model with a colourful love-life on Benedict's page. Only on the telephone, of course . . .'

Framboise clapped a hand to her head.

'It's all gone horribly quiet without Fergie,' lamented Eva. 'She was the one I liked – at least she had a bit of go about her. She's never been allowed to get back to normal after it all went wrong, more's the pity. That story was nearly as good as Dallas, in its day . . .'

'I thought it *was* Dallas, at one stage.'

They continued, companionably, until Framboise said: 'Let's talk about fifty-one years ago.'

Eva studied her son's closest friend with an uneasy sense of the inevitable. 'I was afraid that was why you'd come to see me.'

In an upstairs room, Framboise did not flinch from the crushed strawberry bed. The monstrous pink plastic affair was original 50s. It had long been a talking point at parties, if rather too Diana Dors for most tastes.

'We should have had our cheese and pineapple hedgehog up here and made a theme evening of it,' joked Framboise. 'Played some Liberace, maybe.'

She was trying to lighten the moment, Eva knew. But the heaviness in her heart remained, as she lumbered over to a cupboard and pulled open the door. She tugged at a drawer inside.

'Can I help?' asked Framboise.

'I can manage . . . that's it.' Eva brought the tattered Harrods bag over to the bed. There was nowhere else to sit in the room. 'You might draw the curtains.'

Framboise obliged.

'Has he . . . been talking about me?'

'Some.'

'Only we all make mistakes, dear. Doesn't mean we don't try to put them right . . . in our own ways . . .'

'I know.'

'Only . . . with Tony – he's always been self-contained. Never said much about what's really going on with him. You're the only person he opens up to.' Eva gathered herself. 'In spite of everything, I do care.'

'I know that too.' Her son's *confidante* was letting her proceed at her own pace. Eva had never been one to shirk a confrontation, should the need arise.

'Phil Hawty,' she said, wondering how long Framboise could be strung along. 'It *is* possible, you know.'

Framboise gave her a non-judgemental glimmer of a smile.

'We were young then, and he was attractive enough as a proposition at the time . . .' She was rambling, she knew. Catching Framboise's seriousness, she said: 'We might be able to work it out for once and for all with these.'

Eva tipped up the Harrods bag. From it poured

bundles of scuffed letters. And dozens of tiny scuffed diaries.

'Wow,' breathed Framboise, then she gave a tiny laugh.

'What?' said Eva.

'At least there's no doubt about whose son he is . . . on his mother's side!'

An ominous thud from downstairs interrupted the pyjama party atmosphere. Then a thump.

Framboise visibly jolted. 'What was that?'

Eva studied the floor.

'It's coming from downstairs,' said Framboise.

'Mmm.'

'Whaddaya mean, *Mmmm?*'

'I was coming to that,' said Eva, 'It's a man. He did say his name.'

'A man,' repeated Framboise, still clearly dubious.

Eva nodded. 'He must have come round.'

'Come round – to visit?'

'No-o-o. Well, that is . . . he *did*, this afternoon,' said Eva. 'But I meant, come round from a little something I slipped in his tea.'

'*Wha-a-t?* You're telling me this . . . *man's* been out cold . . . downstairs?' Framboise's painted eyebrows were taking a roller coaster ride around her forehead.

'Under the stairs,' confirmed Eva.

'Oh-mi-gard.'

'I locked him in the hall cupboard.'

'I hardly dare ask . . . Why? And how did you get him there?' Her guest was fairly boggling.

'I wheeled him in.'

'You *wheeled* him?'

'Yes,' said Eva. 'On my hostess trolley.'

46 | *Rosy's Release*

Benedict Pierce was a quivering lip with hairstyle attachment by the time Rosy left him to wallow in his fuss.

She trampolined her way across the plywood floor which had caused him so much anguish, then strolled past the bar and the bulletin board where the latest press cuttings had been pinned. By the main entrance was an exhibition about yet another forthcoming film project, this time a remake of *Tender is the Night*.

Black and white photographs of childlike people in floppy clothes stared out at her. In the background, the beaches were rough-hewn and empty. The caption to the largest picture was 'Riviera Beach Party, 1924'. Intrigued, Rosy drew closer.

'Heat and light, you can feel it can't you?'

She wheeled round to find the woman in red. She was as tall as Rosy. 'Oh, hi . . . Look, I'm, er, sorry about the charming reaction at our table back there,' said Rosy. 'You went down with a real thud. You're absolutely sure you're all right?'

The woman nodded. 'I'm fine – really. You can stop asking now. These shoes . . .' She indicated high-ish courts.

'It isn't a proper floor.'

'It isn't a proper anything here.' The woman chuckled, deeper than Rosy would have expected. 'But I guess it always was that way. Even Scott and Zelda' – she waved vaguely at the grainy exhibition shots – 'they realised that, and they had a vested interest in believing . . .'

'Given that they invented it,' agreed Rosy.

The woman smiled, her strong face crinkling. 'You're involved in this?' she asked, meaning the film.

Rosy shook her head. 'F. Scott Fitzgerald was my first love, you could say.'

'I admire your taste.'

They chatted for a few more minutes. It was only after they had gone their separate ways that Rosy realised that neither of them had given anything away.

In her hotel room, a million miles away from the bright lights, Rosy flipped over the pages of a press release. The six-inch stack of glossy movie brochures contained sheets of sub-journalism, with the odd anodyne quote from an actor or actress, and a fistful of still photographs and transparencies from the work in question.

Rosy's night, in other words, had all the allure and glamour of a pink processed pork pie, with none of the excitement of a risky indulgence. Lying on her bed, the nobbly brown bedspread rough under her bare legs, she could hear the traffic passing outside.

No, she decided, it was more than the traffic – it was Life passing her by.

More than once, she crossed to the dark window and rested her elbows on the creaky sash. But then her unfortunate conversation with Benedict eddied around in her head, until she was forced to find something – anything – else to suppress it. She made a strenuous effort not to think about Lulu Bisset in any shape or form.

And then a picture of Jamie would pop up . . .

She speed-read another press release and chucked it on the floor. It hit the pile. Yawning, she reached for another wedge of potted publicity.

When she hit on the colour transparency of the woman in red, she thought she was hallucinating.

Then she saw it for what it was: the first stroke of luck she'd had in weeks.

47 | *The Liberators*

'But . . . who is he?' asked Framboise.

'He was asking too many questions,' said Eva obliquely. The two women were considering their options upstairs in the bedroom while the thumps grew more insistent. 'Tell you the truth,' she continued, 'I was getting a bit worried about the feeding aspect.'

'The feeding?'

'Would it be peas through the keyhole, or slivers of toast under the door? It's never been a good fit, that door. Not since its days as the bondage grotto, with that chap – I'm sure you know the one – '

Framboise coughed. 'Eva . . .'

More furious thuds and thumps from beneath the stairs. 'I must say, I'm glad you're here, dear.'

'Yes, well . . . I take it you're not intending to keep him in captivity,' asked Framboise, raising one eyebrow sardonically.

Eva crossed her arms.

'I mean . . . I mean, how did you get him on your trolley, that's what I wanna know?'

'I can see you've had no experience of this kind of thing . . . I positioned it casually and coaxed him upright with the pretence of a cream horn for tea at the very moment he was dropping off . . .'

Framboise was agog.

'Timing is crucial.'

'I can imagine,' said Framboise.

'Never mind that now, dear.' Eva thought hard about the next manœuvre, to the counterpoint of an angry roar from the hall cupboard, and heavy kicks. 'As there's two of us, perhaps we should try to liberate him. I did think he might be more docile than this . . .'

'What did you give him?'

Eva shrugged. 'Only two sleeping pills. To give me a chance to think.'

'And have you?'

'You arrived, if you recall. Not that it isn't a delight to see you at any time you choose.'

Framboise beamed. 'So, to the business in hand – '

'In cupboard.'

'Whatever. Liberate, then interrogate?' suggested the singer wryly.

'I think so.'

They pondered a moment.

'Perhaps – ' Eva's plan was forming.

'Perhaps what?'

'Hang on a tick.'

Eva dived back into the bedroom wardrobe and clicked hangers along the rail. She emerged with a black rubber number and a black satin uniform. Framboise's face was a picture when she registered the detailing.

'Eva. *Bad* idea.'

'Not in the mood, dear?' grinned Eva.

'The mood for *what*?'

'A bit o' fun, of course.'

Framboise clunked a hand against her head. 'Dominatrix with cut-outs . . . and whip belt?'

'Just a thought, dear. Went down a treat when that girl . . . Anyway,' Eva stopped herself. 'The last thing our man . . . Crighton Something, that's what he said . . . there! it always comes to me in the end . . . the last thing he'll be expecting . . . is the sheer terror of a bit of unwanted sex, rage and sin . . .'

'No way,' said Framboise emphatically.

Their compromise reception outfits consisted of a policeman's jacket over a serge skirt for Framboise, and a battlescarred housecoat with truncheon and hat pin for the hostess.

Eva sighed sentimentally. 'You know, I feel one of my parties coming on . . . like in the good old days . . .'

'Could we concentrate on present company?' Framboise tried to ease down the straining jacket. 'Feel like a tube of goddamn toothpaste in this . . .'

'You look very nice, dear. Quite the ticket. Don't want to ruin your lovely dress, do we? This could turn ugly. Breathe in, and hold it there.' Eva yanked.

'Thanks.'

Slowly they descended the stairs. The battering and thuds grew louder under the creaking boards, as if a monstrous child were kicking from the inside of a womb. Or so it felt to Eva.

'Lemme out . . . Lem-me-out!'

Standing in the hall they exchanged stares. Then Eva went forward, lethal hat-pin in hand. With one deft movement – or as near to deft as she got these days – she flicked the lock of the cupboard door, and scuttled back.

There was a charged pause.

Then a misplaced kick brought the man out like a cork from a champagne bottle. Almost somersaulting, he rolled uncontrollably against the opposite wall, making contact with his head.

He lay dazed. Eva stood by, motioning at her accomplice to raise the truncheon.

'Who are you?' asked Framboise.

The man rubbed his head. His face was as grey as his hair.

'What do you want here?' persisted Framboise.

'She's a bloody madwoman,' he said at last, in Eva's direction.

'You watch your language in my house.'

He glared.

'He says he's a researcher, if you please,' said Eva. 'Asking questions about my son.' Much as she trusted Framboise, Eva thought she'd leave it at that.

The man was stumbling to his feet now. The two women moved back as one. He wagged a thin white finger. 'I'll have you for assault and imprisonment.'

'Self defence,' said Eva, body language belligerent.

He shook his head disbelievingly at Framboise. He had a long, overhanging nose and a short upper lip: under the crude hall light, its shadow cast him a Hitlerian moustache. 'What the hell do you think you are playing at?'

'Our question exactly,' said Eva.

'I have seen you somewheres before,' mused Framboise.

He stared that down, without responding.

'He's been hanging around here, out in the street,' said Eva, as she made her way over to the telephone under the stained glass window. She began to dial. 'Nine, nine n – '

She was abruptly pushed aside, as the man flung himself at the front door, fumbled with the latch, and rocketed out.

There was a stunned pause, during which the only sound was the clap of his soles on the concrete path to the gate.

'Well . . .' said Eva. She closed the door softly.

'You OK?'

'Fine.'

The exit had been so swift, they found themselves momentarily at a loss. Framboise ripped off the policeman's jacket. 'That really fooled him.'

Eva shrugged. 'Framboise . . . did you really recognise him?'

The singer deliberated. 'Not sure. He didn't like the idea, though. What are we gonna do?'

'He's gone now,' said Eva. 'Let's leave it at that.'

'What? This guy bluffs his way in here – '

'Leave it. That's what I said.'

48 *A Few Theatrical Memories*

Anthony Sword fixed Sir Philip Hawty with his most inquisitorial stare.

'So,' he said to the man who would be his father, 'Talk me through it.'

The famously failed ex-Home Secretary adjusted his position in a deep winged chair at the Beefsteak Club and pushed back a strand of silver hair from his brow.

His handshake had been a damp clench.

'I want to be frank with you,' he replied, in a tone which implied he would be anything but.

Sword noted the flex of the muscles in his jaw. 'Indeed.'

'You are not making this easy.'

'No.'

The consummate senior politician tried again. 'We must try to understand what is meant by this . . . the wider implications . . .'

Anthony Sword made a steeple of his fingers and continued to glare.

Sir Philip's smooth butterscotch complexion was more or less intact, but there was not a hint of the self-assurance which had carried him through forty years of Conservative Party rubber chicken dinners with such legendary aplomb. The watery grey eyes were wandering uncontrollably around the dark leathers and panelling of the room.

'What*ever* possessed you to come to my house like that – unannounced, with your trumped-up charges, like some hideous great *deus ex machina*?'

'I, er . . .'

'With a bloody *chorus* behind you in the bushes?' Sword shuddered at the thought of the *Daily Post* photographer who had materialised from behind his hedge.

'Not much got into the papers, though . . .'

The gossip king was incredulous. 'Do you ever stop to think? Or does the heady scent of publicity overcome you every time?'

'What do you – ?'

He silenced him with a look. 'No one would have been stupid enough, or rash enough, to run it – for starters.'

'Benedict Pierce's people mentioned it in the *Post*.'

'My case rests.'

Sir Philip faltered.

Sword ensured that the message went home. 'They have already heard from my lawyers. It will prove an expensive mistake, I fear.'

'Quite so.'

'I think we both know,' said Sword, making a show of assessing first his own prize girth and stocky limbs, and then his guest's lean and rangy frame, 'that you are not my father.'

'It would not seem . . . likely. Yet – '

'Yet, nothing. For God's sake, man!'

For once Sir Philip seemed speechless, if somewhat relieved.

'And now that I have that off my chest, I would like you to tell me about your relationship with my mother.'

'From the beginning?' The older man seemed to lose any remaining veneer of bravado.

'The very beginning.'

The beginning, as recalled by Sir Philip Hawty through a mist of pathos and a large single malt, was a meeting in a church hall in south west London in 1944. No less obscure was the repertory company – half of the troupe no more than amateurs – that had gathered for a rehearsal.

'Eva was the most cheeky, prettiest, most dimpled girl I'd ever seen,' he reminisced under duress. 'She must have been about twenty and she could dance and she wanted to be an actress. I was younger, waiting for my call-up. Doing whatever I could to make the waiting easier.'

'With a theatrical troupe,' said Sword sardonically.

'Important war work, boosting morale.' He managed to make it sound anything but noble, or indeed selfless.

'Go on,' sighed Sword. 'What were you rehearsing?'

'Can't for the life of me remember. I was backstage working sound effects, prompting, helping with the props . . . whatever.'

'And you and Eva?'

'She was so marvellous. We'd talk and play about. I idolised her, absolutely worshipped the ground . . . She's quite a woman, eh? Still got plenty of the old dash about her . . .'

'If we could – '

'The . . . nitty-gritty?'

'If you could, please.'

Sir Philip took a gulp of scotch. 'She was . . . experienced before I came along. I wasn't her first. We knocked around together' – he had the grace to acknowledge the filial wince this provoked and attempt to repair the damage – 'we were *close* for some months . . . before the show closed . . . and she went off without a word.'

'And then?'

'I was called up. D-Day and all that. I never saw her again until some five or six years later.'

'Where – how?'

'Predictable, really. Another rehearsal room, another theatrical troupe. I'd had this idea that I wanted to be an actor – and at the time I was ASM and understudy. To the chap who became television's Mr Clean, as a matter of fact. And Eva was a fully-fledged actress by then.'

'And?'

'And . . . we've been friends on and off ever since. What more can I tell you?'

'What more? What *more?*' cried Sword, his frustration boiling over. '*Where* did she disappear to, back in 1944?'

Sir Philip was the picture of puzzlement. 'Damnedest thing,' he admitted. 'She never would say.'

49 | *Stars of Staged Success*

That afternoon Rosy had blown her expenses on a new dress and she had found Robert Arden.

The clinging cream dress – far too expensive – was to spite Jamie Raj, the features editor and the world, probably in that order.

The most sought-after star in Cannes was at the cinema on the rue d'Antibes – or a poster of his latest film was, anyway. Rosy was so beside herself at the unexpected breakthrough – the elusive name in great red block capitals – that she ran straight across the road out of Nat's boutique, narrowly missed by a motorcycle and a maniac in a Peugeot.

When she saw that the poster was a painting rather than a photograph, her legs buckled with disappointment.

There wasn't a face on it that looked like his.

There wasn't a name on the credits she hadn't hassled already.

And she had scoured the town in vain for another sighting of the woman in red. The photograph from the film press pack was crumpled and sweaty from an afternoon being hawked around every hotel doorman she could find.

* * *

The red carpet up the main steps to the entrance of the Palais des Festivals reminded Rosy of nothing so much as a great tongue slurping up to an orifice. No doubt, in the circumstances, that was highly apt.

The previous night, Clint Eastwood and Meryl Streep had ascended, fêted like royalty, photographers pressed on either side against crush barriers, blinding the anthill of star-gazers below with the bright explosions from their electronic flies' eyes.

Tonight it was the turn of the brightest and the best of the British film industry. On these same steps Barry Norman, ably assisted by a home-grown queen of the mini-series, gave a cheery wave.

The palm trees on La Croisette obligingly rustled in the balmy evening breeze. Lights from the cars cruising the main drag lit the scene in passable imitation of 1930s Hollywood.

Any commendable effects stopped there, as far as Rosy was concerned. The next star of the show to arrive was Lottie Landor, with her perky blond escort, Benedict Pierce.

The BAFTA dinner was set out in one of the conference rooms in the Palais. The eating and drinking here was even worse than in London, Rosy lamented, giving her waist a rueful squeeze. At least in London you had a few hours' respite each day in the office. Through the dauntingly dim atmospheric lighting, white tablecloths and candles gleamed on the ranks of round tables.

Amazingly, Rosy found her name on the seating plan.

Jamie's name was there too, but he was nowhere to be seen.

The guests – the men in black tie, the women in jewelled colours – surged and chattered towards their tables. Rosy, feeling conspicuous in the new cream dress, merged gratefully into the gloom and watched a group of perfectly formed but three-quarter sized people exchange dazzling smiles. She recognised the stars of a moderately successful ensemble film of the previous year in which old friends at Cambridge had played old friends at Cambridge.

She wondered briefly about the possibility of redeeming herself with the features editor with a piece about them – but she felt too sluggish and, frankly, too implausible to approach them.

On her table, her companions for the next few hours were gathering. Most seemed to know each other.

'Oh, God, Matt Pyne in a film called Chicken and Chips. Where will it all end?' whined a woman television producer Rosy had seen around.

'One of those unanswerable questions, Soph. Like how is it that Arnold Schwarzenegger regards himself as a great comic actor, and whether it was bad luck or bad brooding that made Marlon Brando what he is today,' said a man with a boxer's face under curly hair.

'What are we eating?' asked the woman to Rosy's right.

'Turkey would be appropriate,' smirked a man next to her.

They sat down to a vegetable terrine which reminded Rosy uncomfortably of the bottom of the fridge back in Endymion Road.

She was hauled into the conversation.

'This town is full of the silliest, vainest people in the world,' said the boxer. 'It's the *perfect* setting for all this mayhem.' He was in his late thirties, and said he owned his own production company. Rosy had been in Cannes long enough to know that could mean anything. He was still attractive, though, by which she meant that he took some notice of her and his looks were completely different to Jamie's.

'And many of the silliest, most vindictive people in town are here on a great big freebie from Fleet Street,' cursed the television woman, with feeling.

Rosy laughed guilelessly.

'I thought *you* were a journalist,' said the attractive boxer.

The woman producer carried on regardless, cigarette in red-tipped claws, as she re-ran in some detail a run-in with a princely showbiz writer on the *Daily Mail*.

'I am a journalist,' said Rosy, without much conviction, 'but that doesn't necessarily mean I can't see the wood for the trees.'

'You look far too nice to be a rat-pack reporter.' He reached out a hand. 'Will Buchanan, mainstay of Howling Films.'

Rosy stretched her own hand across. 'Rosy Hope, reporter at the *Daily Dispatch*.' Career hanging by a thread, she might have added.

He read as much on her face. 'That bad, is it?'

She concurred.

'Cannes is a madhouse. If you don't have some kind of breakdown, you ain't been here,' he smiled.

'All the talk, all the publicity – all the *press releases*,' said Rosy, 'and half the films aren't even made yet.'

'Nor will be,' said Will.

'And who *are* all these people?'

'Well, that's just it. No one really knows who anyone is. There are schemes which might happen. There are projects that are sold but not made, and others that are made but not sold.'

Rosy sighed.

'The network is here, and it's out to lunch,' grinned Will.

'And meanwhile,' said Rosy, 'the crowds keep waving at *n'importe qui*.'

* * *

When she asked Will, they were at the coffee and cigar stage. Several of the others had sped off back into the fray and they had moved round the table to sit together.

'You wouldn't, by any chance, have come across Robert Arden at all?' It didn't come out as succinctly as she would have liked.

'Sure,' he said. 'I have a few contacts.'

'I need to contact him somehow.'

'I can help,' said Will. 'No problem.'

They had more coffee and brandy together in a café in the old port. He asked her if she would have dinner with him the next evening, and he would see what he could do. He stroked a light finger down the back of her hand when she agreed.

Rosy left, knowing exactly what the score would be.

50 | *Benedict the Big Shot*

There were aspects of being a social columnist that were akin to the dilemma faced by royalty, Benedict decided.

Social climbers clamoured for you to accept their invitations.

Showbiz luvvies popped up in their droves.

One could be dazzled on a daily basis by Impact Specialists such as Lily Savage and Framboise Duprée.

One was also dimly aware – more dimly than most, in Benedict's case – that the nicest people were not necessarily those who propelled themselves forward.

There was all the excitement of the royal experience without the inconvenience of having to be polite through gritted regal teeth.

Of course, one was criticised constantly. One simply had to learn to live with it.

And one's consort was not always what one had once hoped.

Lottie had made her own arrangements the previous two nights. Which had caused him no pain and left him free to chase an eager German production assistant – eager, that was, until the question of essential peach oil and a black silk dressing-robe had presented itself.

He had slept alone.

In the morning, Benedict had roused himself from his reverie – in which his beautiful and empathetic book, entitled *The Princess and Me*, made him a million the day it was published – to answer the telephone by his bed. There was nothing but an eerie silence. For one crazed second of crypto-optimism, he fantasised that it was the Princess of Wales herself.

Then Bernie Ziegler came on.

'Meeting at 10.30,' he said without preamble.

Benedict was caught on the hop. 'Er . . . yeah.'

But, for a film project of his own, he was more than willing to jump when asked.

First, though, he had a mission: to present himself to Merv.

Benedict prepared himself for the onslaught – the telephone negotiations for his promised interview with Robert Arden having taken on the characteristics of a full blockade – by returning to his earlier thoughts.

He had long been aware that each member of the Royal Family had a distinctive way of dealing with unwelcome situations. Uncomfortably aware, on some occasions.

The Queen gave the cameras one majestic smile, followed by indifference to anything but the duty in hand.

The Queen Mother beamed from her best side like the jolly old trouper she was.

The Duke of Edinburgh grimaced as if regretting he'd not brought his gun for some target practice.

Prince Charles pulled pained, impending tantrum faces.

Princess Anne had her just-swallowed-a-lemon expression of distaste.

Benedict experimented with a combination of them all in the mock-Louis XV mirror.

When he arrived at the makeshift Power Pictures office suite at the Martinez where Robert Arden's man Merv had so often been in a meeting, two heavies on the door stared at him as if he were a nasty strain of the Black Death.

He was contained right there.

An hour later, in a private suite at the Majestic, Benedict took the line of coke Bernie Ziegler offered. The film producer was a grizzled lion of a man, with thick flowing grey hair and a stomach which rose over the waistband of his jeans to speak volubly of addiction to cheeseburgers and other fine LA food.

The *Post*'s man gave his best Michael Douglas as he sniffed and straightened up. He was in the film business now.

If he had discovered anything in his dockside partying, it was that an independent film producer these days would go to any lengths to secure funding for a project. As a past master of the relationship between publicity and pay-offs, Benedict *loved* this idea.

'What we're talking here,' said Bernie, 'is major league social connections. The real people, the real truth.'

'Absolutely,' said Benedict.

When Benedict had met Bernie for the first time – at a party for someone else's movie project, naturally – he had judged him to be yet another shifty hustler. The dark grey, closely cropped beard had reminded him, in a rush of paranoia, of Anthony Sword, and caused a certain Pavlovian jangling of alarm bells. But, in the interests of culture and column inches, he quickly quashed them. This Bernie Ziegler was speaking his language.

Benedict was buzzing.

'We're talking substantial returns here,' went on Bernie. 'For you and for them.'

'And for you.'

'I want to make a movie. Everyone's looking for the next *Four Weddings*. This goes one better . . .'

'With the real people, playing themselves, set on their own territory,' reiterated Benedict. 'Their rambling ancestral territory, although naturally these houses are called rambling only by people who have never had access to really large houses . . .'

Bernie rubbed his tanned forehead in a cut-the-crap gesture. 'We tell the true story, with many of the true people involved. And the best part is . . .'

The gossip was all ears and anticipation.

'. . . they pay for the privilege of appearing!'

There was a stunned pause before Benedict heard his own voice say: 'Masterstroke! I love it! I *love* it! Er . . . how?'

'Think of it as product placement,' said Bernie. 'All the tours they can offer round the homes we shoot. All the coverage on the social pages.'

'The newspapers will go mad for it.'

'You *are* the newspapers, Benedict.'

'Well . . . that's very kind of you . . .'

A strange look from the depths of the producer's armchair. 'What I mean is . . . you can control the coverage, Benedict.

'Ah, yes. I think you may not have understood the essence of British newspapers here, Bernie. But . . . certainly, I could give it a bash . . .'

'Not enthusiastic enough, Benedict.'

'I, er . . . It's a great idea, Bernie. Great, *great* idea.'

It took another line of coke for the gossip columnist to feel truly up to the task. By the time Bernie brought up the question of nude scenes, Benedict could have persuaded the Queen herself to oblige.

'And no body doubles,' insisted Benedict excitedly.

'This whole film is the true story, no holds bared – I mean barred. I get that.'

'A couple of scenes of truly gratuitous sex and violence and appalling bad taste are absolutely vital,' said Bernie.

Benedict nodded vigorously. 'Vital.'

'Not that they necessarily have to be in the finished cut.'

'That's a shame. Why not?'

'Because we don't want an adults-only rating. We want a PG blockbuster. We only need for the censor to see them, be disgusted, and demand these scenes are expunged.'

'Oh' said Benedict. '*Why*?'

'The censor is grossed out – we gross big.'

Light dawned. 'We go to the *News of the World* with the out-takes. Does Lady X get paid for the nude pics as well as us?'

'You're way ahead of me, Benedict. I was only thinking of the *Censored: Sexy Scenes of Raunchy Aristos* headlines. I had no idea you could go so far . . . and I love it already . . .'

Benedict's brain was a fierce furnace. 'Executive producer, you say?'

'If you can deliver.'

At that moment, he could have ruled the world.

'The other element we definitely need,' said Bernie, 'is a charismatic leading man – maybe an unknown. With connections . . . but cheap, ya hear what I'm saying . . . We may be pushing our luck, even with your specialist influence, to expect the anonymous author of *Princess Laid Bare* to play himself.'

'I have the very man,' said Benedict.

51 | *A Friend for Breakfast*

For about the hundredth time, he dialled her Islington number.

'So that's where you are, at last!' It wasn't the most diplomatic opening gambit in the world, but Anthony Sword was not about to let niceties obscure his profound relief.

'Good morning to you, too,' said Framboise.

The arch-gossip clamped the telephone to his hammering chest, and screwed the receiver to his ear like an instrument of medieval torture. 'Look, I know it's early, but what are you doing – '

'I'm having a friend for breakfast,' interrupted the singer pointedly.

It hadn't occurred to him that she couldn't talk.

'Framboise, I really need to speak to you – ' In the background, there was a dense grunt. An unmistakeably male grunt. 'What was that?'

Framboise's warm gurgle of laughter melted his iciness.

'*Wha-a-t* is going on there with you?' Sword demanded.

'I'm afraid your call has coincided with a rather sticky moment . . .'

Sword strained to make sense of the disturbing sounds

in his ear. 'Oh, no . . .' he breathed as he put two and two together with the tinkle of china and a muffled thumping.

'Breakfast in bed,' said Framboise. 'Spelbridge has put his elbow in the marmalade. God, I love you English! You have such wonderfully eccentric sexual dysfunctions . . .'

Anthony Sword, in philosophical mood, sometimes found the cold comfort he was looking for in Kant or Hegel, but would invariably then go instead to his tried and tested tome of inspiration: Mrs Beeton's *Book of Household Management*.

Two plum duffs later, he would usually have found a nourishment both spiritual and physical, and feel he was master once more of his house.

It did not always work.

It was nearly three in the afternoon before Sword arrived at his office. As he was about to breast the corner from the corridor, he heard the shrill tones of his latest girl reporter.

'Sword's detained,' she was saying. 'Somewhere between the gastronomic rigours of an enormous breakfast and an equally vast lunch, I should imagine. Not a word . . . no, not even a burst of incoherent slurping to a background of restaurant chatter . . .' The gossip columnist paused outside. 'The silly fool, I know, I know . . . and as for that idiot Rosy, she's not worth even stepping on . . . you're going to cream them all, darling . . . You've got all you need, then?'

Sword waited a little longer as the monologue wound down. Then he swung in.

Lulu was all angelic innocence.

'Who was that?' he asked, with a casual tone he certainly did not feel.

'Oh . . . just Jamie.'

'I see.'

He also saw several of the huge red leather bound volumes of past Sword's Secrets pages open and slewed across her desk and a table by their bookcase. The books dated back thirty years. They smelled of dust and dry rotting newsprint, and breaths of old scandal.

'Did he want something, then?'

'No-o . . . he was only calling in. In case there was anything he should know.'

He had to hand it to her. She was brazen.

Sword weighed up the various methods of venting his fury – with her insolence, with Framboise, with Eva, with every perfidious woman he had ever encountered. Then he went for the most obvious and satisfying. He planted his bulky legs and broadcast his terrible rage to the world.

'What was she doing there?' he thundered to the column's elder hack Pearson McKnight, when the worst was over and the girl had retaliated with her own tearful rejoinders.

Sword checked over the opened entries. One book contained the very first columns he had written in the mid-sixties. He couldn't bring himself to read them, half-afraid of how bad they might be. Other books, holding more recent editions, were open on pages heavy with his stock ridicule of Sir Philip Hawty.

'Not sure. She must have got the books down while I was at lunch,' said Pearson. 'Not that I could manage much after unarmed combat last night with Muriel's sister's roast beef and bullet spuds . . .'

Sword waved away this tedious repartee. 'So what do we think of Lulu?'

'Not much, to be honest.'

'And the honest is?'

Pearson didn't bother to pretend. 'She's not Rosy, is she?'

Sword shook his head.

'Lulu has all the right contacts,' groaned the older henchman. 'If she knew what to do with them, we'd be getting somewhere. But she goes to every party in town and misses the story at nearly every one. Either that, or she comes in the next morning with selective amnesia. Something involving a mate that she can't stand up. Or can't *quite* remember. Frankly – '

'All right, all right – no need to go on.' Sword stomped back to his seat, somewhat refreshed after the best blow-out for some time.

There was still something in reserve though, for his discovery of Pearson's expenses sheet in an in-tray – an exercise in creativity which managed to rustle up £584.18 for a dubious exclusive on the Prime Minister's overcoat, involving an alleged backhander to an opportunistic cloakroom attendant.

The reprise was ruthless.

52 | *The Carlton Terrace*

If Rosy had felt reassured by the apparently safe choice of venue for her evening with Will Buchanan, her nerves were reactivated only twenty minutes after the first drink on the Carlton Terrace.

She was sipping her white wine and cassis, taking in the last glitter of sunlight on the sea along with the Dutch courage, when he told her that the car to take them to dinner would arrive soon.

'Oh. I, er, imagined we'd be staying in Cannes.'

'I think we can do better than that, Rosy.'

She smiled, feeling like an old hand. 'St Paul de Vence?'

'No-o.'

A clammy feeling rose up her back, but she forced herself to sound as if she went off into the unknown with more-or-less strange men while on foreign assignments every day of the week. 'Where are we going, then?'

'Just along the coast.'

'Ah – far?'

He gave her a disbelieving look, as if she were acting like a paranoid teenager.

I think you should know, she wanted to say, that I am not the adventurous type. My idea of risk is eating an out-of-date yoghurt exhumed from the fridge.

'To Eze,' said Will, with decisiveness.

'I, um – ' Rosy didn't know quite how to put this. 'I – I think I should maybe . . . let my photographer know, in case he . . . needs me for anything, you know . . .'

'You want to call him?'

'To be on the safe side,' said Rosy.

Standing at the telephone in the flower decked marble foyer of the grand hotel under the glitter of crystal chandeliers, her legs were decidedly wobbly. 'Please be there,' she whispered into the mouthpiece, her distress signal ringing insistantly in her own ear.

Not that there would have been any guarantee that he'd know, any more than she did, what or where Eze was. But at least someone would have had a clue where she was.

The only answer from the Beast's mobile was an electronic invitation to try again later.

By the time she arrived back on the terrace, she had taken many deep breaths and resolved to tell this Will Buchanan that she would, regrettably, have to stay in Cannes tonight.

Then she saw the one thing that could have made her change her mind. Jamie and his female entourage.

She slipped into her chair and smiled at Will. He had a nice face, she resolutely decided. The boxer effect was due to the rough-hewn cheeks and brawny shoulders under his striped, open-necked shirt and blue blazer. His eyes crinkled at the corners when he smiled.

The time had come to start living dangerously. Like a real reporter on a national newspaper, even.

'Get through?' he asked.

'Mmm. Everything's fine.'

'Good.'

Rosy dropped her eyes to the table, then gathered herself. She sat back and surveyed the tragi-comedy.

Among the table-hoppers, there were so many sequins and shoulder pads on the women, and such stiff, unlikely hairstyles on the older men, that she had a sudden sense of déjà-vu. Then, with a surge of certainty, she knew where she was. It was a Dynasty barbecue scene.

Her own best olive-green silk top and long sarong skirt flopped disconsolately in comparison, on the edge of the lights and action.

'It's been quite a floor show,' said Will, following her stare. 'Those girls were on the table a minute ago, failing to do the splits. And you missed the leopard on a diamanté lead.'

Three lithe blondes, all tanned expanses of exposed midriff in fluffy pastel mohair suits, were putting on a pert performance for a television crew. 'There's Sophie Brown again,' pointed out Will.

Behind the cameras was the woman from their dinner table at the Palais the previous night. She stood stock-still, miniskirted, legs planted like a victorious general after battle.

'Seems a little downmarket for her,' said Rosy ascerbically.

'She's doing a hatchet job on the festival – and from that body language, I'd say she's got exactly what she wanted,' he reprised. 'You know she's been getting all sorts of fake stories planted to see what rubbish people would swallow – especially the hacks? Star sees UFO, Marv Midas has breast reduction, Queen hooked on video of *Reservoir Dogs*, that kind of rubbish . . .'

'Don't tell me, Batman and Robin's itchy tights.'

'I haven't heard that one, but . . .' He grinned. 'Could be.'

Rosy nodded, tongue in cheek. 'I'll make sure someone gets that scoop. I know the very person.'

'You can tell me something, though – I know who the

fluffy ones are, but who's the idiot in the Armani suit with them?'

'That,' said Rosy, with a squirm, 'is called Jamie Raj, and is a prime example of lengths some people will go to to get on national television.'

'Soph will have him for breakfast.'

'If he runs to form, that may well be truer than you know – but first he'll have her tonight.' She drained her drink. 'Is that car here yet?' she asked.

53 | *Sword Live*

In the predictable furore over the book *Princess Laid Bare,* no public figure rode the rollercoaster of public emotion more adeptly than Anthony Sword. He cranked himself slowly, menacingly, up to the peak of righteous indignation – then let it all go in a frenzy of screaming and arm waving.

When it came to TV, Sword, like a certain soap powder, was well ahead in the whiter-than-white challenge.

He could positively feel the incandescent fury he was orchestrating.

It crackled in the air like static, incensing those who knew his tactics all too well.

He could feel it recharging his batteries.

This evening, his performance was for the benefit of the nine million prime-time viewers and the selected studio audience of *The David Robbins Show.* He was sharing the bill with a lady from Carshalton who had premonitions, a dreadlocked singing group from Middlesex, and, inexplicably, a daytime television talk-show host. A convention of Alan Whicker impersonators from East Grinstead were currently stuck *en route,* due to railway signalling difficulties at Croydon.

To the side of the set – an airport lounge *circa* 1971 – Sword limbered up.

'Do you get nervous?' asked the woman with premonitions. She was less than resplendent in a dress of printed autumn leaves, with hair suitably windswept above a worried face.

Sword bared his teeth. 'Madam, at present I have the same galvanising tingle in my bone marrow as I get when the words "Newsroom SouthEast" are flashed across the small screen.'

She seemed to take that as a yes.

'If the look on your face, madam, is an indication that unsettling sentiments are occurring, then you are highly likely to be spot on the ball tonight. Now kindly leave me to prepare myself.'

'I say, no need for that tone of voice,' pitched in the guesting talk-show host, all screen geniality and unlikely toupée. 'All friends together, eh, eh?'

Sword squared his broad shoulders and glared. 'Were you a last-minute replacement for someone worth speaking to?' he asked.

It was just possible to discern a career structure to frontman David Robbins' rise in television. He had gone from hamburger salesman, to hospital porter, to ambulance man, to AA roadworks announcer, to wacky weatherman, to Prime-Time Bloke. And all with that inane, cheeky-chappie persona and his mouth for the masses.

He got right up Anthony Sword's nose, in other words.

A shop window dummy in a maroon blazer, David Robbins pulled him into position with a handshake and did one of his more ingratiating welcomes. As the star turn, Sword was last up.

'I have to ask,' began the TV host, 'I have to ask about . . . *That Book*.'

'Well that's what you asked me on to speak about,' snapped Sword, settling in.

The talk-show host crossed his hands and acted as if he was listening.

Sword took his cue. 'Like the government, I am committed to the highest possible standards in public life,' he announced, puffing with pomp. There were a few weak titters from the dark rustle of the studio audience, but nothing to indicate any substantial appreciation of his ironic opener. '*Naturally* this book is an abomination!' snarled Sword. 'It is an abomination that tosh like this should be published at all.'

'So you feel strongly that the Royal Family should be subjected to no more of these terrible books,' said David Robbins, addressing this to the polyester and viscose audience. His smile was relentless.

'Absolutely. This has no named sources and provides no new evidence. This is of no use whatsoever. We need names, dates, places. New dirt, not old well-worn mud pies!'

'Absolutely. So, let me get this right,' said David Robbins, the smile drying on his mouth, while the message struggled through.

'Do you ever stop grinning?' barked Sword. The man was a veritable Prozac prince.

'You're saying you think the book is useless,' summarised the popular talk-show host for the benefit of those who, improbably, were more slow-witted than himself.

'Well,' said Sword, 'that depends on one's critical criteria, of course. Compared to the utter twaddle talked on television about the royals, it is edging towards Nobel Prize nomination.'

'Now hang on . . .'

'Give me one example of television providing a detailed examination of one of the pressing royal issues of the day!'

'Well . . . offhand – '

'What I find truly trying about television in this country today is that the only kind of inside information you offer on a regular basis takes the form of revolting operations and grotesque injuries in your endless, mindless sequence of hospital and ambulance dramas. What people want and need is glamour, high-life and intrigue, not 999 reconstructions.'

'Now . . . I – '

'Put it this way,' said Sword, 'The closest the BBC's royal correspondent has come to a royal scoop in recent months is buying an ice-cream cone at a van outside Buckingham Palace.'

'Have you finished?'

'I could go on,' growled Sword, 'but you are staring at me as if I were barking mad.'

'I – '

'I don't think I'm any more barking than the average most famous gossip columnist in the world!'

A cagey tic was beginning to play in the host's chin. Sword decided he was enjoying himself. 'All right,' he said, with an exocet flash of his teeth. 'I will concede that there was a very entertaining documentary on the Abdication Crisis the other night. *Again*. I quote the *Radio Times*: "Contains footage never before seen on television. *Brackets, REPEAT*." '

The BBC man rallied. 'There you go. Marvellous stuff.'

'Marvellous? Of course it was marvellous. *Those* royals cannot SUE. They are *dead*,' pantomimed Sword. 'It is *behind* them.'

'I can see that would help . . . So you're saying here that

a book like the latest one can't give the true picture. Is the threat of a libel writ a real problem for this kind of book?'

'Let me put it this way,' retorted Sword. 'If my Moscow correspondent were to file a salacious story about a contemporary Catherine the Great, it would not be enough merely to have a sworn statement from the lady herself about her amorous activities.' He paused for effect. 'The way things are now, we'd need a signed affidavit from the fucking horse as well!'

In the stunned silence before the signature tune cranked up, David Robbins stopped smiling. 'You said fucking,' he said, ripping off his microphone. And then, under his breath: 'You fucking said fucking! You bloody bastard!'

'Oh,' said Sword, pleasantly. 'Were we live?'

54 | *The Road to Eze*

On the way to wherever it was they were going, Rosy took herself sternly in hand. She was going to act like any other confident, professional woman who was responsible for her own actions.

She kept a keen eye out for roadsigns, and every other kind of vital landmark.

The Cannes taxi sped east in the direction of Nice.

A distinct aroma of coach party lingered about the lower reaches of the rocky mount where they climbed out of the car. A tourist kiosk lurked in the shadows, and next to it a wooden hut with a window showing tea-cloths imprinted with maps of the place. Rosy took note. There was a distinct threat of worse travesties of world travel culture inside.

'We walk up from here,' said Will, steadying her with a hand under her elbow. They began the ascent. 'It's a pretty special place,' he said. 'A medieval hill stronghold.'

And rather further than I expected, puffed Rosy to herself. And if he led her into a private villa, she was fully prepared to scream with appropriately medieval fervour all the way back down to the Corniche. Aloud she observed, gesturing at the tiny shops on the twee twists and turns upward: 'So far, we're in the *centre mondial de l'artifact touristique.*'

They went up and up the steep stony paths.

Near the top was a small scale castle, ruthlessly restored – a Disneyland for rich adults. The stones were so clean they looked like an unconvincing film set. Bright geraniums spilled from terracotta pots, jasmine scrambled up the artful weathering of the stone. It was a tiny warren of a courtyard with black painted doors and wrought iron bars and gates.

They were shown through an archway to a terrace. Rosy's breath solidified. They were on a platform above a vertiginous view of the Mediterranean. Lights twinkled miles below them. Below the cliff where they perched, the midnight blue velvet of the hillside poured down into the sea. The lights were strung like sunken stars along the coast and across a slim peninsula.

'That's Cap Ferrat,' said Will.

Involuntarily, Rosy shivered. 'I feel as if I'm in an aeroplane, not a building,' she gasped.

They were shown to a table where the railings on her side dropped dizzyingly down the precipice. She was given a menu, which she put down on the stiff white cloth, unable to decide what was making her more shaky – the knife-edge drop or the terrifying solicitude of the battalions of waiters.

The establishment, she had noted straight away, was a hotel.

She dragged her concentration back to what he was telling her. It was another of his movie anecdotes. He was big on those, as she had discovered in the car. 'Cap Ferrat was the inspiration for the most successful B-feature ever made. A man called Murray Burnett was there in the late thirties, and he wrote a play after hearing a black pianist in a bar. The play was made into *Casablanca*.'

He reeled off a few more in that vein while the waiting army hovered.

'So which of your films would I have seen?' asked Rosy, uncomfortably aware that this was a question she should have asked a lot sooner.

'I don't know you well enough yet . . . to know what you like.'

'What are we talking, though? Art house, thriller, action?'

'Action would cover it.'

Rosy shrugged. 'Schwarzenegger-type action?'

'Now, if I could persuade Arnie to do it . . .'

'It? It what exactly?' persisted Rosy.

Will Buchanan gave it to her straight, then. 'Porn.'

Mid-way through the food he'd ordered, his career details were still something of a kick in the teeth of conversation.

She struggled on the best she could.

He didn't seem much interested in the vagaries of her life as a roving reporter, such as it was. Disconcerted by his intent stares, which made her feel as if he were stripping off the top layer of her skin, she knew she was prattling but was unable to stop.

Eventually, the producer hit the nail on the head. 'I'm feeling that I mistook you for something else, Rosy. Maybe like someone more . . . professional.'

She stared down the face of her own misjudgement. And she paused a fraction too long before saying: 'That makes two of us.'

He chewed the corner of his mouth in amused contempt. 'You're way out of your league here . . .'

'Oh, puh-lease . . . spare me the bad screenplay,' said Rosy, heart pounding.

Will Buchanan pushed his plate away and stared hard. 'You want to find Robert Arden, don't you?'

She shrugged, not very convincingly. That was the last thing she wanted to remind him.

'Well, this is where he's staying.'

Rosy gazed out over the black precipice, as far as the dark coast stretched. Car headlamps flickered now and then on the winding hill roads and the Corniche below.

'So I've kept my part of the bargain,' said Will, scrutinising her features. 'And now it's your turn.' Under the table, one of his hands found her thigh. He squeezed, hard.

'I'm sorry,' she said with as much dignity as she could muster, 'I didn't realise that a simple dinner with you was some kind of . . . mephistophelean pact.'

His laugh was so harsh that other diners looked up from the most tongue-in-cheek peasant stews and lamb provençal on the Côte d'Azur and even, momentarily, from their gold leafed chocolate desserts. 'I've asked some friends to join us later. We'll have some fun.'

'I don't think so,' said Rosy. Uneasily, she twisted round in her chair.

'Don't you like having your photograph taken?' he asked. 'I've booked the room. Beautiful room . . .'

'Could you take your hand away from my leg, please. You're hurting me.'

He squeezed all the tighter. 'I can't believe they let a girl like you loose! Where did you come from – did the Sunday school crocodile move off without you? Did you miss the turning for girl guide camp?'

Rosy glared. 'I'd like to go now, please.'

He smirked alarmingly.
'Now,' said Rosy.
'No . . . not yet.'

55 | *The Bedroom Pay-off*

In one of the most glorious bedroom suites she had ever seen, nemesis was about to descend. Amid a heartbreaking perfection of palest pink and old gold, Rosy trembled in horrified anticipation, transfixed by the sight in the mirror.

The canopied bed had all the preparatory crumples.

The champagne was open, fizzing in two half-full flutes.

The guy was ready for action.

Rosy could feel her eyes were wild and staring. All she knew for certain was that there was no way out now.

Then, the woman raised her dark head and shook off the last flutter of her robe and Rosy saw her properly for the first time. Under her own labouring breath, Rosy gave a yelp of disbelief.

She closed her eyes against the voyeuristic scene.

It was all the snake Buchanan's fault. Rosy wondered whether 'fugitive from pornographer' would make an admissible defence.

When he had made his intentions clear out on the dining terrace, Rosy had taken the only escape route she could – she had excused herself and run. The place was so damn discreet that, stumbling blindly for the sanctity of the Ladies, she had unwittingly crashed into someone's bedroom suite.

Trembling, her back crunched against the wall around one corner, Rosy was now voyeur to a bed scene starring of one of the most gorgeous and sought-after bodies in Hollywood.

There was no way the man was her equally famous husband, either.

Rosy fled, with a charge for the door that would have sent bullfight spectators into a blood frenzy. It was hard to tell whether having her hands over her face would preclude identification on a pervert parade, but it almost made her miss the top step as she flung herself out into the dark.

She ran as if for her life.

Her path to the summit of Eze came to a sticky end – a six-foot sentinel cactus. The jardin exotique on the top of the medieval mount was almost entirely planted with prickly cacti.

Going up when they'd look down was the only gambit she could think of. She'd seen it in the films often enough.

When she'd heard enough footsteps scuffing across the cobbles below, and muffled shouts had turned to laughter, Rosy eased herself out of her spiky hiding place.

She rubbed the cactus punctures on her arms and trusted her instincts.

Down and round and round and down the hill she ran until her chest was bursting. Blindly, she stumbled on until she hit a winding gravelled road. The occasional lamp burned orange, but otherwise she hurled herself on by the light of the half moon. Panting, gasping for breath in dry heaves, she stopped to check behind her, then raced on.

It was only when she reached a beach – she assumed it

was the beach she'd seen from the terrace high above – that she knew for certain that she'd made a bad decision on the turning.

If they were looking hard enough, anyone up at the hotel could make out a lost figure down there. She hugged the side of the path and cursed herself. In the balmy dark, she felt her way down to the sand to get her breath back in the shadow of a clump of trees.

Under her feet was the crunch of stones.

She lowered herself down on to the pebbles and closed her eyes, feeling she might faint. Cold trickles of sweat prickled her temples and then her cheeks.

Then a man laughed, right behind her.

56 | *Idol Promises*

'Don't say no,' he said. 'Not until you have considered carefully.' Benedict filled his prospective star's glass. 'It would be perfect for you.'

Jamie Raj dropped a lazy arm over the back of his chair and gave his prospective executive producer a crafted smile. 'I would have to consider very carefully,' he said. 'Not least, my position as far as Sword is concerned.'

'I understand that,' said Benedict, before he played one of his very few trumps. 'I could always ask Imran . . .'

'Indeed.'

'But . . . you're much younger . . . more on the scene these days.' Don't make me say better looking, thought Benedict.

'Sure . . .'

'Better looking than Imran . . .'

'I'm most flattered to be asked, Benedict.'

'So?'

'We'll see.'

'You were getting some screen practice here earlier, I noticed. Which was the programme?' Benedict was torn between wishing that he had been filmed for television on the Carlton Terrace – and congratulating himself on his own sure recognition of star quality when he saw it.

'Oh . . . just *The Late Entertainment Show.*'

Benedict whistled. 'Congratulations.'

Jamie raised his glass of champagne. 'I shall think about your offer very carefully indeed.'

That was the best Benedict got for his bottle of Louis Roederer.

Soon after, Jamie scooped up his blazer and disappeared into the soft blue night – in the opposite direction to their hotel. Benedict finished the bottle with only his own thoughts for company.

And the more he thought about it, the more the *Post*'s gossip columnist wished it had been him, on the television. Quite apart from the public exposure he needed if he were to maintain his credibility, it would have provided a neat answer to the increasingly unpleasant tone of the messages he had been receiving from his masters back at base.

They seemed to want more than his usual tittle-tattle to justify his expensive days in the sun. As if all he was doing all day was lying around, eating and drinking!

He took the final swill indignantly, and made sure he took the receipt when he paid.

'Hey!'

Unsteadily, Benedict made for the steps down to the pavement.

'Hey! You Benedict Pierce?'

He stopped, but swaggeringly. 'Who wants him?'

'You the guy who wants to meet Robert Arden?'

Benedict looked round to see one of the heavies who had barred his way to Merv Michelson at the Martinez that morning. 'What's it to you?'

'Simple question.'

'Yeah. I want to see Arden.' That was an understatement. He wanted to tell him, in great detail, the trouble he had caused. Perhaps he would even sue him for undermining a fine newspaperman's professional standing.

Benedict wobbled.

'Got a message for you. From Merv,' said the heavy.

'Oh, yeah?'

'Tomorrow. You get the boat, the Sainte Marguerite. Be there after lunch for ya.'

'And Arden's there?'

The heavy curled a lip contemptuously. 'Nooo . . . a great big clue . . . what do you think?'

'The Sainte Marguerite,' said Benedict. 'Tomorrow afternoon.'

At last.

57 *The Bottom of the Heap*

They must have been about twenty minutes into the conversation when Rosy took stock of the situation and realised that she was surely losing her mind.

Here she was, on a gritty beach at the bottom of a precipice, miles away from Cannes, talking to a stranger. Another stranger.

Having escaped from a gang-bang of pornographers.

Or so the story went, in her mind.

Mortification was such an ice-breaker.

The man was sitting some six feet away from her, smoking. The red-tipped glow of his cigarette rose and fell casually. When they spoke, it was in English. Like many French people, he had an accent which suggested he might have learned the language from American films and tapes.

'I should have known, I should have realised,' wailed Rosy over and over again. Her heart restarted its painful pounding. Perhaps she was in shock.

'You can't always know – '

'The guy was full of movie bullshit.' Rosy didn't care whether he understood the nuances. It was enough that someone was listening. 'He set the scene by telling me it was on one of these Corniche roads that Grace Kelly crashed the car. He seemed to think that was a turn-on,' gasped Rosy.

'Lowlife,' said the man. There was so little light on the stony beach that she could only barely make out his quarter profile.

'Tell me,' he said, after a slight pause. 'Have you ever read any Scott Fitzgerald?'

The question was no more bizarre than anything else this long evening. 'Some,' she said, non-committally. 'Funny, someone else was talking about him the other day . . .'

'That's the movie business for you.'

Rosy frowned. 'What they can plunder next, you mean.'

'When *Tender is the Night* was about to be published, Fitzgerald asked his editor not to refer to the Riviera when he advertised the novel, because the words, he said, invoked a feeling of unreality.'

Rosy knew exactly what he was saying. She had felt it ever since the first party at the Martinez. 'Then you add in the fantasy world of every wannabee who's on the verge of a major deal . . .' Then she stopped, realising. 'Your English is extremely good.'

'Thank you. Some of us speak surprisingly well.'

'Are you an English teacher, by any chance?'

'I'm an American.'

'Oh, God.' Rosy buried her head in her hands. 'Ah. I'm afraid I'm having rather . . . an improbable . . . evening.'

'You're British?'

'Yep. Does that explain it?'

He laughed. 'What are you doing down here?'

Rosy took that strictly generally. 'I'm a journalist, covering the Cannes Film Festival for a newspaper. Allegedly.'

'Having a good time? Apart from this evening, that is.'

'No, not really, to be honest.'

'Oh?'

'I've been sent here to track down a Hollywood star who has made a shrewd career of staying out of the limelight. Someone who is hardly likely ever to want to speak to me, and quite frankly, who can blame him?'

'Not good.'

'Oh, it gets worse. My job back in London now seems to depend on it.'

'You like your job?'

'I thought it was better than my last one. I generally get longer quotes now than "Piss off" with which to build up an in-depth picture of someone. But here all I can see is that there are so many other more important issues than who Robert Arden wants to speak to while he's here – if he is here.'

'Like what? What's important to you?'

'Teenage murderers,' said Rosy, oblivious to how that sounded, until it was too late.

Luckily he laughed unthreateningly. 'You'll have to explain.'

There was nothing else for it. 'Have you been reading the French press? There was another this week, not far from here. A boy decapitated a girl of twelve. He was *fourteen*, for goodness sake. And every time there's another, you get a description of what the child was like, how normal he or she was, what was in their bedroom, you know the sort of thing. But what's the connection, that no one seems to be making?'

'What?'

'All these children – youths, whatever – have been watching videos and films like *Natural Born Killers*. To them, what they are doing is *heroic*! They're nothing special until they get a gun or a knife, and suddenly they can do these sensational, attractive action sequences . . .

It's frightening. It seems to me that they can't tell that it's fiction.'

'Is that their fault, or that of the movie-makers?'

'I don't know,' said Rosy. 'There was an article in one of the papers the other day about a television programme which went out in America. It was a spoof about a massive asteroid hurtling towards Earth. All through it, apparently, the programme flashed up a line of text reminding everyone that it wasn't really happening. The switchboard was still jammed by terrified viewers and there were hundreds of complaints.'

'That's easy to explain,' he said. 'Half of them were plain stupid – and the other half have their trauma lawyers on to the main chance.'

Somehow neither of them laughed.

Rosy clinked a handful of pebbles. 'Not even dust yet,' she murmured. Then, suddenly, a shock of fear galvanised her. What on earth was she doing here, talking with a strange creep on the beach – yet *another* strange creep?

About murders. In the instant the thought occurred, she was on her feet again, scrabbling round for her bag. She grabbed it and was ready to run.

From a standing start, she went for the nought to sixty.

'Wait!' called the man. 'Don't go!'

She didn't look back.

'Hey!' His words carried over the scrunch of her feet. 'Come back!'

She ran all the faster.

58 | *Preparing to Sail*

Benedict made heavy weather of removing the squid from his seafood salad at Le Vieux Port. The rubber rings around his plate made a miniature safety raft.

'Is this supposed to be like . . . er, Freudian?' asked the Earl of Trent, who had declined food in favour of espresso and Marlboros.

Maybe it was. In an hour or so, if all went to plan, he, Benedict, would be exclusively face-to-face with the most famous recluse in Hollywood.

Benedict prodded the fishy arrangement on his plate with a fork. 'Like chewing elastic bands. This stuff bounces back at you. In fact, it reminds me unpleasantly of certain ex-Cabinet ministers . . .'

The earl inhaled deeply. 'He's not taking no for an answer.'

'No.'

'I'm not sharing my billing with Sir Philip Hawty . . .'

'I understand that, Brett.'

'He's way off line, man . . .'

'I will do my best – '

'I mean, Hawty appears . . . and it's a red bus movie!'

Benedict narrowed his eyes quizzically.

'For years and years, every time a director has wanted

to make the point that his movie is set in London, England, he's put in the bus above the words.'

'And Hawty is . . .'

'The social equivalent.'

He waited for his lunch companion to explain further.

'It's post-modernist, man.'

Benedict was torn between pointing out that he'd been spending too much time hanging out with the media studies crowd, and a woolly understanding that Trent could well be right.

The fashionable earl was gushing ideas, many of which Benedict knew that he would soon be only too happy to pass off as his own, but he drained his coffee and stood up abruptly.

'You off?'

Benedict nodded. 'An important meeting.'

The earl pulled a creative face. 'I was flowing, then . . .'

'A very important meeting.'

The columnist turned on his heel, a man with a mission. He walked briskly towards the sea front, pausing only to buy a copy of the *International Herald Tribune* at a corner kiosk. It gave the right impression of a man of the world who never, ever, ran the risk of missing a news angle.

It was a practical move, too. Merv hadn't been too precise about a time for the pick-up.

The whiteness of the boats in the marina dazzled him. Further out was a cruiser he was sure was the one a certain panda-proportioned newspaper proprietor took his last splash from some years back. Hand to his forehead like a sailor boy, Benedict allowed himself some minutes' reverie.

Quarter of an hour later, unable to spot the boat and feeling like an emperor wearing dubious clothes, he accosted an official-seeming person in the tiny marina office. 'Le Sainte Marguerite, monsieur?' Benedict pulled at his cuffs in a self-consciously Prince Charlesian manner.

The man's deep sun-tan split with white teeth. 'You want the Sainte Marguerite?' he answered in English.

'That's right.'

'You go back to La Croisette, and you walk almost to the Palais. Only before you get to there, you will find the Sainte Marguerite boat.'

'Merci, monsieur.'

'De rien, monsieur.'

Benedict glanced at his Rolex as he swung off the timber walkway. It was almost two-thirty. Unless American film stars disregarded all local customs, he was still safely in the after-lunch time zone.

He adjusted his shades and struck out, comforted by the knowledge that his nautical rendezvous was prestigious enough to merit a prime mooring. As he passed the British Pavilion, he automatically turned his head to see who was there.

A group of rowdy photographers crowded the bar, and Jamie Raj was doing his languorous number with a perky PR girl, judging from the amount of papers she had on the table between them. She had her back to the entrance, but it might even have been his party planner Kitten O'Shea. Benedict squinted harder.

'Ah! Watch it, Benedict!'

When he turned to see who it was, all he could make out was a mass of long wavy hair. A slew of newspapers on the pavement was being gathered up by a curvy girl in an understated white shirt and chinos. He made as if to help, then saw that he had walked straight into a red-faced Rosy Hope.

'I could do without this. I really could,' she snapped.

'Temper, temper,' said Benedict, unrepentant. 'What's eating you, darling?'

Her wide mouth quivered. She seemed as if she were about to boil over.

Unable to resist, he needled with a shrug, 'Awfully sorry, Rosy – I'd stay to help but I'm off to get the scoop of the festival, and the yacht has been sent for me . . .' He'd expected a sharp retort, but she merely looked crushed.

Benedict pushed off while it seemed opportune. When he glanced back, she was still outside the pavilion, standing with the papers bunched in her arms as if undecided whether to go in.

She wasn't his problem. The Ste Marguerite was, he realised, as he reached the steps of the Palais without having spotted any white gleaming craft which fitted the image in his mind.

He stood searching, shading his eyes with one hand. Straight to one side of the Palais – where he had been directed – was the yawn of an underground car parking bunker, and then to the right of that, announced by a great fairground sign, the tourist pleasure boats to the Iles de Lérin. Snakes of trippers curled out from a garish green and blue map of the islands which lay out beyond the bay.

Benedict walked back the way he had come around this undistinguished dock and surveyed the scene in vain. Then he retraced his steps again. He swallowed his distaste and went into the Information and ticket office. There was no one else to ask.

'*Excusez-moi*. I am looking for the Sainte Marguerite,' he said. 'Moored near here?'

The woman behind the counter nodded intelligently enough. 'Three o'clock,' she said.

'It will be here at three?' He was relieved already.

'It is here already. Forty-five francs, please.'

'I beg your pardon?'

'The ticket – return – is forty-five francs to the island of Sainte Marguerite, monsieur.'

59 | *Another Kiss Off*

After an aeon of indecision, Rosy went in. In a town where appearances were everything, the British Pavilion was the obvious place to make her silent statement.

The taxi ride back from the far outskirts of Nice early that morning might have cleaned her out financially, but she had survived to fight another day.

Rosy tried to concentrate. The black coffee she bought back to her table didn't help. She was gloomily aware of how little joy cometh in the morning newspapers these days. RECESSION DEEPENS AGAIN, growled the *Guardian*. RENEWED CONCERN AS TRADE DEFICIT WIDENS, hissed *The Times*. MEDICAL EXPERTS PROVE CELLULITE IS INCURABLE, howled the *Mail*.

That was all she needed.

Other reporters – the successful ones – rushed around her, checking their pigeon holes and the bulletin board where faxes of their latest showing in the London tabloids were displayed. Prominent that morning was a page of Sword's Secrets from Cannes.

Soon enough, its author swaggered over to her. Her nerves were too shot to take evasive action. Sitting duck, she lowered her head into a broadsheet. Too late to hide her flaming cheeks.

'Rosy!' Jamie spread his arms wide. 'Where have you been?'

'Where have *I* been?'

'The girls last night . . . it was all a set-up for the cameras at the Carlton.'

'Oh, yeah . . . whatever.'

'And then you left with that . . . whoever . . .'

'Yeah.'

'Rosy, *Rosy* . . . I – you've been avoiding me – '

'Jamie, I'm warning you . . . if I hear one more terrible line from the male of the species in this hell hole . . . Just leave me alone.'

He sat down uninvited and did his stuff with the amber eyes. The *hurt and confused* routine.

She went back behind *The Times*. Now that was an apt position . . .

'What's wrong?'

'Oh, for God's sake . . .'

'OK . . . why, then?' cooed Jamie, raking back his floppy dark curls when he had her momentary attention.

'Because I think you may have mistaken me for someone else,' said Rosy.

He frowned.

'For someone whose feelings can never be hurt, and who will be so grateful for crumbs that they'll do anything for you, and who'll believe any amount of crap,' she explained slowly.

'You don't understand – '

'Jamie, do the words *piss off* mean anything to you?'

He opened his mouth, but said nothing. He didn't go either.

'I can't get over you, Jamie.'

A softening?

'I'm glad to hear it.'

'I mean, where do you get your front from? Sincerity Trading? Vanities R Us?'

He shook his head, acting disbelief that he was hearing this.

Rosy gave him a long hard stare. Her voice came out smoothly. 'I invented you, Jamie.'

She scrutinised his beautiful sculpted face. The only thing that was plain was that he didn't get it, at all.

'Handsome guy.'

Rosy stopped mid-stride. At the entrance to the pavilion, standing by a half-baked attempt to provide a row of rose bushes as an international demarcation zone, was the woman in red.

Or rather, in blue today. A blue suit far too hot for a Côte d'Azur afternoon.

'Can we talk?' she asked Rosy.

Could they? Rosy had never been so pleased to see anyone. The woman in red, who had fallen into Benedict's lap. The woman in the Arden film stills. If she could keep a lid on her desperation, she might even get somewhere.

For some reason, the woman seemed wary of all the usual locations. They pitched up in the garden of Rosy's hotel, in two festering wrought-iron seats, screened by dense pines. Rosy was so far out of it, she felt it was a miracle she was making it through the motions.

'He may be handsome, but he's a creep, by the way,' she said, when the woman mentioned the chance encounter of seeing her again with Jamie Raj.

'You do seem to make a habit of going out with creeps.'

Rosy agreed with her all too readily, then thought about it. 'Er . . . how do you know . . . I mean, oh crumbs . . . is it *obvious* . . .?'

The woman shook her head. 'You're looking for Robert Arden,' she said.

Rosy was infinitely relieved that someone was taking control. 'I've been sent out to fetch the Holy Grail, yes,' she began waspishly. 'And you know what, the longer I stay in this place, the more sympathy I have with the man. He's the only one with the right idea – stay away. And I've got this wretched features editor, all he wants is the impossible . . . and anyway, I'm beginning to think there might be some other trick going on . . . some hidden agenda here . . . and I'm trying to put on such a brave face . . .'

Rosy's misery tumbled out before she could think. Her eyes were as sore as her feelings. 'Sorry, sorry. How embarrassing . . . this is awful for you . . .'

The woman handed her a soft handkerchief. As Rosy took it, cast down, she noticed the woman's hands for the first time. Then she looked up from the square, weathered fingers and blinked.

'You've found your man,' said her companion.

Rosy's head suddenly felt several sizes too small. She watched, aghast at first, then with rising fear for her own sanity, as the person beside her peeled off eyelashes and spun-sugar hair, then drew the back of a thick hand across the immaculate make-up.

Red lipstick smeared like blood.

60 | *The Boat to Ste Marguerite*

Benedict's ocean-going blazer was more than incongruous among the day-glo bermudas and T-shirts of the ferry boat trippers. It marked him out as an Englishman at sea, in all senses.

He shucked it off and folded it carefully.

The wooden seat under his Ralph Lauren casuals throbbed to the juddering of old engines.

The gossip columnist concentrated balefully on the blue horizon swelling the other side of the square windows.

The boat bumped a wooden jetty on Ste Marguerite some fifteen minutes later. His fellow passengers leapt out, dragging bags and towels and beach equipment in a burst of late spring opportunism. Benedict made his descent, slithering as the smooth leather soles of his loafers failed to grip the planks.

Clumps of tanned and reddened sunseekers stood around on the quay, already prepared to call it a day and catch the next sailing back. Benedict, feeling urgent, consulted his watch.

Turning away from the turquoise water, he marched up to a map of the island. It was larger than he'd expected, long and thin, and criss-crossed by paths. Tiny beaches were marked in dozens of shallow inlets. He took stock.

So the Ste Marguerite was not a yacht, but an island.

That didn't alter the premise that the elusive Robert Arden would be on it. The only question was, where?

The pine-needle path to the most obvious starting point became a wood-chippings track after a while. It cut straight to the island's most obvious landmark – the old fort. It was deserted. There was no sight or sound apart from unbroken trees and a Gucci-shredding crunch under his feet. At every junction with another path there was a map logging his progress, and a sign warning visitors of fire hazards.

After a while, Benedict took the shade line at the edge of the path. He must have been almost there when he heard his name.

'Hi there! Benedict Pierce?'

He started, and stared down an intersecting pathway. Two floppy-haired figures in jeans straggled towards him.

'Coincidence, or what?' said the taller one, a studenty boy with a small Shakespearian beard and a bottle of Wild Turkey.

Or what, was the worrying option for Benedict. Although . . . they didn't *look* like rival journalists. He clenched his teeth. They could easily be stringers for a hip film magazine.

The girl with him, he could see now, toted a matt black rucksack and was chewing gum behind scarlet lipstick. He frowned at the couple.

'Toby Weedon,' said the boy by way of reminder. 'We've met through Lottie. Do you know Minky Winkworth?'

'I'm in the film business now too,' said the girl.

Benedict vaguely recognised the face from party spreads in the *Prattler*.

'This is most excellent,' said the boy, despite Benedict's most fervent facial indications that this was emphatically not the case. 'You are going to be very interested in the concepts we have for your treatment.'

'I'm really not – '

'The way we see it, you're making the *Darling*! of the 1990s, and what we can offer is the *cinema verité* of the Notting Hill techno-Bohemian culture with – '

'Look,' said Benedict sharply. 'Another time.'

'We'll talk, then?' urged the boy.

'Weedon, you said?'

The lad nodded. 'Cousin of.'

Benedict sighed. 'I'll be in touch.'

'Yo!' said the girl.

'In this business, you have to push,' said the boy.

As the two made black Caterpillar tracks in the opposite direction, he had the feeling he had made two wannabes very happy. For the time being.

His head full of National Film Institute speeches, he arrived at the overgrown graveyard where the fort should have been before he realised he must have taken a wrong turning. Under a canopy of trees, the grey slabs of stone were hemmed in by the token gesture of a little iron railing, barely a foot high.

Exasperated, Benedict cast round for another of the island maps. For once, there wasn't one. All he found was a weathered plaque commemorating the incarceration of the Man in the Iron Mask on the island.

That was exactly how his head was beginning to feel, he winced to himself as he turned right and scuttled on past rocky dips from the path which crumbled into the sea. It was almost a quarter past four by the time he made it to the Fort Royal. He scanned the sparse groups of strollers wildly, but he was almost sure that his odyssey would by now prove a vainglorious expedition.

'Fuck,' he cursed to the wind.

Benedict hung around on a thin shred of self-regard long enough to do the tourist number. He read every information sign, although it was not until the third reading that he took anything in, and all he found out then was that it wasn't an iron mask they'd put on the poor bastard during his long years of imprisonment in a dank cell in this very fort, but a velvet one. By five, he knew that they took the infamous prisoner off to the Bastille, where he died in 1703, after eleven years in this old-time Alcatraz on the Ile Ste Marguerite. No one knew who he was exactly – some said the illegitimate brother of Louis XIV, but others suggested Louis XIII's son-in-law, although he was held under the name of Eustache Dauger.

Not even the Man in the Iron Mask was all he seemed.

61 | *Idol Chatter*

The latex mask was a limp jellyfish in his hand, bloodied with Max Factor.

'You . . .?'

An affirmative nod.

'I don't – I mean, I can't . . .'

'I *am* Robert Arden.'

The shock had subsided, but Rosy was still babbling inanely. 'I'd vowed that I was having nothing more whatever to do with guys who acted the whole time . . . present company most definitely excluded.'

The film star had produced a pair of old jeans and loafers from his Ungaro bag. The female attire, he explained, was the pivotal point of the next Oscar-winner. He played a transsexual called Maxi.

The real Arden hair was nondescript sandy, his natural face a pleasant yet curiously blank canvas – until he smiled, that was. He was doing it now, and Rosy found herself having to suppress all the girlish manifestations of teenage fandom. Here she was, only feet away from the romantic lead of the previous decade's ultimate feel-good movie. She'd been an impressionable fifteen when she'd seen it.

'How did you know who I am?' asked Rosy. This was

the part that didn't add up. 'When I left you,' she said, puzzled, '. . . the first time after you fell on Benedict, neither of us said who we were. In fact, I was kicking myself, because I saw your photograph in the background of a couple of the Maxi stills in the press release later that very night, and . . . well, I was desperate to get back in touch with you.'

'You read the press release? You *are* serious . . .'

Rosy couldn't stop for the chummy witticism. 'So, when you suddenly appeared in Benedict's lap like that, it was the most incredible coincidence . . . only the wrong way round . . .'

'Oh, it wasn't a coincidence,' said Robert Arden.

'I don't understand.'

'This Benedict Pierce has also been somewhat desperate to talk to me. Very persistent. But after five years out I never speak to anyone – *anyone* – without being sure of what and who they are.'

'You staged the fall?'

He raised his hands in acknowledgement.

'But . . . hang on.' Rosy's mind whirred. 'You hardly know who I am either. Only a brief chat on the way out, by the *Tender is the Night* exhibition . . .' She couldn't read his expression.

'I reckon I know quite a bit about you . . . after last night. I was *mighty* relieved to find that you got back safely,' he said. 'I was pretty worried.'

Rosy's bug eyes popped.

Then, in that same neutral accent he had used then, he said. 'I very much enjoyed our conversation on the beach . . . before I scared you off.'

It took a while for Rosy to get back on track. But the selectively reclusive film star obviously enjoyed being in control. She hauled her voice-activated tape recorder out of her bag, and for the first fifteen minutes it did all the work for her.

'In this business, you are only what you seem to be,' he told her, developing his theme. 'It's completely one-dimensional. You're an actor, you do suave – you have to do suave in every picture you make. We-ell, I can do that, but I can do a lot else besides. I realised pretty early on that the key is not getting pinned down.

'Whatever you do, you get labelled,' said Rosy.

'That's right, because with the millions of dollars involved, no one wants to take a risk. It's all about winning. At the outside, they take a safe bet.'

'But you get labelled anyway,' persisted Rosy. 'You're the Enigmatic Recluse.'

'That, I can live with.'

'It must be useful.'

'Very. When I come back, I can be anyone I want to be. All the industry cares about is inventing people – and not only on the screen.'

'I know exactly what you mean. "Nobodies until I invented them" . . . At least people know what they're getting in the film business.' He waited for her to explain. 'There's someone else who always says that . . . at the newspaper.'

'First lesson in Hollywood. Nothing is real or permanent. There's no problem that can't be resolved in a sitcom twenty-three minutes – otherwise there's gotta be a pill or a therapist to fix that.'

'Acting isn't real,' ventured Rosy.

'No. But it's a fake for honest reasons, or it should be. Like writing fiction to point to the truth.'

She smiled shyly. 'How do *you* see yourself?'

The box office superstar hesitated. 'I'm a cynic. But, hell, I make it work for me.'

Rosy had to agree there.

'You know what's the only story that matters in LA? The gratuitous sex, violence and sycophancy in the process of getting the movie made in the first place. The way everyone is so driven doing their banal routines, yet they talk about it as if it's Shakespeare . . .'

'I see . . .'

'I'm a regular guy, in other words.'

Indeed, he did seem it now, wearing an open-necked shirt and sinking a beer. Apart from the disconcerting reminders, at certain angles, of the cinema's most alluring Wild West outsider.

'Do you have a wife and family?' Rosy took her chance and held her breath as he mulled over his response. There had never been so much as a neighbourhood mentioned in any newspaper article she'd found.

'Sure,' he said, at last. 'Been married fifteen years to the same woman, we got three kids.'

She opened her mouth to speak, but he cut in: 'Her name's Joanna; it's two boys and a girl in that order, eleven, seven and two. She stays home, we're extremely happy and no, she isn't here and she's never been to Hollywood either.'

'How did you meet her?'

'In a burger bar, and that's all I'm saying.'

She got no further. Unwilling to jeopardise what she did have, she reluctantly brought the subject back to his films. 'So . . . *why* do you do it then?'

'I play the game. And don't you think one job every five years beats the hell out of the nine-to-five?'

Rosy had to agree.

62 | *Malice in Blunderland*

It had been weeks since Anthony Sword had felt like a song in the morning. When he had tried his morning workout before breakfast the effect had been less a mid-ocean greeting from the QE2 than a windy parp from his old Vauxhall.

He knew exactly who to blame, and why.

Framboise had staged the definitive disappearance.

He tried calling her again when he reached his red telephone at the office. The jolly rendering exhorting him to leave a message grated on his irrascibility. When, heart in throat, he dialled the number for Spelbridge Place – half-dreading, half-hoping to find her there – he was told that Lord Spelbridge was out of the country. No further information was forthcoming.

So much for the high commander of telephone terrorism.

He got through to an interior designer said to be having an affair with the current Home Secretary. That is, she answered her telephone, but then doggedly pretended to be an answering machine.

The husband of a top-ranking mistress told him to piss off.

And Eva was not answering.

It wasn't the best time for the new features editor to show off what a terminal asshole he was.

'Ah . . . Anthony!' he said, advancing unannounced towards the desk fortress.

'Ah . . . Lunt,' returned Sword coldly.

'No sign of any little featurette for the Happy Families slot?'

'No.'

'That's a shame, I would have been – '

'I am very bored with this conversation . . . and with you, Lunt.' Sword thought how ratty the man was, with his receding mousy hair scrapped back and held fast with wet look gel. His thin face snuffled around at the idiosyncratic diary office suite. 'Have we anything else to say to each other?'

The features editor gave the scene the once-over. 'Your intolerable arrogance and the working atmosphere in here – '

(Lulu was sewing the hem of a cocktail dress. Pearson, surrounded by Alka Seltzer wrappers, was an unhealthy colour, with his nose in the first volume of *Spotlight* actresses. Tina was pinning up gilt-edged invitation cards, and collecting empty champagne glasses.)

' – demonstrates without the need for words the way your staff expect the world on a plate.'

Sword grinned in a way likely to infuriate. 'Your girl Rosy Hope . . .'

Sword gave him a nuclear reactive glower. 'Not *my* girl.'

'Don't be so modest now.'

'Can I do something for you, Lunt?'

'You can tell me whether Rosy Hope was always this useless – or wasn't it her professional abilities which interested you?'

'For fuck's sake . . .'

'You're not going to tell me she was any good . . . as a reporter. I've got the editor on my back because of this job she's gone on, number two can't see that I'll ever pull it off, and number three is making odds down in the Scribblers Club calculating my chances of survival . . .

'So what's wrong? Don't they make sewers like they used to?' Sword sharpened his sarcasm.

The other man ignored him. 'That airhead of yours goes to Cannes and thinks we've sent her to Club Med. What she doesn't realise is, if she doesn't get the goods, she's out so fast her feet won't touch.'

'Get out, Lunt.'

The rat sniffled. 'Who *do* you think you are, Sword?'

The most famous gossip columnist in the world declined to answer. 'The conversation is over, Lunt.'

The features editor looked around again, contemptuously. 'The words piss-up and brewery come to mind, Sword. There are going to be changes around here, you'll see. And I can tell you now. You are being watched. Every move.'

Sword had some forthright advice for the new man at the *Dispatch*. 'Go fuck yourself, Lunt.'

63 | *Connected at Last*

Her luck had turned, she knew, when she was put through – at only the second try – to the features editor.

'Hello, John. It's Rosy Hope.'

A grunt from the end of the line. Rosy hugged herself in anticipation of his reaction. The Arden tape was burning a hole in her hand. 'I've got good news,' she began.

His reaction was nothing like she'd imagined. 'The trip's over, Rosy.'

'Eh?'

'It's been over for days.'

'I'm sorry . . . But I've – ?'

She was answered by the dull groan of the dialling tone.

After three hours her hotel room was a snowstorm of discarded paper, but she knew what she'd written was good. ROBERT ARDEN, EXCLUSIVE BY ROSY HOPE IN CANNES she wrote in block capitals on the top of the first page.

The next part would be the hardest.

Rosy picked up the telephone by her bed and pressed nine for an outside line. Then she clenched sharp fingernails into the palm of her free hand and replaced the receiver without dialling. Much as she disliked the old fashioned art of doorstepping, she felt instinctively that she had no option this time.

She stuffed the sheets of paper into her bag, grabbed her jacket and keys, and went towards the door. Then she hesitated and turned back to give herself a check in the mirror and add some light lipstick before heading out.

It took her a good ten minutes to reach the Sofitel Méditerranée, during which time her euphoria level had slumped. It seemed to be buzzing somewhere around her knees, overwhelmed by nervous anticipation.

As casually as she could, she strolled past reception and straight into the lift up to his floor. She knocked on the door, willing him to be there.

He was.

'Hi, Jamie.'

'Rosy! This is . . . unexpected.' She tried to tell herself that it wouldn't matter if he had company. 'I haven't actually come to apologise . . . for earlier . . . but if you want me to, I will.'

To his credit, he didn't ask the obvious question. 'You'd better come in.'

'Is that OK? I mean – '

'There's no one else here,' said Jamie. He led her in.

'I need to ask you a favour – it's work,' said Rosy, trying not to look at the bed.

'Anything.'

'I need to use your laptop, to send back to the *Dispatch*.'

'Er, sure. What have you got, then?'

'Oh . . . this and that. May I take it back to my room? I mean, you won't need it to send your next column for at least the next day or so.'

'Rosy . . . *This and that*?'

It was a sweet moment.

'Oh, just my Robert Arden interview,' she said.

* * *

In the end he was helpfulness itself, insisting she installed herself at his desk there and then to type it up on the computer link to the *Dispatch* back in London.

When it came to work, he was ever the professional. 'Look, it's up and running here. You don't want to get it back to your place, and find it won't work, or the wires are crossed . . .'

'Thanks for the vote of confidence.'

'I'm just saying. Besides, I'm assuming you don't want to waste a moment putting it through.'

Privately she was relieved, although she wouldn't have told him that.

Rosy tapped in her prize piece.

To her relief, he left her to it, making for the slanting remains of the sun on balcony with a book.

When she had finished she added a second piece for good measure: five hundred words on Rebecca Hunt and Joe Wesley. She wrote a version of the boudoir scene in Eze that was as close to the knuckle as she could manage without getting tacky. As luck would have it, Mr Wesley's press coordinator had been only too delighted to oblige with a happy quote. So long as she mentioned his sincere hopes for the next – unfinalised – movie.

'Hi – again,' said Rosy, leaning on the door frame. 'That's about it.'

Jamie had abandoned his book and was contemplating the sea, his feet up on the balcony rail. 'All done?'

'Yeah.'

'Do you need some help to send it?'

'If you wouldn't mind . . . just overseeing.'

He swung his legs down and stood up. With his back to the light, she couldn't make out his face. He followed her inside. 'How long is it?' he asked.

'Not sure exactly . . . a bit under two thousand words. You know how they like to cut.'

He sat down at the machine and scrolled down part of what she had written. 'Wha-a-t? A man in a mask . . .? A *transvestite* man in a mask! This is incredible.'

She nodded with a grin.

He whistled. '*You* are incredible, do you know that? I mean . . . here's half the entertainment press in the world looking for the guy, big money changing hands, Benedict Pierce trumpeting up and down the bay . . . and then you come along and – '

Rosy looked at her watch. It was probably too late for the *Dispatch* to run it for the next morning, but suddenly it seemed desperately important that she got it logged in as soon as possible.

'Jamie, do you think you could just . . . send it?'

He twiddled with a few keys. 'Yeah, of course. But, I want to hear all about this . . .'

'Sure.'

'Why don't you open a bottle?' He gestured towards the mini-bar.

In these professional circumstances, it seemed rude to refuse. She picked out a half bottle of white wine.

The wariness between them lasted for nearly all of it.

'Sorry, Jamie . . . I'm suddenly feeling really exhausted. I'm going back to my hotel.'

He was still visibly incredulous at her account of the past two days – and she had only given him the briefest version. Needless to say, she had left out the part about being wrung out with hurt and fury at the way he had treated her. 'Bloody hell, I'm not surprised. Eze . . . the beach . . . then getting back here. Then – ' this was the part that was still giving him trouble ' – the major star of the festival stripping off in front of you.'

'So to speak,' said Rosy.

'Even so.'

She got up to go. Weary as she was, she had to ask. 'Why was it so necessary to bother with me . . . the other night . . . when you've been so cosy with Minette?'

Jamie turned his eyes on her like arc lights. 'Minette? Oh, that's not anything – '

'That wasn't what I asked.'

He raked his hands through his hair in his characteristic way, and reached out for her. 'Rosy . . .'

She was on the brink of another empty embrace. Then she gathered herself and walked away. 'No . . . actually I don't want to know,' she said at the door.

Excuses and hollow declarations, she could do without.

64 | *Degrees of Gossip*

There were degrees of gossip, thought Benedict the next morning. There was the everyday variety, without which life would not be worth living. There was the tosh that overcame reason at any good party. There was the calculated political do-over manoeuvre.

And there was the codswallop that Anthony Sword came out with when he clambered breathlessly up on to the moral high ground.

Benedict Pierce snarled at his copy of the *Daily Dispatch* and thought dark thoughts of sabotage.

He didn't trust himself even to begin to address the question of how Jamie Raj had go to Robert Arden and how he, Benedict, had come to be so thoroughly fucked.

To add to his humiliation, his editor was insisting – in the way only a man with a pathological self-regard could insist – on the Pierce presence at the Arden press conference that morning in the Palais des Festivals.

He was not going to hurry.

Approaching the venue, Benedict ignored the ruthless comments of all those other hacks who had expected him to bring the recluse to exclusive after taking up pole position.

The conference room was on the first floor, and the crush started out on the pavement. Accredited journalists and photographers from around the world thronged the wide steps and the cavernous white marble foyer. Crushing them were hordes of the same but without the appropriate passes, publicity hangers-on, film buffs and sightseers.

It took Benedict twenty minutes of jostling through the scrum to reach the foot of the steps to the entrance. Such was the intensity of desire to see the man that a girl reporter thrown against him had her press pass ripped from her by some opportunist.

Crunched with the indignity of it all, Benedict felt a sudden empathy with her. Something similar had happened to his prize interview.

Two hours later, he was reduced to interviewing other journalists as they emerged from the building. He had found his way barred by security staff – on safety grounds, there were no more bodies allowed in the building.

His second-hand version of the Hollywood star's words from a lad on the *Express* cost him a cheque for £250 and a large round of drinks.

He cobbled together a piece, sent it down the wire, and went out to get drunk. He succeeded rather faster than he had intended, on a cocktail of Napoleon brandy and sunshine. Benedict's first steps up to the thoroughfare from the beach bar were ungainly staggers.

A giant merry-go-round sucked him in for a ride.

With painful deliberateness he set his course for his hotel. He could hear the thrilled screams of other riders on the carousel which had supplanted La Croisette. The zoom of cars came from a long way away.

Much later – he must have made it back, for Lottie had

burst in on his siesta – the other iron in his fire showed dangerous signs of leaving him with burnt fingers too.

'I'm not doing that,' pouted Lottie. She was waving the draft script for *Princess Laid Bare.*

Considering the many perversities she had already mastered as part of her career plan, Benedict thought that was a bit rich. Especially as he was doing her a favour, frankly, by finding her a part.

'It's too slutty,' said Lottie.

'I *like* slutty. Lots of people like slutty.'

She threw the script on the floor. 'There is no way I am ever, *ever* going to have any credibility if you make me snog Sir Philip Hawty.'

Privately, he agreed. 'It's only the story . . .'

'Yeah. That is supposed to be a true version.' She crossed her arms, a model of intransigence.

'Well, that's what we *say* . . .'

'No.'

'For me . . .?'

'Especially not for you, Benedict.'

65 | *Cutting Scene*

If ever there were a tasteless scene to be cut, it was this. But Rosy took a deep breath, straightened her back and moved forward as loosely as she could with a body knotted by fury.

She was thinking lithe and confident, straining like hell for Geena Davis – and feeling every inch like the Terminator on a bad clothes day.

With a press conference involving a Marilyn look-alike scheduled for eleven at the British Pavilion, it was a fair bet he'd be there. He was, sitting smugly at a prime table with a stack of papers, ostentatiously reading *Bunte* magazine.

She marched over to him. 'Hello. Jamie.'

'Ah, Rosy! I knew you'd come round in the end. Coffee?'

'Stop it, just stop it!' she exploded. 'What the hell do you think you're playing at?'

The expression of startled innocence he threw out hit her like a brick to the stomach.

At least he didn't ask her what she meant.

Hands on fire with anger, she reached out, trembling, for his copy of the *Daily Dispatch*. It was bad enough that her story about Rebecca Hunt and Joe Wesley at Eze was the lead story, without any kind of acknowledgement, on the Sword's Secret page.

But this! The newspaper ripped as she found the place and spread it in front of him, sick with anger and powerlessness.

The white pages misted over the black print, but not before she had seen it again.

The film stills, and the main picture of another smiling man with a charismatic camera presence.

The bold headline under an Exclusive! banner screamed: ROBERT ARDEN, THE MAN IN THE MASK . . . AND HIGH HEELS. HOLLYWOOD'S MOST FAMOUS RECLUSE TALKS EXCLUSIVELY TO THE DAILY DISPATCH.

The handsome picture of him, and the words 'By Jamie Raj'.

Jamie looked at her for a long time before he answered. 'As someone said to you last year when you joined the Sword's Secrets page, you have a lot to learn, Rosy Hope.'

Struck dumb with fury and resentment, she couldn't even form the words to reply.

Blundering blindly through the streets, tears dissolving the Riviera razzmatazz into pointillism, she realised she had only one option. When vile people fucked you – in this case, in all senses – you first had to restore your faith in your own judgement.

Find a friend who hadn't, in other words.

From a crumpled heap on her prison-block bed back at the Hotel du Jardin, she wailed: 'Emma?'

'Rosy! Where are you?'

'Emma, thank God, you're there!'

'*Where are you*?'

'Still in Cannes.'

'What's wrong?'

Rosy told her, alternatively sobbing and shouting. 'I

mean . . . how could he *do* it to me? What have I ever done to deserve that?'

Emma wisely let her rage.

'It wasn't even as if I'd spurned his advances – and . . . and . . . offended his macho pride. Not here, at any rate . . .'

'Ah, but there you have it,' said Emma eventually, after several reruns of this theme.

'Eh?' snivelled Rosy.

'He can't bear not winning.'

'You mean . . .?'

'You, of all people, to show him up.'

'What?'

'Get the story when he didn't.'

'Yeah, but he wasn't even here for that.'

'Doesn't make much odds. You'd got the story of the year.'

A damp pause. 'Em . . .'

'Mmm?'

'Do you think . . . that . . . maybe . . . getting me into bed after I'd been so cool towards him back home – making me think he really cared and wanted to get back together – was all part of the same . . . *winning* thing?'

There was a long pause.

'I thought so,' said Rosy.

'I know it's not going to help at all,' began Emma hesitantly, 'but it was a great story.'

'Oh, yeah. They only changed two words in the whole thing. The ones after "By" . . .'

'You have told them, back at the *Dispatch*?'

'What's the point? Who's going to believe me?' She hadn't mentioned to Emma about the last unsettling phone call to the features editor, which had strongly implied she was out of a job.

'What are you going to do?'

'Dunno,' said Rosy.
She really didn't.

66 | *A Ripe Raspberry*

Rosy kicked over the traces as she mooched down the street.

Her British Airways ticket was an open return.

She had a Visa card.

She had met and interviewed a man she'd admired for ever, even if no one else knew that.

There were other newspapers in the world.

Several of the French ones carried front-page stories of a teenage Bonnie and Clyde who had stolen a car and a gun and cruised through Cannes in a blaze of glory. Their spree had ended in a hail of police bullets round the headland in Miramar.

Which was all the more tragic, given that the stolen gun, in this instance, was a paint sprayer.

Waiting to cross the rue d'Antibes outside the shop where she'd blown the advance on her expenses on the cream dress – she would count that as her leaving present from the *Dispatch* – Rosy wondered idly if she'd ever be able to afford clothes again.

It seemed as if months had passed since her trudges up and down here those first few days. Now, she was almost inured to the sight of slinky French women with their squeaky toy dogs passing by with their bags full of famous names.

Rosy couldn't help but notice this one, though. She steamed out of a boutique. She was so huge and so laden with bags that as the names passed by – Christian Lacroix – Escada – Yves Saint Laurent – Salvatore Ferregamo – Gucci – the effect was that of a goods train chugging by at a level crossing.

Then Rosy saw her face.

'Framboise!' she cried out.

An hour or so later, the singer had disposed of her purchases and cantilevered her ample form into casual wear, and was already at the appointed venue by the time Rosy arrived.

'I can't tell you how pleased I am to see you, Framboise!'

'I think you already did,' said Framboise, beaming.

She was soaking up the sun beyond the shade of Martini umbrella at the Carlton beach bar, dressed to arrest in Pucci leggings and a vast red T-shirt on which the name of its designer strained and flashed in the sun. 'I'm incognito now,' she buffooned. 'What do you think?'

'Very, er . . . camouflaged, in the circumstances,' said Rosy, taking in the rest of the local colour.

'It's kinda the equivalent of, "My man went to Cannes, and all I got was this lousy Versace." '

'Aaah!' Rosy leapt on that. 'Your *man*?'

Framboise popped on a pair of jazzy shades before she said, 'Think of that as a figure of speech.' She assessed Rosy closely.

'I look awful, I know,' said Rosy glumly.

'You look tired. A little pale and interesting, perhaps, but that's OK. It's all the vogue these days – anywhere but here, at any rate. Look at any of the royal family, top-ranking mistresses, those skinny bandy models, Mr Jackson . . .'

'But they're all suffering the aftermath of some terrible trauma,' said Rosy. 'Mind you . . .'

'So traumatised is *in*,' drawled Framboise, blasé as ever in matters of taste. 'What was it Princess Diana once said? "You got to suffer if you wanna be like me." Fancy is as fancy does.' She pulled a moony face.

Rosy had to laugh.

'That's ma girl,' said Framboise.

It didn't take long for the floodgates to open. 'Sword jokes about inventing people – but that's exactly what I did with Jamie. I had this idea of what I wanted, and dreamed him into having all those qualities.'

'That's not his fault,' pointed out Framboise.

'His own self-regard helped,' said Rosy bitterly.

Framboise conceded that one.

'The problem was, we were both in love with one person,' said Rosy. 'Him.'

They both laughed.

'He and Sword, they're both the same,' ploughed on Rosy, recklessness overwhelming tact. 'They're actors. They both play at being something they're not – well, not really.'

Framboise's faint smile was inscrutable.

Not that Rosy could have stopped. 'The nearest Jamie ever got to the truth was when he'd phone me and simply say: "It's me." '

'It's not him you're mad at, it's you,' diagnosed Framboise. 'Anyhow, the way I heard it, it was *you* gave Mr Raj notice to quit.'

'Only on a technicality.'

'So what are you saying – he's a cad and a bounder?'

'He'd probably take it as the greatest compliment to be called either. Those particular terms imply such *prestige*,' said Rosy bitterly.

The singer pushed her sunglasses up into her hair and fixed Rosy with a stare which brooked no misunderstanding. 'For someone who thinks too much, you show a surprising reluctance to reach Conclusion One.'

'That being?'

'Men and women speak different languages. To illustrate,' expounded Framboise, 'I would suggest that, in local parlance, "*Je t'aime toujours*" would accurately translate as "Wanna fuck?" Am I not right?'

Rosy chewed a fingernail.

Framboise brought her pale blue lagoon eyes to bear on a floppy-haired Frenchman at the next table. He responded shamelessly.

'You're incorrigible,' sighed Rosy.

'I'm thinking of getting married,' said Framboise.

'What, really? When you said you had a man . . . I mean, congratulations. That's wonderful. To Sword?'

She cast down her eyes. 'I don't think so.'

'But?'

'I may not even have found the lucky man yet.'

'But . . .' Rosy remembered a snippet Jamie had let slip. 'I heard that you were quite keen on British citizenship!'

The singer managed to give her admirer a tragic Piaf gesture with her false eyelashes. 'Yeah, that's true. But as I'm here, I figure I might as well allow myself the fantasy of a European Union scam . . .'

Rosy smiled indulgently.

67 | *Raging Bull*

His long years of specialisation in *diablesse* had made Anthony Sword an acute sensor of a kindred spirit invading his personal space. So it was the purest good luck that Jamie called him from the South of France just when the Sword's antennae were twitching.

'James,' he bellowed. 'What did you tell Lulu when you phoned in last?'

'Tell Lulu? Nothing. I didn't speak to Lulu.'

'Ah. You're sure about that?'

'Of course. Why?'

'And when you spoke to her the other day, when she was reading out extracts from Hawty's early cuttings and Eva's file? What was all that about?'

'I didn't speak to her the other day.'

'No?'

'Absolutely not. What's going on? Did she say she'd spoken to me?'

'She did. What is more, I pushed the redial button on her phone when she finished the call and went out of the room.'

'And?'

He let Jamie wait for a moment. 'The last number she dialled was your number – or rather the hotel number you left for us.'

Sword noted the sharp intake of breath at the other end of the line. 'You may be right, in that case,' said Jamie, perceptively. 'If you have your doubts about Lulu.'

'Tell me.'

'I am not the only gossip columnist staying at this hotel. Benedict Pierce is in the room next door.'

'A moment on the lips – a lifetime in the cuttings library,' said a grand lady who knew better than was good for Sword's business.

He was at a stand-up lunch in Cadogan Square for the crestfallen. The guests were a mixture of Lloyd's names, death-duty do-gooders, and upper-crust estate agents. The occasion was the launch of an upmarket bed and breakfast network by which the unfortunate wretches could turn a penny in their desirable old country houses. They were calling themselves upper middle class as an egalitarian gesture.

And the great draw was supposed to be the healthy traditional food they would offer on their refectory tables.

So naturally, the directory of these fine B & B addresses was called *The Oat Monde*.

'Whatever we may call ourselves, paying is still not the same as being invited,' grumbled Lady X.

Sighs of resignation all round.

'It's the eternal problem, isn't it? Letting the money in without the parvenus.'

'I am wary of decadence . . .'

'I am weary of decorating . . . England seems to expect these ghastly little cupboard bathrooms which are known as En-Suites.'

'So *difficult* to know what to do, eh, Mr Sword?'

'Terribly difficult,' he agreed.

'I mean, I mean,' said Lady Y, 'Much more of this and

we may well be forced into the gutter. What do you suggest, Mr Sword? Shall we all become gossip columnists?'

His best decision of the day was leaving the lunch abruptly. He arrived back a good hour too early for Lulu, who replaced her telephone receiver with an unmistakeable expression of guilt.

The truth fell like a guillotine.

Sword raged in like a bull. 'Since when did you work for Benedict Pierce?'

There was a nasty pause which indicated the game was up.

'Since last year,' she replied with a simpering smile.

Her dismissal was instant and brutal. By the time he had finished, smoke alarms were wailing throughout the building, all production was suspended, and an ambulance crew was hurtling towards the epicentre of the blast.

The air took some time to clear.

'Give me a list of the messages you've passed on to Lulu in the last couple of days,' he barked at the hapless Tina when it had.

His secretary flipped through her notepad. Five minutes later, she gave him a sheet of paper with a column of names. There were only three marked under the day's date: Eva Coutts, one of Eva's as-yet-unknown actresses, and John Crighton.

'No number for this Crighton?' demurred Sword.

'He said she knew it.'

68 | *Framboise's Invitation*

Framboise's phone call came at exactly the right time.

The dilemma had reached the when-in-doubt-eat stage.

'Lunch?' said Rosy. 'Framboise, I'd love to. How did you know that lunch was going to be my last request before they finally kill me off?'

The singer laughed. 'You may have to explain that, when we get there.'

It sounded like the venue was a definite booking. 'You may regret saying that. Where are we going?'

'A little place in the hills,' said Framboise.

'Wonderful. To get out of this place . . .'

'OK. We'll be round to collect you at . . . let's see, is eleven-thirty too early?'

'Fine.'

'Great. We'll be outside.'

That was the second time she'd said it. 'Er, Framboise . . . *We*?' If there were going to be any other guest, especially in the form of a certain dark, handsome gossip gatherer . . .

'Relax,' said Framboise, apparently reading her mind. 'The *we* is purely good news.'

'Oh?'

'I'll tell you all when we get there.'

* * *

At eleven-twenty-five, Rosy was scrubbed and freshly laundered at the steps of the Hotel du Jardin. If only the clothes service were available for worn and crumpled spirits.

A parp-parp sounded from a white Renault bowling towards her on the wrong side of the road. A substantial black arm waved cheerily from the far window. Rosy ran down, as the car pulled in.

She took off her Wayfarers as the driver emerged on to the pavement. Even without the highway code clue, there would have been not a jot of doubt that he was English. The familiar mould was country: sludge green and brown clothes, ruddy cheeks. He was tallish and well-built, with owlish eyebrows. His bearing suggested a transplanted Life-guardsman, or some other variety of smart military sort. Despite the heat he was wearing Church's brogues, she noticed.

'Hi, Rosy!' called Framboise from inside. 'I'm not sure . . . have you and our driver today met before?'

He had tipped his seat forward to allow her to climb into the back. A little nonplussed, Rosy smiled shyly at the Englishman, now ramrod straight again. 'Spelbridge,' he said.

'Lord Spelbridge! Of course . . .' Rosy felt herself colouring.

No wonder he seemed even more familiar than his stock type.

'The charming Miss Hope of the *Daily Dispatch*,' beamed the baron. 'Are you still working for that dreadful gossip column?'

Rosy's smile turned into a slight cheek-ache as she shook her head.

Framboise gave them one of her rich chuckles. 'So you *do* know one another!'

'It's been a while since I lost a housekeeper to a drunken neighbour at a party,' said Lord Spelbridge. 'But let me reassure you that I have managed to rebuild my life after all the dramatic weeping and wailing.'

Despite the merry twinkle in his eye, Rosy hesitated to defend herself.

'Sounds kinda intriguing,' said Framboise, turning with a wink as Rosy clambered in behind her.

'Um, it wasn't quite as it seemed,' said Rosy. 'I suppose it's too late to say that I felt terrible about that for quite a while.'

'About what?'

Lord Spelbridge took over. 'Story in the papers had me inconsolable at the loss of the good woman I had cherished as a wife in all but name for twenty years. At one stage I was supposed to have gone mad with grief in the West Wing.'

'When all she – '

'Mrs Padget,' supplied Lord Spelbridge. 'Wonderful woman, that part was right.'

'When all Mrs Padget, the housekeeper, had done was retire because Spelbridge Place had got too much for her,' explained Rosy uncomfortably.

'Which I *did* tell you, when you tracked me down at Claridge's,' he said.

'Which *I* did tell them back at the office . . . only . . .' Here she almost gagged on the words. 'Only . . . the editor of the page decided his version was more entertaining. I'm really, really sorry to have offended you . . .'

'Ah, well . . . water under the bridge,' said Lord S good-humouredly.

'You didn't sue?' asked Framboise, as they started off.

Rosy was relieved to see that they were on the right

side of the road. Even if she wasn't on the right side of her host.

'Never explain, never complain. Only way to deal with the buggers.'

As their captive guest, Rosy remained silent on that one.

The unasked question pressed down on her as they crawled the esplanade out of town. It seemed far too rude to enquire – with him present – how Framboise knew the Kentish peer.

As they headed east into the ridged blues, mauves and rust of an Impressionist landscape, it became disconcertingly clear that she was being taken over more recent old ground. They were following the signs for Vence.

'I think I've guessed where we're going,' said Rosy.

'You have?' asked Framboise.

Lord Spelbridge seemed to grip the steering wheel tighter, but that might have been a reaction to the white delivery van tilting, Prost-like, in their direction. On the side was depicted a huge chocolate-dipped strawberry, which seemed to confirm her theory.

'Let me see . . . a place full of good food, little art galleries and *chocolatiers* . . . where the main stars are the Michelin ones . . . ?'

'You've been already?' Framboise sounded disappointed.

'Not properly,' Rosy assured her. 'I was in the wrong company.' She put aside her disappointment at not having Framboise's company to herself.

The hire car rattled ever upwards.

In the daylight, the medieval fortress town of St Paul de Vence was besieged by coach tours. Eventually, they found a parking place outside the walls, and went through the gateway and portculis on foot.

'There you are,' said Lord Spelbridge, when they reached the fabled restaurant.

'The Golden Dove,' translated Framboise. 'Do you suppose it's any relation to the goose that lays the golden egg?'

'You can give me your verdict when I get back.'

Get back? Rosy's spirits leapt.

Framboise nodded. 'Good luck,' she said, with a friendly squeeze of his hand.

Their hands clasped for only seconds too long. A message hung, unspoken, between them.

'Have a good time, both of you,' he said, with a brief wave.

69 | *An Artistic Lunch*

They were snuggly ensconced under a Picasso inside the restaurant before Rosy could give full vent to her curiosity. She looked up from the menu to find Framboise staring expectantly, head cocked.

Rosy laughed. 'I'm not sure I'm up to asking . . .'

'Call yourself a reporter?'

A wide grin. 'Who, what, where, when, why, how?'

'Let's assume the "who".'

'Then what about the – '

But Rosy's interrogation was postponed by the arrival, apparently unbidden, of a bottle of champagne. The business of popping the cork, towelling the bottle, pouring, and repositioning in the ice bucket seemed to take for ever.

At last, Framboise raised her glass. 'Here's to it,' she chortled. 'Bottoms up!'

Rosy joined in the toast with a quizzical solemnity.

'Hey . . .' Framboise reprimanded her. 'It's a celebration!'

'It is?'

'The "why" – in case you don't get around to asking – is that we are going to get married!'

Rosy put her glass down in amazement. 'Framboise! I –

I . . . well – congratulations, I mean, I don't know what to say. You and – '

The singer nodded heartily.

'It's . . . wonderful.' Then, as it sunk in, Rosy clapped her hands in rapture. 'Framboise, Lady Spelbridge . . . I *love* it!'

'Has a kinda ring.'

'I hardly dare ask how . . .'

Her companion dropped her saucer eyes. 'He came around a couple of times, backstage, at the end of a show. To talk, you know. He's kind of a fan.' She looked up and seemed to gather herself. 'It's a green card wedding – or it would be the other way round,' she explained a little too glibly.

'I get the gist,' nodded Rosy. 'But are you absolutely sure? I mean, how well do you *know* him?'

The older woman was bashful suddenly.

Rosy thought she read the signs. As she remembered the hand squeeze outside.

'I'm really, really happy for you,' she said.

Midway through their jolly lunch, Rosy got round to asking where the titled bridegroom-to-be had gone.

'He has a mission of his own here.'

'Oh?'

'It's quite a story. I can't tell you everything, but he has family who live close by.'

'He's gone off to tell them the good news about the new addition to the family?'

Framboise gave her a long evaluating stare. 'A fair guess.'

For a terrible moment, Rosy thought she'd said the wrong thing. She was convinced of it when Framboise – oddly flustered – changed the subject.

'Do you reckon Spelbridge and me could make the gossip columns?'

All through the exquisite hors d'oeuvres, Rosy had fought shy of even mentioning Sword in the light of these unexpected wedding plans. But here they were, half-way through the lobster, and the bride was hemming her in.

'You could have a wonderful time showing off your lovely home to *Ciao*! magazine,' ventured Rosy.

'That wasn't exactly what I was getting at . . .'

'No,' said Rosy, heart sinking. The last thing she wanted, ever, was to offend this warm, open woman. But she wasn't at all sure what she ought to be saying.

'Sword . . . It'll be a big shock.'

'Hmm,' said Rosy. Then all thoughts of the mastergossip's deadly reaction to this marriage of more-than-convenience flew out of her mind. After days of intermittent irritation when the puzzle had returned to irk her, its pieces suddenly clicked into place. Perhaps the key had been coming back here. 'Sex, rage and sin,' she said aloud.

She was about to run her conclusion by Framboise, but the singer's face was a mask. 'Oh, all that and more,' she said tersely.

After lunch – which was concluded over safer conversational subjects – they wandered out and joined the tourist flow. Meandering through the cobbled streets, each seemed instinctively to understand that the other was preoccupied with her own thoughts.

A pamphlet they picked up outside an Information point said that the nearby village of Tourette-sur-Loup was built on a rocky plateau some one thousand feet above a valley full of violets. Rosy wondered whether a rocky plateau was what you went through in bad times and relationships – like a weight-loss plateau you had to battle over, only without the fifty-calorie treats.

She didn't ask when the elderly fiancé would reappear, even when the cue presented itself with a visit to a gleaming white chapel at the foot of the hill which went up to the larger town of Vence.

The stained glass windows of heavenly blues and greens were by Matisse; the smiles they exchanged there were strictly small, shy Renoirs.

Rosy was absurdly relieved when Framboise linked an arm with hers for the slow walk back.

By a chocolate shop, the pallid gills of Lord Spelbridge told their own story. The baron was a shiny pale Meissen figurine from the neck up.

A sideways glance at Framboise told Rosy she was *de trop*.

Which solved her first problem.

'I – would you mind if I disappeared for half-an-hour?' she asked, seizing her chance. 'There's something I have to do.'

70 | *Benedict's Beach Party*

Benedict's beach party had very few of the traditional trappings: it was too late (both in the day and in the twentieth century) for bikini girls; there was not a grain of sand visible; nor any close approximation of Cliff or Elvis with an undersized guitar.

Early evening found the guests arriving via a staircase leading down from La Croisette, but the floors were solid and a roof blocked any view of the sky and the stars.

The lack of terrestrial stars shooting his way was another bummer for Benedict.

The worst prophesies of Kitten O'Shea, Practitioner in Public Relations, had come to pass. He was in celeb crisis – at the very moment that TV people from *The Late Entertainment Show* had been persuaded to acknowledge his standing.

Apart from the woman in radical chic.

'Benedict?'

He spun round.

'Could we get a shot of you by the entrance?' asked Sophie Brown. Her television crew hovered, sullen and heavy as late summer wasps by the food table.

'Fine,' said Benedict.

'And, er . . . that woman over there . . .?'

Benedict followed her gaze, taking in the shredded skirt, the tie-dyed shirt, and the long frizzled blondish hair above a face of genuine St Tropez leather.

'She's not . . .?' went on Sophie Brown.

'No,' said Benedict. 'Not unless she's shrunk six inches.'

'Shame.' She was clearly reluctant to lose another name, especially one as big as that, in the circumstances.

Benedict thought better of saying, Tell me about it. But then, it was his party, after all. And he knew better than almost anybody that successful appearances counted for everything.

'So . . . who is she then?'

'Ah.' The very question he couldn't answer. These TV people were so direct.

He was rescued by Jamie Raj, of all people. The Lothario of the *Daily Dispatch* cruised in, Armanied to the teeth, set off by the stunning Minette de Pots de l'Argent – or whatever her name was – on his arm.

The collapsed look on the television woman's face was a live version of the reception going on the blink.

'One of the stars of the show,' cooed Benedict.

'Have you heard the latest?' hissed the Earl of Trent, in high agitation.

'Good or bad?' Benedict had never had the greatest faith in Trent sources.

'Fucking brilliant.'

'Go on, then.'

'There's a rumour going around . . . that the Princess of Wales is utterly fed up with being likened to a Hollywood covergirl . . .'

'Unlikely, but . . .'

'Well now, she thinks she's been acting all these years – she might as well *be* a film star!'

'Hell's belles.'

'She went to LA, didn't she?'

'Yeah, but – '

'You haven't got it, have you? Diana wants to be in *Prisoner of the Palace*!'

'*WHA-A-T?*'

'With Elizabeth Taylor as the Queen,' said the earl.

Benedict gave him a look which Trent seemed to translate as 'That's intriguing casting.'

'For the US audience. Isn't it amazing? Diana with *us*! Can you believe it?'

There was a silence which could have curdled milk. 'Brett . . . our film is *Princess Laid Bare*.'

A pause. 'Fuck.'

'Exactly.'

'So what do we do now?'

'We ignore the rumour. No, better . . . we launch an immediate rubbishing campaign. We get serious publicity for our project.'

'But – a Hollywood film, with US backing?'

Benedict ground his molars and admitted it. 'You can see her logic.'

'But, but . . . not even a British Film. I mean, that's her duty, isn't it?'

A pained silence. 'If it's true,' the columnist eventually threatened, 'there will be *big* trouble.'

More silent pain. 'How are we doing here?' asked the earl.

'So-so.'

'Shall I do it now, then?' Trent ascertained rather obviously that a battery of bored photographers was in attendance.

Benedict noted, in particular, the Beast of the *Dispatch* hoovering up all the best canapés. 'Do what?'

Brett Trent drew several bottles of brightly coloured

pills from inside his dark jacket (somewhat sandy) and smiled.

'My Norma Jean.'

Benedict managed to persuade the aristocratic liability of his film project to defer the suicide scene until the stellar quality of the evening had been given every chance. 'Bigger audience, dear boy. That's what you need,' he assured him.

If the event needed artificial respiration, he would know where to turn. The last time Trent had pulled a stunt like it, at an Ascot gathering, he'd made the front pages of all the tabloids and the *Daily Telegraph*. It could work again.

As long as the dramatic moment didn't come over as just another party piece.

71 | *The Camp Follower*

Rosy found the Montée de Casse-Cou without too much difficulty, and hurtled down the crumbly steps. When she reached the sign for brains, she was out of breath. To her relief, the door to the restaurant opened smoothly at first push.

Armand was wiping glasses behind the bar.

'Armand?'

'*Oui, mademoiselle*?'

'*C'est Rosy . . . vous vous souvenez – l'autre soir*?'

'*Aaah*!' He opened his arms in recognition – or so she hoped.

'Armand . . . is your father here? I . . . I must ask him something.'

'*Ah non*! My stories of Cannes are not interesting enough for you?'

Rosy bit her lip. 'Your stories are *very* interesting. But there was a phrase your father used . . . the other night . . . that has been on my mind.'

The restaurateur folded his cloth deliberately. 'Well . . . I donno whether 'e is 'ere . . .' Then he must have registered the dismay on her face. 'I will go to see . . .'

While he was gone, it was impossible not to gaze at the table where she and Jamie had sat – so ecstatically, she had imagined. There it was, still in the corner, in categorical existence while everything that had played out around it had vanished as if it never happened.

Apart from one phrase.

The elder man wore the rear tufts of his grey hair sticking up – showing all the signs of having been aroused from a long afternoon slumber. But he greeted Rosy and her profuse apologies gamely enough, even if he didn't bother to hide his bewilderment at his summons.

They were still standing when she got straight to the point. 'I know this must seem a strange question, Monsieur . . . but have you ever known an Englishwoman called Eva Coutts?'

He was assessing her, spider to fly. 'I will get some coffee,' he said reverently. 'Please – '

Rosy took a seat at the table he indicated, and waited until he shuffled over with two shots of espresso. He sat down opposite her.

'This is a strange question, yes,' he said. 'There are not now many people . . . I am asking myself 'ow you should know to . . .'

'Ask it?'

'C'est juste.'

Rosy took a breath. 'I picked up the code, you might say.'

'Ah.'

'Sex, rage and sin.' She scrutinised the old restaurateur for a reaction.

He pulled down the corners of his rubbery mouth and nodded slowly. 'You notice much detail, Mademoiselle. This is very good.'

'So, you do?'

His rheumy eyes were far from focused.

Rosy had the same feeling she had had when she'd finally met the ancient theatrical tipster to the Sword's

Secret's column the previous year. The only possible feeling, when confronted with a seventy-year-old woman in draped crêpe presiding over kinky party games for consenting adults and networkers only, in a suburban semi in East Sheen.

Curiosity mingled with preparation for the worst. 'You do know Eva, then?' she prompted.

'Eva . . .' said Xavier. 'The naughtiest girl in the world.'

He pronounced it *now*-tiest.

Over more coffee, he told her the story.

'At the beginning of the last war, there were many English and Americans in Nice. Most of them went back, but not all. For some, life went on almost as normal. But, you know, the coast was mined. There was little fishing, but still . . .'

'It was occupied, though . . .'

'Yes, by the Italians. Compared to . . . other places, we were lucky. The Italians, they were not so bad, under Vichy.'

She scrapped together some historical logic. 'But then . . . when they surrendered, what . . .?'

'Then the Germans moved in. In 1943. The Resistance was very strong in this area. My brothers and I were involved, and this café was one of the places where we would meet others like us.'

Rosy took in the rough walls and varnished dado and tried to imagine.

'The leader of the Resistance here was Jean Moulin. He used an art gallery in Nice as a cover. But . . .'

'What happened to him?'

'He was arrested and murdered,' spat Xavier.

There was nothing she could say.

'Later on, when it was near the end of the war, after the British and Americans and Canadians had come over the Channel to liberate, there appeared a young Englishwoman – very beautiful, laughing, and always with this way of speaking . . .'

'Not . . . Eva?'

'Yes . . . Eva.'

'Why was she here?'

Another great all-encompassing Gallic shrug. 'She was a dancer.'

Rosy didn't follow.

'She was young, and like many young people she was tired of waiting. She wanted to be a part of this. As a dancer, she had met many soldiers, in the clubs and the cabarets . . .'

'You mean, she came down with the army – as a kind of camp follower?' frowned Rosy.

'*Non. Non*!' Xavier took visible umbrage at that.

'Then . . .?'

'Eva was how they called . . . go-between.'

Eva Coutts as Mata Hari – now Rosy had heard everything.

As it turned out she hadn't, quite.

As the Peugeot sped back towards Cannes, she had much to mull over. From the silence in the front seats, she deduced that she wasn't the only one.

By the strangest coincidence, the route Lord Spelbridge took out of Vence went as near as the winding road allowed to one of the places Xavier had shown her on the map.

72 | *Fashionably Late*

'Where have you been?' were Benedict's first words to Lottie when she arrived. His party was failing to swing to an accompaniment of worn Beach Boys hits. She looked rumpled, her make-up was smudged, and he suspected the worst.

'Thank you *very* much for your support on the most important night of the festival,' he bleated into her ear while fighting to keep a waxwork smile.

'I was on my way, Benedict . . . when Pierce Brosnan fell on me.'

'Oh great, just great.'

'A twenty-foot-high Pierce Brosnan.'

The columnist snorted his disbelief.

'The cut-out hoarding at the entrance to the Carlton. There was a huge gust of wind. It blew down and *I* was in the way . . .'

Young Wardour St – as evidenced by the pile of near-identical leather flying jackets – needed no encouragement to get down and network.

After his weeks in the fray, Benedict had worked out that making films was to this generation what success in the City had been to their older brothers and sisters, and what being a Lloyd's name used to be to their parents.

How apt, then, that beneath their feet there was shifting sand. Even if this was one of the few beach parties in the world to boast a cloakroom attendant.

The gossip columnist had come to the conclusion that accents could reveal a great deal. The great ideas came with Scottish and Mancunian accents; the money and front with indelible Kensington. The theory was holding fast here, as a Débutante (Type A) with thick, smooth blonde hair and a challenging jaw assured him that success was open to all. 'We've never been class-conscious. My mother once spoke to Arthur Scargill and she wasn't *nair*ly as rude as she could have been.'

'So . . . who *is* she then?'

The Beast was so objectionably persistent that Benedict wondered whether he might recruit him to the *Daily Post*. 'Well, if you don't know . . .' he sneered.

The woman in shreds – who *wasn't* Bardot – was proving thorn-like. Depending on which person he asked, she was variously a director, a former *inamorata* of Roger Vadim, producer of a Vanessa Paradis commercial, and even costumier to the *Jean de Florette* films.

It was unthinkable, naturally, not to know.

When Benedict went off to speak to her himself, he discovered only that she possessed a stony stare worthy of the Princess Royal, and the chattiness of Garbo.

The television crew took several long shots of her, he noticed, with mounting excitement. Finally, when they were packing away their equipment, he could bear it no longer. 'You've got all you need then?' he asked Sophie Brown.

'More than enough, thanks.'

'And our French guest over there?' No point in sounding too impressed.

'I beg your pardon?'

'Our French VIP . . .'

The TV presenter switched on the largest smile he'd seen all night.

'What?' he demanded.

'She came from the railway station, Benedict.'

'Loads of people hate to fly!'

'No. She lives there.'

'I'm sorry?'

'She's a tramp, Benedict.'

'All actresses are tramps,' he spat bitterly.

'A real tramp. A down-and-out. A person of no fixed abode.'

He reeled back.

Her laughter was a shower of tinkling broken glass. 'I'm telling you this so there's no grounds for complaint to the broadcasting standards people.' The meaning could not have been clearer. He had been set up.

'A tramp.' Benedict assimilated this. 'Not . . . not a Romanian gipsy . . . heartbroken and hoping for a part in the new gritty, grainy realism that is Post Art House?' He was pleading, he knew. They would show no mercy, he was equally sure. 'A . . . a Bosnian refugee of grand family . . . maybe?'

'Uh-uh,' Sophie shook her head.

'Shit,' said Benedict.

'Apart from anything . . . the sheer ghastliness of the cliché,' said Benedict.

The leathery woman had departed, paid off by the perfidious Ms Brown.

He was telling Nan Purchase a little later, attempting to give the disaster an advantageous spin.

The Manhattan millionairess, in her turn, was putting a brave face on the sheer collagen-deflating horror of it all. 'Now, Benedict, you gotta keep focused. Centre yourself on your achievements so far and think positive. Positive Mental Attitude, that is the key.'

Benedict suspected this was what had got him into trouble in the past. 'Maybe I should get away . . . go to your Grasslands place for a while . . .'

'It could be a very healing experience,' said Nan, in soothing tones at odds with her starved racehorse body and tight face. The party had thinned, along with the supplies of drink.

'What the – ?' Benedict flinched as the late arrival hesitated in the doorway. 'What is *she* doing here? Get her out!'

His imprecation fell on deaf ears. Nan deftly excused herself as the little figure in Chanel homed in on him, her light spun-sugar hair glued up in a cage, her tiny raised hand sparkling under a massive diamond.

'Benedict, darling . . .' cooed Bea Goff.

He was caught in the headlights with nowhere to run as flash bulbs popped.

'Benedict . . . I have a wonderful surprise for you!'

He opened his mouth to let her know that he doubted that.

'After all these years, at last . . . he has come to me and acknowledged the truth!'

Was she talking about him, or to him?

'Look, Benedict!'

And behind her, another uninvited guest had materialised, as if on telepathic waves of his dread. 'What's *he* doing here? I told him not to come out here . . .'

Sir Philip Hawty advanced, nevertheless. The former Home Secretary had a sickly grimace plastered on his once urbane face. A few more flash bulbs popped.

Benedict attempted to distance himself, but Hawty's approach widened into open arms of a most chilling familiarity.

Still he advanced.

'You,' said Benedict, beyond politeness.

'Benedict,' cried Sir Philip Hawty, making sure of his audience. '*Son!*'

Cornered, the columnist surveyed the wreckage of his party.

The only sound – suddenly – was the tinkle of broken glass, followed inexorably by the hiss and spit of a Pentax motordrive, as Keith 'the Beast' Silver did what he did best.

Over by the mauled trays of food, the Earl of Trent slumped forward into the guacamole, an explosion of pills and bottles at his feet as he made his bid to be fashionably late.

73 | *The Flight Home*

The next day Rosy checked out of the Hotel du Jardin, leaving her bags with the concierge. She went first to the police station, then to a bleak apartment above a row of shops on the outskirts of town, and then to a peeling local cinema in the vicinity of a goods yard.

She sifted through her notes, junked some, and added a relevant article ripped from *Nice Matin*.

At two o'clock, she left a farewell message for Framboise, hauled her bags to a taxi rank and set off for Nice Airport and the plane home.

She took the tube from Heathrow, changing at Earls Court. On the walk from Fulham Broadway, the shops and houses seemed as familiar and small as forgotten toys. The flat upstairs at 24 Endymion Road was empty of everything but mess.

It was *flatshare verité*.

Rosy threw her bags into her bedroom, made herself some coffee and crashed on the sofa.

She was still there some hours later when Emma returned.

Picking her path across the complex tangle of clothes, coffee mugs and chocolate wrappers, like a fastidious old-fashioned lady explorer in her long straight skirt and lace-up boots, her flatmate frowned. 'What is this?'

'*Dolce far niente,*' said Rosy from under the cushions. 'Sweet doing nothing. It's so much less demanding than the Dolce Vita.'

'Be my guest.'

'Yah.'

'Exhausted by the bright lights?' Emma twisted a red curl around a finger.

Rosy groaned. 'The *poseurs*, the frauds and bad acting. You have no idea.'

'All the film people?'

'No, the press.'

'That bad?'

Rosy nodded.

'I hear Quentin Tarantino won the Cannes jury prize for best film,' said Emma.

'Did he?'

Emma gave her a probing glance, then made some tea before she was subjected to the whole story.

Half-way through, she wandered over to the window and drew the curtains. 'What are you doing?' Rosy wanted to know. 'We never draw the curtains. It's not even properly dark yet.'

'Hmm . . .' Emma looked troubled for a fleeting moment.

'Emma?'

Her flatmate tweaked a fold with uncharacteristic fussiness. 'It's probably nothing,' she said.

Oh, great, thought Rosy. 'It's probably nothing,' she repeated. 'One of the great worrying phrases of the world.'

'It probably *isn't,*' insisted Emma. 'It's just that there's been this person – this man – who has been sort of . . . hanging around here . . .'

'Outside?'

'Of course, outside.' Emma frowned indignantly.

'Emma, this window looks out over the garden, not the street.'

Her friend made a mock now-you-tell-me face.

'He's been round the back in the garden?'

'I'm not sure . . . I thought I heard something the other night.'

'Well, what kind of man?'

'Difficult to say, really. He seems to wait until it's dark. After work kind of time. I mean I haven't actually shone a torch on him and subjected him to an interrogation!'

'Yes, but . . . what does he look like, how old is he?'

'He's . . . well, pretty nondescript really. Average height, average build, average age . . . dark hair, dark clothes . . . a kind of grey man.'

'But, but . . . how often have you seen him?'

Emma bit her lip. 'I thought I saw him in a car, as I came in.'

'Stationary car?'

'Yeah.'

'Well this is just great,' said Rosy. 'Nowhere to run. I come home from the fiction factory to find home has turned into *Nightmare on Elm Street*.'

That didn't raise a smile.

'OK, it wasn't funny. Sorry, Em. You've just seen him waiting around out in the street, though, nothing worse than that?'

'Well,' said Emma. 'He rang the doorbell once . . . early last week. I went down to answer it – I was expecting someone else.'

'And, what did he say? Did he know your name?'

'No.' Emma took an audible breath. 'He asked for you, Rosy.'

* * *

'Before you go into full seclusion,' said Emma later, after a summit conference on life and its shittiness, 'there are messages for you on the answerphone.'

'Wipe them.'

Emma stood firm. 'One of them is from Anthony Sword.'

Rosy slumped.

'It sounds important.'

'Then, your mother wants to know whether you can go home for the weekend and give her a hand with the vol au vents for the Chislehurst Golf Club ladies' night,' said Emma with a wicked grin. 'She says you should never pass up a social event as you never know who you might meet.'

'Crumbs,' said Rosy. 'That'll change my life.'

'She didn't actually come out with the phrase *nice young men*,' said Emma. 'But it was there.'

They giggled.

In the end, Rory decided she might as well face all the unpleasant surprises in one go. The mysterious Crighton number that Tina had passed on to her in Cannes was one of the first messages. Sword's was a bald request to call him. Various friends – including Tom Matthews – had asked her to events she'd now missed.

Among her post, there was a long white envelope containing a brief missive from the features editor informing her that her services would no longer be required at the *Daily Dispatch*. She was unmoved.

She had been fully expecting it.

74 | *A Union of Spirits*

'I'm back,' she said simply, when he answered the telephone.

Sword was torn between relief and fury. His morning voice was thick with coffee grounds as he rasped a grudging acknowledgement. It had been days and days since he had joined the dawn chorus for an aria.

'I wondered, perhaps, whether you'd tried to call me, A.'

Sword's reaction came out squeakily. 'No, no . . . why should I?'

Her sigh sounded gale-force. 'I've been to Cannes.'

'I know.'

'Oh. Since when?'

'Since Benedict Pierce treated the world to a few less than charming lines about you and your . . . elderly paramour. Personally, I could have done without knowing about your romantic dinners in the hills, still less the damage inflicted on one king-sized bed at the Hotel Gray d'Albion.'

'We have to talk, A.'

He didn't suppose that the *we* was confined to the two of them.

Sword insisted they spoke there and then. 'I hate bloody surprises,' he snarled.

'Fine,' said Framboise. 'Vivian Spelbridge and I are getting married.'

It wasn't that much of a surprise, in the event. Anthony Sword had always been one to suppose the worst.

The hastily arranged pre-nuptual meeting – he wasn't going to call it a celebration – fell flat as soon as he entered the Palm Court at the Waldorf. As he had known she would, Framboise had extended the invitation to her elderly intended. Lord Spelbridge sat stiffly amid the Edwardian splendour, as uncannily accurate in the setting as a BBC period-drama prop. He should have brought his flower girl mannequin, Sword thought, and made it a foursome.

A tiered tray of tea-time sandwiches and fancy cakes sat between them on the table in grotesque parody of a wedding cake. They had eschewed China tea in favour of champagne.

Sword did his damnedest to rig up a greeting smile.

Mentally, he ripped up his prepared speech.

'Oh, it's more than love,' said Framboise, when he, she, and Lord Spelbridge had reassembled at the table. 'It's a union of spirits.'

Exactly the way, in fact, that he felt about her.

Sword fought to remain non-committal as the singer spelled out for him the way she felt about Vivian Spelbridge.

'Or a *re*union, in fact.'

'What?'

'Oh, yes, we first met in eighteenth-century France, where we had a wonderful time . . .'

'Oh, come on – '

Framboise beamed, but slowly. Then she roared.

'What?' he asked tetchily.

'Haaa . . . I can never resist,' she chortled, wiping an

eye. 'Don't you remember the New Life therapy at Grasslands Hall – the regression afternoon?'

Sword would never forget. 'Hmm,' he said. He knew exactly what she was doing.

Framboise positively sizzled with the excitements of her new country life, and she spared him nothing.

'We were in the Porcupine – the pub, you remember?'

Sword nodded.

'I went inside to the bar . . . and the place is full of these guys in big black hats and wearing sashes and knickerbockers, and carrying these *blunderbusses*! I thought, *boy*, this place is *haunted* today . . .'

'It *is*, dontcha know,' chipped in Spelbridge.

'Well, that's right, he told me it was. So there I am, waiting for my pint of Old Codgers – in this *time warp* – and this guy comes up says, "Good day, my lady, for 'tis the day we shall cream the Roundheads, yet now I shall wetteth my whistle before the battle commences!'

'How much Old Codgers had you sunk?' growled Sword.

'I just could not believe it!' went on Framboise, overriding his resistance to her tale. 'This ghostly apparition goes on to say that the armies were meeting on the Lower Field, and would I like to see the regimental garrison to bless the etchings, whatever that means . . .'

Sword glanced at the Kentish baron for corroboration. Spelbridge shrugged indulgently. 'I would have advised you to say no,' said Sword.

'Hey – he said it was for charity,' replied Framboise with a great wink. 'When we got down there, there was a sight you never seen the like! Flags and tents and mud and canons and smoke and guns pounding . . .'

Realisation had dawned on Sword long before Spelbridge slapped the tablecloth with roaring glee.

'Sealed Knot! She'd never seen anything like it – all the chaps dressed up playing old armies in my old field!'

'Isn't it *wonderful*!' cried Framboise.

Sword smiled weakly. 'It's good to see some people still get off on surprises,' he said leadenly.

He couldn't do it. He could see no way of treating this as any other social occasion.

75 | *Rosy Dispatched*

Rosy made the most of being curled up in her own bed when she woke the next morning.

For about ten minutes.

If anyone thought that she was going to curl up and go away anywhere else but beneath the duvet there, they would be sadly mistaken.

Dressed for action, she fired up with a jog around the Bishop's Park.

By ten-thirty she had a Sunday paper commission to write the article she'd worked out on the French teenage killings and what they all had in common.

Like Rosy, the kids had seen too much blood and revenge in the cinema.

She was a free agent now – comparatively. To mark the moment, she left the red light blinking on the answering machine. She would call Anthony Sword and whoever else had called while she was out when it suited *her*.

On the floor, she spread her research notes and plotted her comeback.

She snatched up the telephone, though, when she heard Framboise's voice coming through her machine.

'Framboise!' cried Rosy, delightedly.

'How ya doin'? Got back OK?'

'Fine. On both counts.'

'What about you?'

'I'm home,' purred Framboise.

'In Islington?'

'I didn't say that.'

'Oh.' Rosy's private smile was involuntary.

'I heard what happened. Jus' thought I'd call to tell you Sword feels terrible . . .'

'Oh, yeah . . . hardly.'

'He's very fond of you. He cares, you know.'

'But when it came down to it, perhaps he just didn't care enough. And why should he?'

'He had other things on his mind, Rosy.'

'Hmm.' He had also effectively condoned Jamie's sabotage of her Arden interview.

'Which you know as well as I do.'

Maybe better, thought Rosy.

'Look . . . have you spoken to him yet?' asked Framboise, sounding urgent.

'Who, Sword? No.'

'Not Sword. *Crighton.*'

Rosy was perplexed. 'Crighton? Who *is* this Crighton? I keep hearing this name, and I haven't a clue!'

'It might be best if we met somewhere,' said Framboise cagily.

They arranged to have lunch the following day.

'Sounds mysterious,' Rosy stiffened.

'I'll take the train from Tunbridge Wells,' said Framboise.

'Aha . . . a Lady who Lunches,' quipped Rosy, determined not to be thrown.

Framboise chuckled. 'Almost.'

Rosy gave in and ran the answering machine tape. To her relief the bleep was followed by Tina's voice.

After some minutes of indecision, she called her. Mercifully, Sword's secretary said she was alone in the office. 'It wasn't his fault, Rosy. When John Lunt came in . . . he was ever so upset about something. He has been for weeks . . .'

Rosy sighed. She could do without the constant excuses, she really could.

'And he was going spare not being able to find Framboise . . . and then Lulu tried to stitch him up, and he sacked her . . . and what with Pearson's lunch with Amy Burton which lasted six hours and the expenses situation . . .'

'Sacked? Lulu's sacked?'

'Days ago. There was a terrible scene . . . the worst you can imagine . . .'

'There *is* a God,' said Rosy. Although she didn't suppose that He'd managed to see to Jamie as well. She wasn't even going to mention his name.

She hardened her attitude. 'Was there anything in particular, Tina?'

'Messages for you.' The secretary reeled off a list of two. One was by way of a personal request from Tom Matthews. The other was from a woman from one of the big ITV companies she had met briefly at a press conference in the Palais des Festivals. 'And some man phoned wanting your address . . . Sword said it was all right to give it to him.'

'What?' Rosy was incredulous. Was this the strange person hanging about in Endymion Road? What did Sword think he was playing at? 'Why would he do that? – I thought that was the first rule of respect for – '

'Rosy . . . calm down. I'm sure it was all right.'

'And if it's not . . .?'

There was a fretful silence.

'You didn't ask,' said Tina, her puzzlement clear.

'Ask what?'

'When I told you about Lulu. There's a *vacancy* here . . .'

No way. 'I couldn't, Tina. Not now.'

'But – '

'Really.'

The secretary sounded dumbstruck. 'You . . . I mean, you don't need your old job back? Only, I'm sure Sword would have you back like a shot . . . And, you know, Jamie has put the most massive payment for you in the book for the story about Rebecca Hunt and Joe Wesley that you got. Plus another £500 that must be for something pretty special.'

Rosy was not at all sure that money would do it. 'It's a very, very kind thought, Tina.'

'But – but you will keep in touch?'

Rosy nodded to no one but the faces in the photographs strewn about the carpet. 'You can count on it,' she said.

One more phone call and she would crack on with her murderous French film fans.

The number the ITV woman had given Tina was a direct line. 'Thank God you're back in London,' she said.

She came straight to the point. 'I work with Sophie Brown on *The Late Entertainment Show* – she says you met in Cannes. We're doing a piece about Robert Arden.'

The name alone was enough to initiate a stress reaction in Rosy's chest. Now, no doubt, someone else expected to feed off her hard work and lucky break.

'And as you are the only journalist in Cannes he spoke to one-to-one . . .'

'You've heard about that?' It was a minor consolation, Rosy supposed, that the news had spread this far. 'How on earth . . . I mean I was sure no one would believe that it was me . . .?'

'We know.'

'Don't tell me that my former colleague is a born-again gentleman . . .'

The producer laughed two notes. 'There must have been at least two people who knew first-hand.'

'Yeah, but – '

'Robert Arden told us. And there's some more good news for you, Rosy. When I say that *we* are doing a piece . . . what I mean is that *you* will be doing a piece.'

Rosy faltered. 'For you?'

'Please. Just agree. We can't lose this.'

There was true desperation at the end of the line. And if anyone would recognise that . . . 'I – I don't understand . . .'

'Arden. He says he'll do the interview – the only condition is that you do it.'

The doorbell made her jump out of her skin. Rosy went first to her bedroom window and peered down at the street, but it was impossible to see much of the person waiting on the doorstep. She went downstairs with a hammering heart.

Through the spy-hole in the front door she could see a man in grey. 'Who is it?'

'Flowers for Miss . . . Rosy Hope.'

A large bright package was waved the other side of the glass eye. She opened the door cautiously and received a cellophaned bouquet.

Upstairs again, she opened the card. It read: 'Don't get mad, get even. RA.'

76 | *Benedict Gets First Blood*

Benedict arrived back from Cannes to find that his new film industry contacts had no intention of letting him go without a fight. Four invitations on his desk at the *Daily Post* requested the pleasure of his company at the same bloodbath of a party.

The event was a homage to the cult status of a supposedly ironic shoot and splatter film which had run on and off for almost three years at the Prince Charles cinema off Leicester Square.

A sartorial note advised: Dress to Kill.

He had barely scanned *Private Eye* to assess the extent of his savaging *in absentia* – that the magazine would have savaged him was not in doubt – when the telephone pleeped. He tossed the rag aside.

'Hi, Benedict – it's Lulu!'

'Hello, darling. How are you doing in the lion's den?'

'If you mean Sword's office, I'm no longer there. The man is quite impossible.'

'Ah. That's a great shame . . . but still. Thank you for what you did manage to get while I was in Cannes. The cheque, as they say, will be in the post soonest.'

'Goody. All those phone calls! Phew!'

'We only spoke once, Lulu.'

'I know. I thought that was awfully clever of you, to set up your middle man like that.'

'Middle man,' said Benedict. 'What middle man?'

'Crighton, of course.'

'Crighton?'

'Yes, him. I was a bit wary at first, but he seemed so on the ball – '

'Lulu . . . I have no man called Crighton.'

'You don't?'

'I haven't the foggiest what you're talking about.'

'Oh damn.'

'Quite.'

'Does that mean I don't get paid for the stuff I've passed to him?'

'Not by me,' Benedict assured her. 'Are you saying there is some unknown man going around claiming he's working for me?'

'Well . . . he didn't exactly put it like that.'

'How did he put it, then?'

'He just wanted to know what you wanted to know. I just . . . assumed . . .'

'Strange,' said Benedict. 'Oh well.'

'Oh well,' said Lulu.

'So . . . what are you up to now then? Enjoying a break?'

'No. I'm a PR now.'

Benedict chortled. 'Figures.'

'In fact, I'm calling about the Doggies do.'

'I beg your pardon?'

'The *Reservoir Dogs* party.'

'Oh, that.'

'It's going to be the most amazing event . . .'

Benedict had to hand it to his former secretary. She had all the phrases off pat already.

'And as you know, Tarantino won the jury prize at Cannes . . .'

He didn't, as it happened.

'The cult followers get into their Tarantino black suits and pack plastic guns whenever they see the film, and shout their favourite lines at the screen like they do at the *Rocky Horror Show*. The girls are all done up as white trash – leopard print minis and satin bras. Big hair, frosted lips. Then they add weapons: chainsaws, hammers, baseball bats . . . Last year they held a convention, and they all got commemorative presents.'

'Don't tell me.' Benedict shuddered, imagining every kind of tastelessness.

'Severed ears,' Lulu told him. 'Dripping blood!'

Benedict said nothing.

'They *were* fakes . . . Isn't it too, too much!'

The gossip columnist thought it probably was, even for his page.

His first lunchtime engagement back in harness was on more familiar ground, at Peppers, a Covent Garden café of the polished wood floor genre. No restaurant re-opening was complete without a minor celebrity or two and a flurry of freeloaders. Benedict justified his attendance as a proclamation of his return.

The first person he saw was Sir Philip Hawty, happily ringed by journalists in search of a quote.

'How bad *is* this for the Government?' the television newsreader had asked of the parliamentary correspondent with undisguised relish that morning.

'*Very* bad for the government, Michael,' had come the equally gleeful reply.

Sir Philip Hawty was less Tory wet than Chinese water torture for his masters. His latest announcement was that he would play himself in a docu-drama detailing the downfall of the monarchy, although he denied vehemently that he had been present at the beach party in the South of France where a peer of the realm had made a botched suicide attempt with a cocktail of Junior Disprin and M & Ms.

Benedict was keeping out of it. He turned on his heel without pausing.

It had taken more than a year to come to terms with Bea Goff as his mother. To be found by a father – by which he meant *this* father – was more than a man could bear. The prospect of Sir Philip Hawty as a parent was marginally less appealing than major surgery.

It may have been the seductive way ignorance sometimes paraded as bliss, or it may have been squeamishness, but Benedict had no desire to get to the bottom of the situation.

It had to be a sick joke.

77 | *Lost and Found*

Officially, Anthony Sword was at a Royal Academy preview, but the man who mooched into Burlington House clutching the invitation which bore his name was in fact a tweedy, starstruck individual sent there by Sword in retribution for the lunches which had paved the way for so much damage.

The fool's lovelorn lingering with would-be starlet Amy Burton had given his ex-junior reporter ample time to pursue her own interests.

Not to mention those of Benedict Pierce.

'You went for lunch at twelve o'clock,' Sword had thundered when Pearson eventually found his way back to the office. 'The day before yesterday!'

The most hungover gossip columnist in the world was staying at home today. And he had spent the previous evening in alone. His shop window mannequins gazed vacantly at him, especially the Victorian flower girl. The little madam wore her dead bird hat at a tipsy angle, and the empty bottles he'd left at her feet made a positively Dickensian picture of his dipsomania.

They arrived unannounced.

'What's this – a deputation?' grumbled Sword, as his mother and Framboise trooped in.

'I suppose it is, dear,' said Eva.

'Straight talk,' said Framboise.

Neither of them mentioned the bottles, which was a bad sign.

Eva began to fiddle with her beads. 'It's about your father, dear.'

A shaft of pain threatened to explode his head. Sword sat down, and they sank down too, on either side of him.

'Straight talk?' asked Sword weakly.

They nodded in curious unison.

'You're going to tell me who he was . . . or you've decided on a candidate?' he sneered, sarcasm gaining over vulnerability.

'More . . . he who was lost and is found, dear.'

'*Found*?'

His worst fears were realised. Any moment now, he would be staggering around the drawing room squawking, '*A Handbag*?'

'Preserve us . . .'

'A . . . I know this is hard . . .'

He gave Framboise the full benefit of his most granite-like glower.

'And *how* . . . might I ask,' he thundered, turning to Eva now,' did the old fellow come to be *found* after all these decades so conveniently . . . misplaced? In an old trunk? A bottom drawer? In some forgotten box of tricks?'

'Now, Tony, dear . . .' She looked helplessly to Framboise.

The singer reached out and took his hand in hers. Sword shivered. His mother's gaudy make-up seemed to expand her features, clown-like, until they spread wider on her face. It was some seconds before he realised that they were distorted by his own tears. 'I mean . . . I mean, you seem to forget that we have played this scene already! Have you got some other despicable old rake sitting outside in a limo waiting for his big moment in front of the press corps?'

There was no answer.

'I think I should make us some coffee,' said Framboise.

At crucial moments, Eva was capable of lucidity.

'I met him during the last part of the war,' she said. 'I'd been entertaining the troops, as you know.'

He stared at her, sceptical but weary.

'I've never lied to you. Whatever else I've done.'

Sword wondered into what category of deceit obfuscation and evasion came. 'Straight talking, you said.'

'Yes.'

An uneasy pause.

'He was . . . you know, SOE, special operations. It's a long story how, but all you need to know for now is that I went abroad with him. We ended up in the South of France. For me, I was only nineteen, it was a big adventure. Hardly knew what I was doing – it was only after that . . .'

He spurred her on with a glare.

'We were involved with the Resistance, right at the end of the War. When they needed some new blood.'

Sword clutched at reality in the form of the sofa arm. From anyone else this would have been impossible to swallow. 'Spying?'

'Official secrets,' confirmed Eva, with a tiny smile. 'I was a go-between.'

Only *his* mother . . .

'Parachuted in.'

Good God.

'The point is – ' said Eva.

'Thank you.'

'That he was the love of my life at nineteen, as they are . . . and we were married out there, as you know. Part of the cover, really, only I thought it was the real thing. The War was all over bar the shouting by then.'

Sword was stock still. 'You always told me you married a soldier.'

'He *was* a soldier.'

'Yes, but . . . in my mind you were . . . knitting socks for the front and dreading the day the telegram came.'

'Me – knitting socks?'

She had a point.

'No . . . we were together. But . . . it was the age-old story . . .'

Sword ran his hands over his beard. Few of Eva's stories were ever age-old, exactly.

'We were too young,' she reprised. 'Never stopped arguing. We lasted about six months. He hated me talking to other men . . . and there were some lovely Free French . . . there was one . . .'

Sword sighed.

'Anyway, by the time I fell pregnant with you, it was obvious it wasn't going to work. And after one terrible, terrible row, I got myself back to Paris. Then back to Blighty only weeks before you were born.'

'And what about him? Did you let him know?'

'Well, there's the rub, dear. I sent letters back to Vence, and I never heard a word. Not a dickie bird. And there I was, same as thousands and thousands of other women – on me own to bring up a child.'

'But . . . surely you must have been able to contact his family here?'

'Oh, I tried. But they didn't want to know, either.'

'Why not?'

'Thought I wasn't good enough, you see. Little actress-dancer from Mitcham,' Eva sniffed. 'Thought I wasn't *quait raight* for a son of theirs. Least said, soonest mended, and I'd just disappear. So I did lose him, you see.'

Sword shared a watery smile with his mother.

'You'll be pleased,' she said, gamely. 'They're awfully grand.'

He snorted.

'I think you might even get along with him.'

Wha-a-t?

Framboise chose that moment to re-enter with the coffee on a tray. She glided silently as a well-trained butler, wearing an inscrutable madonna expression.

'You mean . . . he's still alive?'

'And very much kicking,' said Eva. 'I can assure you.'

'I don't . . . I never expected . . . how did you find . . .?' It was too much.

'Well, dear, you have Framboise and Vivian Spelbridge to thank for that. They went to France.'

The singer gave him a dipped beam of a smile.

'So. When you were away . . .'

She nodded.

Sword sank back into the deep cushions of his sofa. Then the furies began to catch light again. 'You and Spelbridge! What does our business have to do with him?'

The two women exchanged a glance.

'It's taking you a long time to ask,' said Eva. 'Or have you got used to the idea that he doesn't have a name?'

'I . . .'

At the last, the question wouldn't form.

78 | *The Bride's Tale*

Framboise was showing no signs whatsoever of bridal nerves when Rosy finally caught up with her at Joe's Café in Harvey Nichols. Bunkered by bags, the singer was obviously taking to the trousseau part in a big way.

'You *are* serious,' said Rosy, kissing her soft cushiony cheeks.

'I always wanted a traditional wedding.'

'All the trappings?' Rosy produced a kitsch reproduction Victorian silk-bound horseshoe. 'I couldn't resist . . .'

'*All* the trappings,' confirmed Framboise. 'I shall treasure it.'

'You needn't go that far.'

They laughed in unison.

'You know . . . I was thinking,' said Rosy. 'If it's not rude . . . I suppose children are out of the question? I mean, you're one of these people who don't seem to have an age . . .'

'Much as I relish the idea of a young black Baron Spelbridge lording it over the wassails or whatever . . . I can't see it happening, not at our age. Although, with my style and Vivian's aristocratic bearing, he would be more than cute . . . he would be goddam irresistible . . .' Framboise drifted off dreamily.

Rosy reeled her back. 'I want to talk about Sword, Framboise. There's something I want to ask you . . . What have you said to Sword?'

'Oh . . .' she said. 'A's cool.'

'I don't think so. I had a message from him on my answering machine. There was a definite edge to his voice.'

'Rosy, trust me. Everything will be all right.'

'Hmm.'

'I can't say too much, but . . .' A mysterious smile spread across her jolly jowls. 'By the time I'm finished, Sword and I will be closer than ever.'

'*Fram*boise . . .'

The singer was suddenly utterly serious. 'I've found someone far better for Sword than a wife . . .'

'What? Who?'

'I've found him a father, Rosy.'

Rosy honoured the moment with a respectful pause.

Then she said: 'I had a feeling you had, and I think I know where.'

'You do?'

Rosy nodded. 'If I'm right, we got there within hours of each other, as well.'

Framboise urged her on, first with a puzzled frown, then a creeping grin.

'The day we went to St Paul de Vence, funnily enough – the day you told me about you and Lord Spelbridge,' said Rosy. She knew she was right when Framboise waved away a waitress with the menu. 'Lord Spelbridge went off to meet him, while we had lunch at the Colombe D'Or, didn't he?'

A sigh from Framboise. 'Did you know that at the time?'

'Of course not. Although it was clear as anything

something was going on between you and Lord S,' smiled Rosy. 'I put it down to wedding intrigue at first.'

'It was, in a manner of speaking.'

'Funnily enough, it was a way of talking that gave it away . . .'

Framboise cocked her head. 'You're riddling me.'

'All right. When I went up there with Jamie, we went to a little restaurant which is famous for all the Cannes gossip, on account of the proprietor, Armand. Anyway, while we were there we met the old guy, Armand's father, who used the phrase "sex, rage and sin" . . .'

The singer's puzzlement lingered.

'Who do we know who always uses that phrase?'

Realisation dawned, a fat summer sunrise on Framboise's face. 'Eva . . .'

'Right. It was only later, when . . . I didn't have other priorities on my mind . . . and I went up there with you, that I realised. We walked around the Matisse chapel, and got back to find your intended, looking fretful. When I disappeared for an hour, I went back to see Xavier.'

'The old guy.'

'Right. He told me some wonderful stories about the Resistance during the war, and how Eva appeared, introduced by the Englishman who still lives in the hills, working a vineyard. Then, he had been in the army, survived various escapades – which I imagine were well embellished by Xavier – and joined their band of Resistance fighters. That part is all rather hazy . . . but apparently he had good connections.'

Framboise cleared her throat.

'But the important part is that . . . all the dates match. It was Sword's fiftieth birthday earlier this month, wasn't it? And Eva was there for at least six months at the vital time . . .'

'You know his name, then?' asked Framboise.

Rosy put a hand under her face and smiled coyly. '*L'Honorable*, that's what they call him.'

'You do know – '

'The Hon. Frank Spelbridge. Why he's even in the family business, isn't he!'

They finally ordered some lunch.

'What an amazing coincidence,' said Rosy. 'I still can't get over that . . .'

'Coincidence had nothing to do with it,' said Framboise. 'Frank L'Honorable is not the only brother with a nose for intrigue.'

'You mean?'

'Vivian Spelbridge picked me, don't forget, not the other way round. He came round backstage, got to know me . . . I hate to admit this, but my charms were a secondary consideration . . .' She gave Rosy an absurdly coquettish look. 'At that stage.'

'Why?'

'He found out that I was a good friend of Sword's. That was hardly low-profile.'

'Suppose not . . .'

'And last year, when Sword's Own Secret came out – '

Rosy smiled at their shorthand for the public revelation that Eva Coutts, the dotty theatrical tipster and party girl of dubious repute was, in fact, Sword's own mother. A mother he had kept, if not hidden, then publicly unacknowledged ever since he had become Anthony Sword, master of other people's hatches, matches and dispatches. Until Rosy had blundered in.

Framboise smiled and continued. 'The Spelbridge family got to thinking . . . well, they were mostly distant relatives and old retainers, but they remembered Eva, you see. That she was a war bride once.'

Rosy doubted she could take another unlikely bride. 'Eva was *married* to Spelbridge?'

'*Frank* Spelbridge, yes,' said Framboise. 'The younger brother.'

'Blimey.'

'And the family – for that read Lord S – set about tracking Eva down, verifying the connections . . . and other investigations. Their secret operative was this old housekeeper, Mrs Padget. Jeez, what a character . . .'

'So, why . . .?'

'They need a male heir, Rosy.'

It wasn't until they were heading out on to Sloane Street, and she saw the grey pavement, that Rosy remembered with a sudden tingle of fear.

'Framboise . . . you haven't told me what you know about this Crighton person.'

'Oh, *him*.'

'He's been hanging around outside the flat – at least we think it must be him. It's creepy. What's going on?'

'It's OK. He's a private detective.'

'What? Why -?'

'He's a specialist in his field,' said Framboise. 'A genealogical private detective. Very thorough, by all accounts.'

Rosy was dumbfounded. 'I still don't – '

'Hired by the Spelbridge family. They had to know what kind of person was underneath the terrible Sword persona. Before they found him . . . officially.'

79 | *Two Peas in a Pod*

They drove down to Spelbridge Place in near silence. Sword, at the wheel of the Bentley, fixed his mind on the A21. Framboise had made one caustic remark about his gruntfest, then left it at that.

Her smart purple suit with gold buttons said it all: it was Meet the Family time.

Primed as he had been with promising biographical details, Sword knew that meeting his father for the first time could prove the toughest social event of his life.

They turned off the main road and motored on through the curves and tree-tunnels of the lush Kentish countryside. He could feel her mounting excitement as surely as his own dread. As they slid through the last village before Spelbridge, past the Porcupine pub where they had been only weeks before – it seemed like a hundred years ago – Sword spoke at last.

'Did you know, then?'

'Know? That Vivian was your uncle? Of course not!'

'But he did.'

Framboise pulled down the corners of her brightly glossed lips. 'We know that *now.* At the time, I guess . . . I just thought he was this nice old guy who liked my shows. Then, when he asked me to come on down and see his house in the country – he *said* he wanted me to do a turn at one of his soirees, if you remember – he joked that I should bring a friend who liked wine . . . as a safety precaution . . .'

'Very clever.'

'Sure was.'

Sword steered around a flower festooned corner and shifted the car into a determined gear to tackle a winding grind of a hill.

'He also got a lot more than he bargained for!' said Framboise, flashing a ruby the size of a quail's egg on her left hand.

He declined to comment on that.

'So who sent the photograph of Eva standing outside the Porcupine?' Piecing together the information supplied by his mother, Sword realised the black and white scrap of a picture must have been taken some time before she and his father left for France.

'Vivian did – via his man Crighton,' said Framboise. 'I think the idea was to see how you'd react, whether it meant anything to you.'

'How much Eva had told me, in other words.'

A tiny silence, as if in honour of Eva's long reticence.

'And the Spelbridges think *they* have family pride . . .' said Framboise, rolling her eyes skywards.

The Bentley swept through the ancestral gates, into the drive and across a sullen moss-green moat to the house. Sword had expected some awkward ceremony choreographed by servants, but the two elderly men appeared right on cue at the grand entrance and came down the stone steps to greet them.

One was tall and patrician in his English countryman's tweed. Lord Spelbridge gave Framboise an affectionate embrace and stuck out his hand to Sword.

There was no mistaking the other.

Frank Spelbridge was shorter, round and ruddy cheeked even through his baked-in tan. He sported the dark checked jacket and linen trousers of the off-duty Continental man. Pepper and salt hair curled and frizzed above blue eyes which shone with a familiar piratical humour. A fine double chin and impressive girth spoke volumes of a stubborn geniality that any son would be proud to inherit.

On seeing Sword, his noble face split into an identical smile.

Their introduction was a hug which must have looked like two great grizzly bears locked in combat.

Words came later.

After a celebratory lunch of some splendour, Framboise and her wine-maker sloped off in the direction of the tasting pergola that Lord Spelbridge had recently installed.

'Damn fine woman,' said Frank Spelbridge. 'Proper shanks on 'er, not like all these stick people nowadays, eh?'

His son agreed heartily.

'Can't be doing with folk who don't like their grub.' His language had an arcane quality, as so often among long term ex-patriots. Sword found it endearing.

The gossip columnist was profoundly cheered by the way his father – from the first minute there had never been any doubt about that – had excelled himself at the table. His *embonpoint*, Sword decided, was both stately and delightfully self-indulgent. And most importantly, the man's evident good health boded excellently for his own prospects on that score.

'You never wanted to come back here?' Sword asked him, as they began a leisurely perambulation of the gardens.

'No, never did. Beautiful place, don't get me wrong. But it was always going to be Vivian's, as the eldest son. I liked it where I was. I still had an interest here, though. I found the vines and sent them to start the vineyard here.'

'Good man,' smiled Sword.

'My life's work is in France, though.'

'I'd like to see it.'

Frank clapped his arm around his son's shoulders. 'Oh, you shall . . . you *must*. And, then, when you take over here I shall keep a very firm eye on what you have learned.'

Sword did a dizzying double-take. 'What?'

'When you take over here.'

'That's what I thought you said.'

The older man stopped and turned to face him. 'They haven't explained? Good Lord.'

Sword shook his head.

They stood, belly to belly – unnervingly, two round peas in a pod – on a gravel path.

Frank sighed. 'Vivian, as you know, is a widower. Without issue – he and Elizabeth had no children. Terribly sad business, and all that. As younger brother, therefore, I am heir to the barony and the estate . . . but I am a mere two years younger than he, and . . .' He shrugged in the gallic way. 'However, I have been married – three times, as a matter of fact – '

The gossip columnist grinned, to imply that he would take those details soon enough.

'I have four children. But only one son . . . my first child.'

The question was almost too big to be broached. It took a while. 'Why did you never look for me before?'

'I never *knew* about you before. Not until . . . last year.'

'When it came out publicly that the one-time actress

Eva Coutts was my mother . . .' Sword shuddered to recall how many years he had fought to keep that under wraps.

'Vivian recognised her in a newspaper article. He didn't even tell me what he was up to until he and this genealogist-cum-private detective he hired were as certain as they could be that you were my son – and could inherit.'

Sword could hardly restrain himself. He had not dared think it – Lord Spelbridge-to-be! 'And I *am* legitimate?' he asked.

His father grinned. 'You can thank your mother's deeply suburban streak for that. Now . . . shall we find another drink?'

There was no need for words.

Sword had a feeling that he couldn't have invented anyone better.

80 | *A Country Wedding*

Two weeks later Rosy rejected the dress she'd bought in Cannes as too glamorous for her bleak mood, and too clinging for her brand new personal philosophy of standing solidly on her own two feet. Then she relented.

It was a wedding, after all.

Her grand invitation to Spelbridge Place at four o'clock had been additionally engraved with a green ink scrawl from Framboise: *Bring a friend!* Rosy had resolutely ignored the social euphemism and asked several.

A whole TV film crew's worth.

She'd needed all the moral support Emma could provide before she set off. But during the drive south to Kent, pepped up by James Brown Feeling Good, she knew that she would now.

She parked the Renault in a field designated Guests' Parking, clamped on her wide-brimmed summer hat and joined the line of well-dressed people striding towards the tiny village church.

From its square Norman tower, to the lichen on the gravestones, to the bower of blooms around the lych-gate, the church and its setting on the edge of the Spelbridge Place estate was an English country dream.

The bells had begun to toll jubilantly. A small crowd

had gathered on the road outside the entrance, straining for a glimpse of the wedding party.

'Bride or groom?' an usher asked her as she went inside.

'Bride,' said Rosy firmly.

From her pew halfway down the nave – she was placed, happily, between a well-known woman agent who had known Framboise for years, and an amusing saxophonist – Rosy could glimpse Lord Spelbridge's grey head bobbing nervously.

When Framboise arrived, beaming widely at the oak door, at ten minutes past four, there were gasps and even a smattering of clapped hands.

Rosy failed to suppress an unseemly grin at the singer's interpretation of a white wedding. It was the essence of the phrase, it appeared, not the literal application that Framboise meant.

She was swathed head to toe in scarlet silk.

Then, with the prickle of a happy tear behind one eye, Rosy realised that all was right in Framboise's world.

For, taking her arm tenderly, a morning-suited Anthony Sword, with a red rose in his lapel, began to lead her down the aisle.

Rosy had long subscribed to the view that nothing happened but the unexpected – but never when Jamie Raj was involved.

'I saw you on *The Late Entertainment Show,*' he said, cool as ever.

Drinks were flowing on the grey stone terrace at Spelbridge Place. Beyond the clear primary colours of wedding finery and explosions of June flowers and the deep mossy greens in the moat, were still waters running deep.

Rosy said nothing.

'You were very good. Robert Arden really opened up.'

Don't get mad, get even.

'Thank you,' said Rosy. 'The producers thought so too, as a matter of fact. They were pleased with it.'

There was a definite edge to his voice when he said: 'Quite right, too.' He cleared his throat. 'Rosy . . . I know this isn't enough . . . but I am sorry . . . for what happened . . . I don't know what I was thinking of when . . .'

She had waited for this.

'When you filed the piece on my computer . . . they automatically thought it was from me – it wasn't as though it was a preconceived plan. The subs just assumed it was mine. I didn't put them right in time . . . and I'm sorry.'

Rosy fought her stubborn remaining feelings for him. 'Don't be. You did me a favour.'

'Oh?'

The scene was getting sweeter. She wondered whether he would mention her full-page piece in the *Sunday Times*, or whether that was just too choking.

'If you hadn't stitched me up, I would never have found out that not all idols fall,' said Rosy. 'I wouldn't have been in a position to have Robert Arden himself take a hand and show what a more than decent person he is,' she added when she saw him frown. 'He refused to do the television interview with anyone else but me.'

Jamie was green.

'It was also his way of showing me, in practice, something we'd talked about in France. About why he hardly ever does print interviews – because he reckons they very rarely give the true picture.'

She didn't labour the point.

'And you had your fifteen minutes of glory,' said Jamie.

'It might . . . be more than just the fifteen.'

'Oh?'

Rosy was loving this. '*The Late Entertainment Show* have asked me to do some more pieces for them. Starting here.'

'I have been filmed from every angle on the ancient showstopper,' Lord Spelbridge reported, an hour into the outdoor reception, after Rosy had repeated her heartfelt congratulations and good wishes.

Rosy smiled warily.

His bride in scarlet laughed heartily. 'The *house*, Rosy. He means the house.'

'It *is* wonderful. This is the most gorgeous place.'

'Great place for a party,' smiled Framboise.

'A fine traditional house,' said Lord Spelbridge, with a look at Framboise which implied a private joke.

She shook her head. 'No . . . I draw the line at that. In fact, I have to say I almost didn't wear this dress because of what people would think. I hate to worry people unnecessarily.'

'What . . . that it's not white?' asked Rosy. 'I wouldn't have thought anyone would be put out that you aren't wearing white . . .'

'Everyone always has it at weddings,' said Lord Spelbridge.

Framboise roared with laughter. 'Not the dress – what it implies. The *song*. I just know that when the band strikes up half the guests will be cringing in readiness for *The Lady In Red*!'

81 | *The Biter is Bitten*

Dinner was served in the Great Baron's Hall. On the top table, Anthony Sword was barely conscious of the fine foods which appeared so efficiently beyond the napkin over his great belly.

Candles flickered.

Silver gleamed.

Under the high vaulted ceiling, the hall was filled with guests, lit up here and there by glow-worm lights from lower candelabra.

Beside him on one side sat his father. On the other side sat Eva.

Sword sighed with the inevitability of it all.

The two hadn't stopped arguing since they sat down.

'You always were in the right, weren't you? Everyone else could be wrong – but not you, Frank.'

'Well, that's typical of you, Eva. You always were . . . a right little madam, I believe is the phrase.'

'And what about the time you insisted – *insisted!* – that we move to Paris? Lasted a fortnight on black bread, we did, and not a sniff of what we went for . . . and that chap, you know . . . what's his name . . . the one who was always going on about – oh, you *know* . . .'

'*And* there's another thing . . . you could never

remember anybody's bloody name! Used to drive me insane.'

Nothing had changed, it seemed.

It was a pretty unseemly floorshow to be recorded for family posterity when the inevitable video cameras came around.

After dinner there was a mellow drift towards the dancing. The night was so warm that the band had begun to play outside, where a dance floor had been laid around the giant chessboard in the gardens beneath the terrace. Already, entwined couples were moving across the black and white squares.

Sword strongly suspected Framboise's hand in the symbolism.

'Mr Sword?'

She emerged from an arrangement of heady lilies and lisianthus, startling him. 'Rosy!' he said, making to kiss her cheek. 'Since when have I been *Mr* Sword to you?'

She gave him a characteristically uncertain glance over her smile.

'I must say, you look absolutely stunning in that dress, darling! Enough to turn an old man's head . . .'

'It's quite an occasion, isn't it?'

'It certainly is.'

'Good to see Eva again,' said Rosy.

Sword took a belt of the Armagnac he had brought out. He had pushed the discomforting knowledge to the back of his mind that Rosy had been the first, indeed the only member of his staff to penetrate the walls of his mother's house in East Sheen – and that while one of her unspeakable parties was in full swing. 'She's . . . a game old girl.'

'Of course . . . some people might find it strange that

your mother was invited to this wedding,' said Rosy equably.

'Not at all. She and Framboise have become great mates.'

He could have sworn that his former reporter winked at him. 'Ah,' she said ripely.

Sword was uncertain where this was leading. 'Saw you on the telly last week. I was proud of you.'

'Thanks.'

'You didn't return my call. If it's any consolation Lunt's a fool and a flash in the pan. He'll be out on his arse any day now. I was going to offer you your old job back.'

'That's OK.'

'I got rid of that pest Lulu.'

'So I heard.'

He wasn't going to push it. 'What are you up to now?'

'Um . . . I've got another television commission from *The Late Entertainment Show.*'

'Well, good . . . good.'

He was genuinely pleased for her. The news assauged the residual guilt he felt for having colluded – even passively – with his deputy editor's disgraceful purloining of her scoop. Sadly for Rosy, the way of the world was that Jamie Raj was too good an operator to risk losing.

And she was enough of a professional to realise that, it seemed.

'We're filming here, in fact,' she told him.

'The new Lady Spelbridge – you have to hand it to Framboise, she's got style!'

'No,' said Rosy. 'The new Lord Spelbridge-to-be.'

82 | *Explosions*

There was a charged pause, during which bass notes boomed and Rosy feared her former boss would go up like dry tinder. She trod carefully around the UXB of his need to be in control.

'*What*?' he uttered, with seismic resonance.

Rosy held her breath, and her ground. 'We are making a documentary slot on the Spelbridge story. Lord Spelbridge and . . . your father . . . have given their full permission,' she said. 'Naturally, you are part of that story. It's your choice whether you speak to us or not.'

Sword continued staring at her, nostrils flaring, shoulders as square as the house behind him.

She stared back.

Then he threw back his head, and roared. The music from the band missed a beat, dancers faltered and guests ceased milling.

Once the laughter had started, it was as unstoppable as the Amazon.

Sword clapped one arm around her, still braying. 'I have taught you well, Rosy. I'll say that.'

She smiled.

Arm-in-arm, they walked back to the house.

'There's one more question I need to ask,' said Rosy,

when the impromptu filming session with a royally gracious Sword in a quiet drawing room had been accomplished.

He had even thanked the camera and sound crew, as well as exhorting the director to help himself to more wedding fare.

'Shoot,' commanded Sword.

'Benedict Pierce,' said Rosy, as they began walking back towards the celebrations.

'Ah, Benedict. Some men might be considered over-qualified for the job. He is merely over-coiffed . . .'

Rosy laughed, briefly. 'I missed his party in Cannes' – she wondered whether to tell him why, but decided against it – 'but I heard there was the most extraordinary scene at the end, when Sir Philip Hawty appeared, and claimed he was Benedict's father!'

'Where did you get that from?'

'One of the TV crew was still there.'

'You must introduce me. I'd relish the details.'

'You didn't know?'

Sword gave her a glare. 'Of course I knew. But I savour every nuance.'

'I'll bet.'

'It was I who activated Bea Goff and coerced Hawty into co-operation.'

Rosy grinned. 'But *is* he Benedict's father?'

The rival gossip columnist had once told her himself the fact of his adoption. Then, Rosy had heard the stubborn rumour that Bea Goff, the dedicated attention-seeker and serial wife, was his birth mother. She had reserved judgement on that.

'You know, I rather think he is,' said Sword.

They reached the threshold of the Great Baron's Hall, still magically cavernous by candlelight. Rosy could have sworn Sword physically puffed with pride.

'There's a certain look, in a certain light – don't you think?' asked Sword.

'That's substantial evidence?' said Rosy.

'My mother has always said' – they exchanged looks – 'that she knew Bea Goff when she was an actress. They were in the same theatrical company for a brief while at the dawn of time.'

So the Bea Goff rumour was true. Sword seemed to take it for granted that she knew.

'Eva wasn't impressed, I take it,' said Rosy, taking a flyer.

'To put it mildly.'

They stopped by the top table.

'Eva has always known more than she's let on,' said Sword.

'Masterly understatement,' said Rosy.

They faced each other over the artful debris. 'When Bea Goff was going around last year, trying to get close to Benedict, it was Eva who told me she'd stake her life – well, to quote exactly, her suggestive telegram from Orson Welles – on the wretched woman being Benedict's mother. She also told me, and again these are her own words, that Bea got herself up the spout by the assistant stage manager of the company, if you please.'

'That was a cover-up?'

'No,' said Sword. He poured two glasses of claret from an abandoned decanter on the table. It was masterly, thought Rosy, how he sucked people into his game. 'Haven't you ever suspected Sir Philip Hawty of being a man who was a little too fond of stage-managing his own publicity?'

'Or trying to,' she grimaced. She was remembering something now.

'It turns out – or so Hawty himself tells me – that he too was a part of this theatrical troupe.'

'Which is how he knows Eva!' cried Rosy. 'You know, that always bothered me. When I was on the column, she often phoned in with stories about him, and I *did* wonder . . .'

Sword managed to convey with a gesture that this was barely the half of it.

'You know . . . I don't think I ever told you this but . . . that party Eva gave . . . in East Sheen . . . Hawty was there. I was there.'

'I know,' said Sword. 'I watched you go in.'

Rosy didn't want to ask why or how. She took it as read that somehow he knew everything. There were also more pressing lines of inquiry.

'So . . . Bea Goff and Sir Philip Hawty did know each other, back then?'

'He *was* that assistant stage manager,' said Sword.

Rosy was stunned. 'Poor Benedict.'

'Indeed,' said Sword, clinking her glass.

On the brink of the fray outside, Rosy cranked up her courage to look him in the eye and ask.

'You are all right, aren't you – about Framboise and Lord Spelbridge . . . all this . . .?'

Sword nodded.

There was a bright sparkle in the corners of his eyes which could have been the light from the revelry, and there again, not.

'I know,' said Rosy cautiously, 'that she thinks the world of you . . . and that she thinks she's done her best by you, as a friend.'

There was little she could say, and that was probably too much.

'She has,' said Sword.

A rush of tearaway guests passed by, and disappeared shrieking into the dark maze.

'And what about you, Rosy?'

She knew he meant Jamie.

'In the end, he did his best by me too – in a way,' she said. 'It's all you can ask, isn't it?'

'Mmm,' said Sword. 'You make a good couple.'

Rosy shook her head.

'You and your handsome television director, I mean,' said Sword.

'What? How did you know? It's only been . . .'

Stymied, Rosy gazed at the most famous gossip columnist in the world. Then they exploded together.

83 | *Party Chatter*

'Benedict! What are you doing here?'

'Sssh! If you don't mind . . . it's all rather awkward. Whose are those cameras?'

'They're with me, as a matter of fact.'

'Well, well . . . Rosy, darling . . . you wouldn't want to point them anywhere near my direction now would you . . .'

'Not in the slightest.'

'Thank you. I mean that.'

'So what *are* you doing here, Benedict?'

'Editor's orders. Believe me, I don't want to be here. But it's a good story.'

'Talking of which . . . they tell me that a certain ex-Home Secretary has been more than usually embarrassing.'

'These matters are all relative.'

'My point precisely.'

'Another two weeks, Jamie, and all the finance will be in place for the British film of the decade . . .'

'I thought the idea was that the cast put up the money and opened their lovely homes for the cameras?'

'Yes . . . but you know what they're like . . . they're all so tight!'

'And Brett . . . I don't want to take anything away from the extravaganza here . . . but I did hear that there was another consortium doing a very similar project. In Hollywood. With a Very Important Person on board.'

'We-e-ll . . . it's possible.'

'I think it's more than possible, I'm afraid.'

'It'll never get off the ground.'

'So you're not giving up with *Princess Laid Bare*, then?'

'Certainly not. We're auditioning for a man with a megaphone to direct it next week at the Savoy.'

'Brett . . . have you ever heard of a chap called Pedro Almodovar?'

'Come again?'

'He'd be perfect. Take it from me. He's big on great, colourful, messy lives . . .'

'Give me the name again . . .'

'Tssstup, tsstup, stssstupp!'

'Do you *have* to?'

'I am merely tasting professionally the quality of my excellent Spelbridge Müller-Thurgau 1990. Does it bother you?'

'It reminds me of that chap . . . mmmm, agh! you know the one . . . in the film, in the leather mask, lots of close-ups and blood . . . Hannibal Lecter. Quite puts me off . . .'

'You don't change, Eva.'

'I shall take that as a compliment. Neither, for the records, has *he*.'

'Still hammer and tongs, eh?'

'Humph . . .'

'*They* seem to be getting on all right. Look at them. Two peas in a pod.'

'St Emilion?'

'1961, 1970 or 1982.'

'Fair enough. Not a Châteauneuf-du-Pape?'

'No . . . not as fine.'

'I couldn't agree more. It's the restraint of the gravel on the fruit.'

'My dear boy! You have it precisely!'

'And you would serve?'

'Ah . . . a sautée of wild mushrooms and the creamiest garlic . . . perhaps a slow-roasted side of *sanglier*, with truffles . . .'

'Aaaah . . . it's such a relief to find that we can at least talk . . . could have been such an awkward moment . . . To find a *bon vivant* is almost too much . . .'

'Talking, yes . . . but *eating*, that is the grand pleasure . . . You *will* come to my table – '

'Set on a steep vineyard, with the scent of thyme and rosemary?'

'You must come.'

'It will be like coming *home* . . .'

'Historically, this is a most sociable area, Lady Spelbridge. In the eighteenth century, noble men and women would come to the Wells and it was a very fashionable place for gossip.'

'I just *love* it!'

'You see the man over there? He's the Dipper.'

'The Dipper?'

'He serves the spa water to tourists at the Chalybeate Spring at the end of the Pantiles in Tunbridge Wells.'

'Spa water, health food – filthy stuff. Never touch it, I'm afraid.'

'Oh, but you must . . .'

'This isn't some kind of *health* town is it? Only, the last time I went to a grand house in the countryside, it turned out to be the most God-awful inner transformation, no-food place . . . Did I tell you I make the most wonderful soul food, you just would not believe . . . do you think your parish council would like it if I made that for the village get-togethers . . .?'

'Just who *does* Sword think he is?'

'Why, he's the future Lord Spelbridge. He's absolutely one of us, darling.'

'According to the long-lost Frank?'

'According to *Debrett*.'

'How absolutely extraordinary.'

'I always felt there was more to Anthony Sword's commanding presence than met the eye. It's so reassuring to be proved right.'

'Breeding will always out.'

'And the new Lady Spelbridge?'

'She's rather a find, actually. I asked her about her antecedents . . . and she told me that her father was a real prince . . .'